COLTONS *of*
GRAVE GULCH

UNCOVERING
COLTON'S FAMILY
SECRET

LINDA O. JOHNSTON

HARLEQUIN
ROMANTIC SUSPENSE

Danger. Passion. Drama.

These heart-racing page-turners will keep you guessing to the very end. Experience the thrill of unexpected plot twists and irresistible chemistry.

AVAILABLE THIS MONTH

COLTON 911: DESPERATE RANSOM
CINDY DEES

OPERATION WHISTLEBLOWER
JUSTINE DAVIS

UNCOVERING COLTON'S FAMILY SECRET
LINDA O. JOHNSTON

UNDER THE RANCHER'S PROTECTION
ADDISON FOX

ISBN-13: 978-1-335-75946-7

EAN

At age thirty-seven, Oren had been in law enforcement over a dozen years. He had learned a lot—and he could tell something here definitely wasn't right.

Should he speed up to get far ahead of that driver? But this car, though it drove well, wasn't exactly built for speed. That was one reason he'd stayed in the right lane.

Should he slow down? No. That would make it too easy for the other driver to reach them, if that was what was going on. That tactic would definitely suss out whether they were the target—they might get hit or forced off the road.

And even though he was armed, Oren wouldn't attempt to use his weapon with Madison in the car unless it became absolutely necessary.

"What's going on?" Madison demanded. "What's with your driving, Oren? Are we okay?"

"Yeah," he said, hoping that wasn't too much of a lie.

* * *

The Coltons of Grave Gulch: Falling in love is the most dangerous thing of all...

* * *

Dear Reader,

This is my third book in the wonderful, long-running Colton series.

Uncovering Colton's Family Secret is book number ten in the new twelve-book Coltons of Grave Gulch miniseries, in which many Coltons are in law enforcement—and there are some murderers out there whom they need to identify and catch.

In *Uncovering Colton's Family Secret*, though, Madison Colton isn't in law enforcement. She is a kindergarten teacher, and while visiting a town not far from Grave Gulch, she sees a man who appears to be her father, Richard Foster—who has been dead for twenty-five years.

Before she can approach and question him, she is arrested by US marshal Oren Margulies for jaywalking. Was that man her father? Couldn't be. But why is she now being watched so closely by that handsome but difficult US marshal? Is it because she suddenly seems to be in danger? Their mutual attraction doesn't seem to be the only reason Oren's remaining so close to her.

I hope you enjoy *Uncovering Colton's Family Secret*. Please come visit me at my website, www.lindaojohnston.com, and at my weekly blog, www.killerhobbies.blogspot.com. And yes, I'm on Facebook and Writerspace, too.

Linda O. Johnston

UNCOVERING COLTON'S FAMILY SECRET

Linda O. Johnston

Special thanks and acknowledgment are given to
Linda O. Johnston for her contribution to
The Coltons of Grave Gulch miniseries.

HARLEQUIN®

ROMANTIC SUSPENSE™

Recycling programs
for this product may
not exist in your area.

ISBN-13: 978-1-335-75946-7

Uncovering Colton's Family Secret

Copyright © 2021 by Harlequin Books S.A.

This edition published by arrangement with Harlequin Books S.A.

For questions and comments about the quality of this book, please contact us at CustomerService@Harlequin.com.

Harlequin Enterprises ULC
22 Adelaide St. West, 40th Floor
Toronto, Ontario M5H 4E3, Canada
www.Harlequin.com

Printed in U.S.A.

Linda O. Johnston loves to write. While honing her writing skills, she worked in advertising and public relations, then became a lawyer...and enjoyed writing contracts. Linda's first published fiction appeared in *Ellery Queen's Mystery Magazine* and won a Robert L. Fish Memorial Award for Best First Mystery Short Story of the Year. Linda now spends most of her time creating memorable tales of romance, romantic suspense and mystery. Visit her on the web at www.lindaojohnston.com.

Books by Linda O. Johnston

Harlequin Romantic Suspense

The Coltons of Grave Gulch
Uncovering Colton's Family Secret

Shelter of Secrets
Her Undercover Refuge

The Coltons of Mustang Valley
Colton First Responder

Colton 911
Colton 911: Caught in the Crossfire

K-9 Ranch Rescue
Second Chance Soldier
Trained to Protect

Undercover Soldier
Covert Attraction

Visit the Author Profile page at Harlequin.com for more titles.

Of course, again and as always, this story is dedicated to my dear husband, Fred. I also once more want to thank all the other authors in this enjoyable series, as well as Carly Silver, our wonderful editor for the Colton books.

Chapter 1

Now what do I do? thought Madison Colton. He just went inside—I'll stay out here. She stood on the sidewalk in the downtown shopping district of Kendall, Michigan, ignoring the small but flowing crowd around her—not far from where she had been this time last week.

But for a very different reason.

At the moment, she watched the door to a coffee shop, waiting for that man to come out. The person she had come to Kendall to see. And observe closely. Just in case her imagination had a sliver of reality to it.

She had been lucky. She'd seen him already today, not long after her arrival, near where she had seen him before. That was on the next block, across the street, and he had come out of the bookstore there.

She had followed him. Unobtrusively, of course. His goal appeared to have been a chain drugstore a few blocks away. He was only inside for a few minutes and came out holding a bag, then headed back in this direction. He'd stopped in a couple of other shops on the way, and she'd waited for him each time.

At least she wasn't attempting to find a wedding gown here in Kendall right now. That was why she had come last week.

Now, he was in this café. The idea of caffeine sounded good to Madison, but she didn't want to mess things up by getting too close. Not yet.

She wanted to watch him awhile before...what? Confronting him? Not likely. She couldn't exactly walk up to a stranger and challenge him just because he reminded her of her father who'd been dead for twenty-five years. But hopefully she would decide soon what to do.

She knew she appeared very different this week. Which might not be necessary—or it might be very necessary. A kindergarten teacher among a family of mostly law enforcement, she was the last person who'd be expected to be doing this. She certainly hadn't expected it herself.

Yet here she was. Not that she was likely to need to look different, but she felt comfortable in her kind-of disguise—large black sunglasses and a big sun hat, over her charcoal sweatshirt and black jeans, along with similarly dark-colored athletic shoes—not the kind of outfit she wore most days. Not as a teacher in her hometown of Grave Gulch, about a two-hour drive from here. But today was Saturday—and last Saturday was when she had been here before, to visit the bridal shop on the other side of the street and about a block down.

Then, she had been dressed up, wearing a lacy blouse

and flowing skirt, because it had felt appropriate for her goal here.

That had been Madison's intention when she had made her appointment there. Before seeing that picture of the dress in *Lake Country Brides* magazine, she had begun wondering if failure to find the right dress had meant something. Something she hadn't wanted to think about. But this dress? She had fallen for it immediately. To prepare for her upcoming wedding to dear Alec, a teacher at the same elementary school.

That had been then.

And now? Well… She'd been thinking about the gown and more. Hard. Especially after her serious conversation in the car on the way home with her cousin and dear friend Grace Colton. The conversation that had made her question… Never mind. The questions had already been there about Alec, though she hadn't wanted to think about them. And she also didn't want to think about them now.

But what had happened then, what—who—she'd thought she had seen, had caused her to skip the appointment, without explaining it to Grace, who'd assumed it was because Madison didn't really want to marry Alec—which, she'd realized, was actually true. Oh, as they'd walked along, Madison had made herself laugh as she mentioned to Grace that her imagination was in overdrive, that she thought she'd seen someone resembling her long-dead father, then went on to talk about what she was seeing in store windows or otherwise, not indicating she was fixating on that illusion in her mind. And the sudden pain it had caused.

She didn't want Grace to think she was delusional. Was she? Well, she hoped to find out. She hadn't bought the dress then, and that wasn't the reason she was here now. But now she'd returned in this probably unnecessary disguise.

Around her, people continued to walk by, so she backed up toward the curb to get out of the way. To her left were two parents with kids at their sides, and the younger child, a little girl, appeared kindergarten age. She pulled at her mom's arm for attention, and her mother laughed and shook her head. Madison figured she knew what it would be like to teach that insistent child.

Madison always suspected that she'd chosen to teach young kids as a result of wishing her own family had been different when she was younger—like, that it had included her father.

When she looked away, a young couple slowed in front of her as they held hands and stared into each other's eyes. "We're almost there," said the girl, a pretty blonde with flowing hair. "You can't come inside with me, you know. It's bad luck. But I'll see you later. For now—let's hurry to the shop so I won't be late."

"Of course," said the guy, smiling at her, twentyish, somewhat handsome, with short but shaggy facial hair.

Madison couldn't help smiling herself. Wryly. She suspected this couple was heading for that bridal boutique, and she wished them well. But her own regrets started pouring through her once more as she stared at the door of the coffee shop.

Ever since last Saturday, she had been thinking a lot about why she'd not chased down the man, chastising herself about it while refusing to ignore the highly unlikely possibility of what she'd thought she'd seen. *Who* she'd thought she'd seen.

Was it possible? No way. And yet…she had to be certain.

She'd had to find the person who had triggered this absurd obsession, see him again, so she could wipe it permanently out of her mind. Not that thoughts of her growing up without a father around would ever completely stop eating her alive inside.

But even though she had spotted that man again here in Kendall, she'd put off doing what she needed to: talking to him.

Maybe this was all wrong. She considered pulling her phone from her purse and looking at the picture she'd taken last week—very surreptitiously. She had pretended to talk to someone on her phone but had instead snapped a photo.

One she had looked at often since then. Studied. Analyzed.

And still not been certain.

Well, how could she be, without talking to that man? Asking him questions?

Today, that changed.

But so far…well, she had to continue her observation first. It all seemed so potentially surreal…

Even though she had come all this way, and she'd actually seen that person again, she'd told herself more than once to forget it. Forget who she thought he looked like. Forget her absurd impulse to check it out like this, in disguise, and just go home.

After all, just standing here, ignoring people's glances, watching that door… It now felt weird. She was thinking way too much. She needed to take hold of herself, her emotions, go home and get back to her normal life.

What she'd imagined had to be impossible. Just a result of her own ridiculous thoughts.

Her father was dead, after all. He had been for years.

The man she'd followed could not possibly have been him. His resemblance to her brother was totally a figment of her imagination—despite that photo she'd taken, and studied…and not dared to show to her mother.

But… Well, for now, she'd wait till she saw him leave the coffee shop and follow him one more time—even knowing this was all a farce, a way she'd allowed herself to avoid the real issue in her life.

Her urge to end her engagement to Alec.

Thanks, Grace, she thought, recalling their conversation last week. She found herself twisting the engagement ring on her finger now and made herself stop. Again. Her stomach churned the way it did when she'd talked with Grace—and her cousin reminded her that happened a lot when she tried to visit bridal salons. But while Grace had focused on her assumption about getting cold feet, the question Madison attempted not to deal with was *Did she really want to get married?*

Okay, maybe she wasn't madly in love with Alec. But there was no one else, she was getting older, and he checked the boxes for a perfectly nice life with a husband and children.

And yet…

The chill air penetrated her thoughts, and she tucked her hands into her pockets. There wasn't a lot of traffic, yet she smelled a bit of car exhaust.

Near her, a couple of young boys dashed away from their parents, yelling and pushing each other. Madison reeled in her urge to catch up and gently scold them. She wasn't in her classroom now.

Instead, she turned slightly and watched as the minimal traffic passed both directions. Main Street, of course.

But this was getting ridiculous. He might stay in

there all day. People kept sending her curious glances, and no wonder.

Maybe that was the place to start chatting with him, after all.

But when she tried to rev herself up to go into the coffee shop, its door opened. There he was! He had a medium-sized cup of coffee in one hand and the bag he had gotten before in the other.

She maneuvered in the small crowd and began following him again. Fortunately, he walked at a relatively slow pace, and she did the same, trailing him only slightly, on his right side.

He wore a red plaid woolen shirt over jeans. His outfit last week had been somewhat similar, loose and casual.

But it wasn't his clothes that had drawn Madison's attention. It had been his height, his somewhat familiarly muscular build. And, mostly, his face.

She wished she could just stop him, stare at that face, assess it thoroughly. It still appeared as she'd thought last week: intense eyes beneath shaggy black brows. Blue? Yes. She could tell from the picture she'd taken, though she wasn't close enough to see those eyes now. But he did have a high forehead. Dark lashes. Lips that were rather narrow. Pale skin. A somewhat-pointed chin. Ears that hugged his head. His hair was rather light but she saw dark roots in her photo, as if it had been dyed. And…

Okay. Analyzing all his features wouldn't do her any more good today than it had before. The thing that was important was that this guy looked like her brother, Bryce Colton. A lot like him—if Bryce was maybe twenty-five years older. There were some lines and wrinkles in his face.

But heck! To her, he appeared like her brother's doppelgänger despite the difference in age and hair and eye colors.

Was she imagining it? That was what she had come back here to find out. And now, here he was again, not far from her.

What was she going to do about it?

She had an urge to sidle up to him. To talk to him. To ask him a slew of questions.

But not here. Not at this moment.

Next store he went into, though, she'd do it. She hoped he would return to the bookstore. That block, at least, was around the store where she had first seen him today. Did he work there?

She decided to let him get a little ahead and follow him. See if the bookstore was his goal this time. If not— well, wherever he went into, she'd go talk to him there.

She just hoped he didn't get into a car and drive away. No, despite her procrastination out of fear, or whatever, she wanted to talk to him. Needed to talk to him.

And why did she care?

Because he looked so much like Bryce, even with the different hair and eyes…perhaps most importantly, he also looked like the pictures of her long-dead father, Richard Foster, that their mother had kept all these years.

Of course. Richard Foster, who'd had no similarly aged brothers or cousins who might resemble him, had been the love of her mother's life, even though the childhood sweethearts had never married. He'd been a soldier then and frequently shipped out. But he had spent time with Madison's mother when he was home on leave, and he had managed to father Verity's three children: Madison, Bryce and their sister, Jillian.

Their parents had planned to marry when he finally was sent home...but that never happened. He had been killed in action. Their mother had always teared up telling that story, and no wonder. Her description of their dad indicated he had been a wonderful, caring, good-looking man who was eager for his last tour of duty to finally end.

But he had never come home. He had died overseas. *Allegedly.* Was it possible this man actually *was* their father?

He couldn't be. She knew that. Official notice of his death had been provided by the military, and his remains had been sent home to his parents. And yet...

On a lit pedestrian signal, the man crossed Maple Street, at the intersection, to the next block of shops directly across from the bridal boutique. Madison went that way, too. He then appeared to prepare to cross Main Street at the same intersection, but instead, he pivoted and headed into the nearest outlet, a liquor store. Madison went in, too, following him.

What kind of alcohol did he like, this man who so looked like Bryce? Madison knew that Bryce was a beer fancier. And it seemed highly appropriate that this man also headed to the area where crates of beer bottles were stacked.

But he didn't buy any. Maybe he'd changed his mind, or who knew why he'd come in here? But he had a short call on his cell phone. Then, after talking briefly to a clerk who'd asked to help him, he was soon back out on the sidewalk.

With Madison behind him. Without trying to talk to him. Yet.

Where was he going? Should she stop him, after all?

But she hoped that watching where he went would help her find him again in the future. That took precedence.

He headed into the small pharmacy next door. Madison did, too, watching him out of the corner of her eye as she fiddled with her purse so anyone watching might think she was looking for a prescription or a list of things to buy.

He didn't stay in there long, either. In fact, his arm nearly brushed hers as he left. He didn't seem to notice her, which was a good thing. But she certainly noticed him.

There were still quite a few people on the sidewalk when they returned outside, but the guy eased himself into the crowd so Madison had to as well. Then, after glancing toward another store, he turned and headed toward the street, but not the signals at the intersection.

There weren't any cars going by just then. Instead of returning to the corner and waiting, the man started jaywalking, right in the middle of the block, as if heading toward the bridal boutique.

Madison realized she might appear too obvious if she followed him that way. But she felt she had no choice. Not if she wanted to be certain of knowing where he went. She wasn't sure what she'd say if the man asked why she'd followed—but she did so anyway, taking a step down at the curb and walking across the smooth paved street.

He walked briskly, and so did she. A light changed, and cars began moving in their direction, worrying Madison, but she fortunately reached the next curb and stepped up, breathing a sigh of relief as she looked around and saw the man continue in the direction of the boutique. She prepared to follow again.

And then—

"Ow!" she exclaimed and pivoted to look at whoever had grabbed her arm.

"You're under arrest," a voice growled at her. She turned to see a man flashing a US Marshals badge.

She stared at it for a moment to memorize his name on the ribbon it was attached to: Marshal Oren Margulies. Then she looked up at him. He was tall, wearing a gray sports coat over slacks. Dark, windblown hair matched his facial hair that formed a mustache and slight beard. He glared at her with deep blue eyes, his lips puckered in apparent anger.

Glaring at her? Angry with her? Why the hell did this guy feel anything at all toward her—and why was he trying to arrest her?

This was one of the few times in her life that she greatly regretted not having any of her law-enforcement family nearby.

"Why are you arresting me?" she demanded in a hiss. "What's the charge?"

"Jaywalking," he responded curtly. He handcuffed her, her arms in front. *Handcuffs?* Then, his hand on one arm, he led her back down the street toward the intersection.

She wanted to scream, but she was in such shock she couldn't even speak as they passed the few shoppers on this part of the sidewalk. Parked at the end was a navy SUV with the US Marshals logo on it.

That made Madison feel slightly better. He apparently wasn't just kidnapping her off the street. Right? But still—what was happening? And the man who resembled Richard Foster had now disappeared. Could she ever find him again?

As the marshal opened a back door and manipulated

her inside, cuffing her to a seatbelt buckle, she got her voice back.

"Why the hell would a marshal arrest an American citizen for jaywalking?" she demanded, knowing she sounded as furious as she felt.

How could she make this marshal let her go? And how would she locate the man she'd been following once she was free?

Okay, so this woman was clearly angry. Oren understood why. He'd caught and arrested her, though not exactly for what he'd told her.

But he wanted some answers himself.

Outside the back of the SUV now, he whipped around and stared back inside the open door, watching her squirm on the seat with her cuffed hands to one side. He'd noticed as he cuffed her that she wore a ring on her left hand.

"Why were you following that man for the last couple hours?" he demanded. "Were you stalking him?"

"What?" Her voice squeaked. Odd, but Oren found her surprisingly attractive, even with that strange outfit she wore, complete with large dark sunglasses beneath an oversize hat. But her face beneath it was smooth and pretty, what he could see of it. He wondered what color her eyes were. And her hair… Some waves of red spilled out from her hat. "I…uh, I was… How would you even know I was around here for a couple of hours?"

"The man you were following told me. He works near here, saw you walking around for a while, then said you definitely started following him. A woman in disguise. Right? *Were* you following him?"

"I…I was doing some shopping, and…I was looking—"

"You were looking. For hours? That's what I was told. When I got his call, I had to drop everything to investigate. So I was looking, too. And saw you, watched you for a while."

"But…why?" Her head shook, as if she was puzzled.

He was getting nowhere. Enough of this. He had to do his job: protect Wes Windham at all costs. Oren needed more information. He stepped back into the SUV and grabbed her compact black purse.

"What are you doing?" she demanded. "Give me back my property."

"After I check your ID," Oren said. He'd have to call the information in to headquarters, to have them run her name.

"It's none of your business who I am," she spat. "This is all a farce. Let me go now."

But he removed her wallet and looked at her driver's license. Her name was Madison Colton.

Colton? "Why is the name Colton familiar?" Oren said softly, thinking aloud.

Colton. He definitely needed more information, both about her and about what she had been up to.

Oh. Right. Colton. Dread settled in the pit of Oren's stomach as he recalled how he knew the name. The witness he was protecting had had some connection to the large Colton family. And the fact this woman was one of them—well, it could mean danger to his subject, if this meant he'd actually been found. Others could wind up at risk, too.

In any case, this was the kind of situation he'd become a marshal to deal with: witness protection in any kind of circumstance, no matter how unusual, no matter how odd.

Sure, he'd handled plenty of other situations since

he became a marshal, although none with a potential suspect as beautiful—and apparently determined—as this one. Most had been closer to his headquarters in Grand Rapids. Coming to Kendall like this? Well, he would go wherever he was needed. But would this set of circumstances have a happy ending—with the man under his protection remaining safe?

That would depend on why this woman was following him and what Oren could do about it.

This gorgeous, clearly opinionated woman.

Well, Oren might even enjoy himself as he questioned her further. But one way or another, he would continue to do his job, and do it well.

And keep his witness safe.

Chapter 2

This was unbelievable. Madison just sat there, itching to somehow ditch these handcuffs. Itching to run away. Under arrest for jaywalking? By a US Marshal? Why here? Could the Kendall Police Department help her?

Maybe she should call Bryce. He was an FBI agent, after all.

This marshal apparently recognized the name Colton. That, at least, wasn't a big surprise, since most of the family was in law enforcement.

But could there be any other reason the Colton name was familiar to him?

She could ask, but—

Well, maybe she was thinking too much, even now, and probably not clearly enough. Talking about this situation might be a lot better, more productive. Apparently, jaywalking or not, her arrest was somehow involved with her following that man who'd called the

US Marshals Service for help. Maybe she could just give this marshal an explanation—modified or not—as to why she might have appeared to be following him. But how would she phrase what seemed to be impossible?

The whole thing made no sense. Jaywalking? Not stalking? Sure, this marshal might have assumed she was following that man, since that was what he asked, so why arrest her instead on a different charge?

She'd figure out what to say as she spoke.

She tried to fake a smile toward the marshal who remained outside, regarding her from just beyond the SUV's open door. Her purse was now on the floor. He'd put her wallet on top; possibly he could grab it again, or so it appeared. In case she tried to run away? Or to keep her identification close to him?

"The thing is…" she said. "Well, what I was doing might have looked a little strange, wandering these streets for a while like I did. I live in Grave Gulch. I'm sure you saw that on my license. I came here last Saturday because I wanted to go into the bridal boutique—" she pointed to the shop near where the car was parked "—because…because there was a dress there I wanted to try on. I'm engaged, you see."

She watched his face. It was a good-looking face crowned by wavy dark hair, enhanced by trimmed facial hair, but she shouldn't notice such things. He probably didn't give a damn, but… Well, there actually was a change in his expression. It had been somewhat neutral as she'd complained and yelled at him and all, but now he looked…a little angry.

Because she was engaged? Because she was talking?

Still, she continued. "The thing is, I'm kind of second-guessing getting married, thinking about what it would be like to spend the rest of my life with my…

fiancé. We're both educators. I teach kindergarten. We see each other a lot at school, but I'm still deciding if more is a good idea."

She elaborated because she'd seen another change in this Oren's expression. But why was she blathering that way about her engagement? She needed to approach her explanation about why she was following that man another way.

"So you're around kids all the time," he cut in.

"That's right." Did he have any kids? Was he married? She couldn't see his hands from here, but she hadn't noticed a wedding ring—which didn't necessarily mean anything, anyway.

Why had he asked about kids? He was off on a tangent like she was. But did she give a damn?

"Interesting," he said, not sounding particularly interested at all. "But I'd rather hear about why you were following that man."

"Maybe," she said. "But…okay. It's ridiculous, I know, but let me tell you why I came back here this week." She inhaled but kept on talking. "I'm not a cop or otherwise in law enforcement. Even so, I tend to be observant. Kindergarten teachers have to be, after all, to keep an eye on the kids. So last week when I was here and outside that bridal shop—well, as I said, it's ridiculous—but I happened to see a man who looks like my younger brother, Bryce."

She was telling the truth, although she knew it probably sounded absurd.

But, looking down at her cuffed wrists, she continued, "The thing is, the man I saw looked like Bryce thirty years or so older, or how I'd imagine he'll look. Also like some photos our mother has of our father, but also thirty years or so older than those pictures. He was killed overseas in combat years ago. And, well, it's impossible of course, but I wanted to try to find that man again. Look at him. And, if my opinion didn't change, talk to him, so I could get over this idea and get on with my life and not think about it again." Maybe. Unless she wasn't delusional, after all. "I saw him go into the bookstore then, and he went into it earlier today, too. Maybe he reads a lot. But—well, after all this time, no matter what or who I saw, Richard Foster can't possibly be alive."

Madison suddenly stopped talking as she saw Marshal Margulies's expression shift. He'd looked annoyed and dubious before but to—well, she didn't exactly know what it was now, as soon as she had said her father's name.

She couldn't help it. "Okay," she said, "what's going on? Do you know that name?"

He didn't reply. Upset, she forced herself to stand as much as possible in the rear seat of this SUV. Enough of this. She had an urge to jump down, slam herself into this Oren and run away.

To get out of this terrible situation.

Right. With handcuffs on.

But she needed answers, this marshal's cooperation, his release of her. Something. She was scared of this man having control over her the way he did.

Still nothing. Although, instead of looking straight at his good-looking face that irritated her, she found herself glancing over his shoulder. Toward the boutique and the used bookstore beyond.

And there was that man again. Amazing! Or not. He exited the bookstore with a bag in his hand and handed it to one of the people on the sidewalk. Then he ducked back inside.

"He's right there," she breathed. "Beyond part of the crowd on the sidewalk and going in and out of the bookstore—again. He's the man who called you? Please tell me why, what you know about him. And please, let me go talk to him!"

Okay, what now? Oren didn't turn to look in the direction Madison faced. He knew where she meant. And she might well have seen the current subject of his witness-protection services.

Wes Windham. The man had been Richard Foster, before.

Oren needed to stop this all, right now, before it became any more complicated. Any more dangerous to Wes—or himself.

And so, he would appeal to her better judgment—and offer her a deal. If she promised to leave right away, not mention any of this to anyone, he would let her go.

He closed the back door of his SUV, then went around to the other side and got in. He gestured for her to settle back into her seat, and he sat beside her. She immediately leaned toward him, eyes wide, brows raised as if she was filled with hope about what he'd say.

She even thrust her handcuffed hands slightly toward him, resting them on her knees, as if reminding him what she wanted: to be released.

Well, it wouldn't—couldn't—be that easy.

"Look, Ms. Colton," he finally said.

"Madison," she corrected with an eager smile, as if trying to become his friend and thereby get him to do as she'd asked.

"Madison…" he echoed, a lot more gruffly. He considered telling her to call him Oren—but Marshal would be more appropriate, if she called him anything at all.

"You're right that there's more going on here than you breaking the law against jaywalking."

The happy, expectant expression on her face melted a bit into annoyance. "So tell me what's going on," she said.

"That's the thing. I can't—or at least probably not enough to satisfy your curiosity. But you should understand this if you talk at all to your relatives in law enforcement about what they do. If I describe all I know about that man, as you asked and, furthermore, let you go talk to him—well, I'd be risking not only his life but yours, too."

"But why? How?"

She wasn't giving up. And she was pushing him for answers he'd already hinted he couldn't provide her.

"Never mind. But it's true. Let's just keep you both as safe as we can, all right?" He didn't wait for her answer. "You need to get out of here, return to your home in Grave Gulch and forget you ever saw that man, no matter who he looks like—or doesn't. Otherwise, well… you're actually risking a lot of lives, not just your own and his. Got it? If you agree to head home right away and never speak about this, I'll uncuff you and let you go. Do we have a deal?"

He watched her lovely face for a few moments and wished he could read her mind. Her mouth pouted, her red eyebrows arched a bit more over her amazingly green eyes, and Oren wished for a moment that he could take her into his arms and try to convince her with a sexy but meaningless kiss.

Which he, of course, wouldn't do. He had to stay professional. Remote. And, hopefully, convincing.

And it had been a while since he'd kissed any woman.

He'd had a few relationships, sure, but they'd gotten nowhere, and he was glad to remain on his own.

Her shoulders finally slumped, and she looked down at her wrists. "Okay," she said. "I really wish I knew what was going on, but I know from my own family that when someone expresses concerns like that, other people need to listen. And so I'll listen to you. I won't talk about this, even to my family, since I understand what you mean. Please remove these cuffs, and I'll go to my car, which is about a block away. Then I'll drive home. I'll give you my contact information, though, so you can let me know if things ever change and you can give me more information about this. Okay?"

"Sure," Oren said, figuring he'd just tear up the paper. Or not. He'd never contact her again…no matter how tempting it might be. And he certainly wouldn't keep her informed about anything regarding the person he was protecting.

Could he trust her to do as she'd said—never speak about this and just drive home? Well, he couldn't keep her here forever, despite the fact he'd claimed to have arrested her. He certainly couldn't take her to his office.

No, he would let her go—and he'd keep an eye on her as long as he could. And assume she would talk, despite her promise, so he would have to deal with that possibility with his subject.

He first pulled the key from his pocket, then reached over and uncuffed her, temporarily feeling the warmth of her hands. He again had an inappropriate urge, this time just to hold those hands for a minute, allow himself to imagine what it would be like to spend more time with this beautiful—but difficult—woman, touching her more, in even less appropriate ways…and her touching him back, with no cuffs on.

He shrugged off that idea as he unfastened the manacles, and she reached into her purse, wrote down her information and handed it to him.

"Thanks," she said and stood in a crouch in the back of the SUV. After thrusting the card into his side pocket, Owen exited his car, then went around, opened the door on her side and held out his hand to help her out.

"Now, where is your car?" he asked.

"Just around the block there." She pointed in the opposite direction from the bookstore, and Oren glanced that way, wondering what vehicle this beautiful teacher drove.

Bad decision. As he looked away, she started running along the sidewalk, ducking between the pedestrians.

In the direction of the bookstore. Where else?

"Stop!" he shouted, running after her. He wasn't surprised when she didn't obey, though. He, too, jammed his way through the shoppers, many of whom had turned to watch Madison run. They wound up getting even more in his way, damn it.

He didn't want to charge into anyone and knock them over. That would slow him, maybe even stop him.

But how was he going to stop Madison, keep her from reaching that store?

Madison didn't even glance toward the bridal boutique as she dashed by as fast as she could in the crowd. The name over the door she targeted was Books of Kendall, and large picture windows showed filled bookshelves on both sides of the entry.

She knew she had done something really wrong. She had lied to a US Marshal. But how could she possibly stay away from the man in the bookshop before she could confirm he wasn't her father? How would she deal with that for the rest of her life? What would she tell her siblings?

So Madison didn't stop. She pushed the metal-framed glass door open and hurried inside, unsure where Oren was behind her. Probably close. She just hoped she saw the man right away in here.

Which she did. There didn't appear to be any shoppers in the store as Madison glanced down the nearby aisles. But just ahead, near a counter where there were a couple of cash registers, that man had stopped.

Madison stared at him. Oh, yes, he did look like her brother—amazingly so. Sure, their hair and eyes were different colors, but his blond looked partly dyed, and some parts of him indicated age, like the gray strands in his hair, as well as the wrinkles on his face. But everything else, even the somewhat-muscular build, the way he held himself, his hands that held a book—they also seemed really similar.

Before she said anything, though, she realized he was staring at her, too, his mouth agape as if…as if he, too, recognized her. That wouldn't be possible, even in the unlikely event the guy was her father. They hadn't seen each other in twenty-five years, and she'd just been a child then. Not to mention, Richard Foster had been presumed dead.

But hell, Madison had been told by so many people, and she recognized it herself. She really looked a lot like her mother, except that her hair was red, not blond.

He's staring at me because I look so much like my mother.

What should she do? What should she say? Should she leave?

She heard a noise behind her that didn't sound like

any crowd murmurs of customers that she'd anticipated in the shop. She turned.

Oren stood right inside. Yes, he had followed her. No big surprise.

But she had done what she'd promised *not* to—come here to see the man she had been looking for. She hadn't spoken with the look-alike. Not yet, at least. But Madison knew Oren wouldn't be at all pleased with her.

Why did she care? Because he was in law enforcement, like much of her family?

Because he was so good-looking?

Of course not. But what was he going to do? Right now, he just stood there, shaking his head. He then pivoted, turned the *Closed* sign around on the door and locked it. Her heart thumped. There was no turning back now.

Chapter 3

Oren attempted to hide his angry scowl. This wasn't at all the way he wanted things to be. Not only had Madison lied to him and slipped away when she had promised to drive off—for her own safety, even. But she'd run straight here and dashed into this used bookstore, where the subject of Oren's witness-protection assignment now worked—using his new identity, of course. But he was still in jeopardy, and this woman's actions might endanger others, too.

At least the moderate-sized shop, fairly organized with books and somewhat musty-smelling, had been empty when they'd entered, despite the abundance of shoppers on the street on this fall Saturday. He didn't even see the owner. Nor did he see other clerks, although there weren't many. But how would he get Madison out of here while keeping this witness safe?

Only… Well, unless he resorted to taking control as a

domineering marshal, which wasn't the worst thing but might not get the ultimate result he wanted, Oren had no choice at the moment except to watch. Right now, the man under Oren's protection, whose current identity was Wesley Windham, stood near the cash-register counter, fists clenched at his side, still staring at Madison—and more. Trembling, his eyes welling, Wes said, "You look… you look so familiar to me. Like someone I once knew. Only…only your hair is so beautiful and red, like— Are you…my daughter?"

And here was that potential consistency, Oren thought. Could it be true?

Madison appeared highly emotional, too, also with tears in her lovely green eyes. She leaned on a nearby glass-topped counter that had books shelved below, and she looked straight into Wes's face. "I think so," she whispered hoarsely. "If you're Richard Foster."

Wow! It was true—probably. He remembered more about the Colton name now. Richard Foster had left behind a girlfriend, Verity Colton, and three young kids.

The guy's smile appeared wistful, almost sad. "That hasn't been my name for twenty-five years."

"But why?" Madison burst out, taking a step toward him, then stopping herself—which was good, because Oren would have had to do it for her, otherwise. "Why didn't you…why didn't you come see us during all that time? Or at least contact us, visit when you weren't on duty in the military or whatever? We missed you—my mother, my brother and sister…me. We thought you were dead. Mom was told you'd been killed in combat."

And, after all that time, what was it about him that she had recognized? She'd mentioned that he resembled her brother, who was undoubtedly near her age. But what about this man looked similar?

This wasn't the time to ask, though. In fact, Oren stepped forward to try to stop the conversation. This man wasn't Richard anymore, not while he was in witness protection, and to bring back that identity could bring back a lot of danger.

But to Madison, this *was* Richard, and while all of them were together, Oren would have to get used to thinking of him that way, too, and not only as Wesley—which was how he knew him. He would have to continue to refer to him, to think of him, as Wesley when Madison wasn't involved.

"Look," Oren said. "No matter who you each think the other is, we need to stop this and separate right now. This is too dangerous. Let's leave, Madison." But she didn't move. She still watched that man.

"Believe me," Wes—no, *Richard*—said, looking at the floor and not toward Madison, "I would have been there if I could. But you see, I stayed away to protect all of you. Myself, too."

"What do you mean?" Madison's tone seemed chillier now, as if she didn't believe him. It would have sounded a bit odd to Oren, too, if he hadn't known at least some of the background. Richard's life had been threatened, and even after all these years he could remain in peril.

Richard looked back up at her. "Please, come over here." He pointed to a circle of chairs used for book clubs. Oren attended now and then to make sure the people there did not appear to present a threat to Richard who, as an employee, was frequently around during the late hours the store remained open for the meetings. Even though his office was in Grand Rapids, Oren visited here often to ensure Richard was doing okay.

In some ways, he hoped to engage in whatever conversation they were going to have. He found Madison amazingly lovely.

Right or wrong, Oren would continue to do all he could to protect his subject. It was his job. And right now, that protection could be even more vital, since Wes's true identity had become known.

Oren took a seat facing the door so he could look outside and make sure no one attempted to get in, although he could understand if people wanted to come and buy some books.

They'd have to wait until later, though.

Right now, he was interested in what Richard had to say, even though he knew at least some of it.

The other two sat down beside each other, to Oren's right. Richard clasped his hands together but looked straight into Madison's face.

"My dear little Madison," he said, his voice choking. "It was…it was horrible. All of it. You see… Well, it happened the night I last came back from overseas. I was on the way to see your mother and you kids just for the weekend, the way things always seemed to work out, but I never got there. I—I witnessed a murder right on the outskirts of Grave Gulch."

"What?" Madison exclaimed. "Who? What happened?"

Oren considered ending this conversation, but then, he'd known what would come out if father and daughter got to talking.

"I didn't know either of the men involved, but… Well, it was so strange. I had stopped to run into a fast-food place for some coffee before I headed to your mom's house. It was fairly late, but the restaurant was still open. I parked under a light near the end of the almost-empty lot, and there was an open area just beyond the curb. I heard some guys yelling at each other right there, so of course I had to look. They both held guns. I was freaked out and was about to get back into my car when one shot the other. I must have made a sound, because the shooter turned and looked straight at me." Richard's voice had risen even as it turned gravelly. "I'll never forget that face—and unfortunately, the guy must have realized that. And he stared right back, memorizing my face as well."

Madison grabbed her father's hand and held it to her face. "Did he shoot at you, too?"

"Yes, but he missed, and I managed to get back in my car and drive away—fast. And I zigzagged so he'd have a hard time following me. When I stopped, it was at a busy gas station across town. I parked and hid behind the building and called 9-1-1. And then...well, it all got even stranger."

Oren knew this part of the story, too, although he listened as Richard told his daughter. The killer had turned out to be a gunrunner the feds had been after for a while. After local authorities went to the place Richard described, found the body—the victim was dead—and chased down and arrested the shooter, the US Marshals then took Richard Foster into protective custody. They needed him to confirm the identity of the perpetrator.

"The thing is," Richard continued, "the feds came right away and took me into their custody, too, so I never did get a chance to go see your mom and all of you. It was for my protection, they said. Not contacting you at all was also for your protection. The feds then insisted that I testify against the shooter in a closed grand-jury hearing. His name, by the way, was Louis Amaltin."

"How awful!" Madison exclaimed. "And it wasn't

fair that you couldn't contact your family. We didn't have a father because of them."

"As it turned out, it was fair. Very fair. Safer for me, and safer for all of you."

Madison's head was shaking. "But how?"

"The good thing," Richard responded, "was that my testimony helped to get the gunrunner convicted. But that damn killer yelled right there in court that he'd find out my identity and kill my entire family and then rip the witness—*me*—to shreds. And of course…well, yes, he was in custody, sentenced to prison for the rest of his life, but what if he got out? Or had accomplices who were still free who would do as he asked?"

Richard stood then, pulling his eyes away from Madison. He began pacing in the center of the circle formed by the chairs. Madison joined him, taking his hand as he continued talking.

"I was scared, Madison. Very scared. I was young then and wanted to live. And absolutely to make sure your mom, you and your brother and sister—my kids— lived, too."

Oren maintained his seat and kept watching them and the window beyond them.

Yes, he'd been helping in Richard's protection for a while. He knew the basic story.

But even Oren had to admit to himself that Richard's description, and his apparent scared and sad state of mind, hacked at his emotions.

The upshot of it was that Wesley—Richard, then— had further attracted the feds. They agreed to provide him with additional protection in exchange for that testimony. For one thing, he'd gotten them to make a deal with the army to announce that he was presumed dead overseas. And then he went into witness protection.

"I did it to protect Verity—your mom. And you, and your brother and sister. I swear it, Madison."

"I understand…sort of," she whispered. "But… what's going on now?"

Madison realized she should be happy with herself, even thrilled, that despite how ridiculous, how impossible, it had seemed, she'd been right.

She had seen, and recognized, her father.

Still alive? In witness protection all this time?

Unable to contact the woman he had promised to marry all those years ago—and their children?

She wanted to grab him and hug him. And smack him.

She realized she was in shock. She had to calm down. Figure out a way to deal with this.

Figure out how she would connect with this man in the future.

Or not.

First things first, though. She moved around Richard—she could hardly think of him as *Dad*, at least not right now—and planted herself in front of him, stopping him from continuing to circle and forcing him to look at her.

She glanced then at Oren. Unsurprisingly, he was watching them, his piercing blue eyes seeming to dig inside her—and her father—as if he was attempting to listen to what was really on their minds.

The fact that this marshal was so good-looking, even sexy, was totally irrelevant. Especially since he had attempted to force her to leave without even meeting this man who apparently really was her father. By *arresting* her, of all things.

She looked away from Oren now and back toward

Richard. "Okay, then," she said as he stared down at her with a puzzled expression, but she refused to look away. She was the one who was surely the most confused, after all, not him. "As you can imagine," Madison said, "I'm worried for you—and for Mom and Bryce and Jillian. Are we all still in danger? Could that gunrunner still come after us—that Louis Amaltin? Is he still in prison?"

If they weren't just confronting each other here, Madison realized she would do what she nearly always did: research on her smartphone for information she was seeking. Looking up the name *Louis Amaltin* online, for example. She would do that later. But for now, she wanted to hear what her father told her.

Couldn't he have come out of witness protection long before, while Amaltin was in prison?

He didn't answer. Instead, he turned away from her and sat down on the chair farthest from them. What was going on? What was he thinking?

Madison suddenly—or not so suddenly—wanted to hear it all.

She approached him yet again and also sat down. She considered reaching for his thin hands, holding them, encouraging him to look at her once more and provide more answers. At least he faced her.

"Please. We really do need to know if we're in danger," she said, although if they were, wouldn't they have gotten at least a hint of it long before now?

He looked in her face at first, as she'd wished, and then down again at his hands. "You—we—should all be fine now," he said. "Maybe, although I still worry... The thing is, Amaltin was killed in prison five years after I testified against him. He had a life sentence."

Madison couldn't help gasping, pain—and sorrow—

rocketing through her. "You mean he died, what, twenty years ago? And you knew about it and still didn't contact Mom? Or even get out of witness protection?"

She glanced toward Oren. He was clearly providing some of that protection, or he wouldn't have told her to go home and stay away from Richard—her father. But Oren's bland expression didn't change, and he once more looked over her shoulder toward the display window and the door into this store.

Why? Was there still some danger they simply weren't telling her about? There had to be, somehow, or why would Oren be watching over him? Were they going to tell her?

Darn it. She wanted to go kick Oren in the shin or even someplace more sensitive, somehow get his attention. Sure, he looked sexy—a whole lot sexier than Madison ever found Alec, unfortunately—but he was annoyingly remote when she still needed answers.

"Look, Madison," her father finally said. "It's a bit complicated. Maybe…maybe I could have come out of protection a while back, even now—but it's been so long. I'm a different person now than who I was way back then. I'm no longer in the military and haven't been for ages. For a long time I stayed away, mostly for Verity's protection, since I wasn't sure what would happen. But I got so used to my new life, even as a bookseller here. And, well, rational or not, that murder scared me a lot. Changed me. I did a lot of checking into gunrunners like Amaltin, and arms dealers like that seldom work alone. Sure, he was dead, but he was bound to have some associates, and I figured there would still be animosity toward me for outing Amaltin and getting him sent to prison. More than animosity. And so—I just stayed away."

Madison's turn to look away, not stare Richard in the face. Protecting her, her mother and her siblings—or just himself?

Or maybe he just got used to having no responsibilities to anyone and just didn't want to come home to his family. Would he ever admit that? Unlikely.

She just felt sad now, and tired. And sorry she had even started this.

She just wanted to go home, to her house, and life, in Grave Gulch.

"I get it, Richard," she said sadly to the man who had fathered her all those years ago.

And who, no matter what his rationale, had wanted nothing to do with her and the rest of her family.

"Like I said," he responded, "I barely know the name Richard anymore."

"I get that, too," she said, then stood up again. She glanced at Oren, who was watching her. He was protecting Richard—or whoever—from her, maybe, as well as other people.

Well, they wouldn't have to worry about her any longer.

"It's been good to meet you," she lied, "but I think I'll just head home now."

And never see him again, most likely. It was better that way.

But he said, "Just so you know, the identity I adopted twenty-five years ago is Wesley Windham. That's the name I've answered to for ages. And...well, I'll be here if you ever want to talk more about the past, and if your brother and sister want to meet me."

Oren interrupted. "Forget that. Bad idea."

But Madison chose to ignore him. "And our mother? What if she wants to see you?"

Richard—no, *Wesley*—grimaced. "Sure," he said anyway. "It would be good to see her again."

Yeah, right.

But just in case, it wouldn't necessarily make sense to drag her mother here, or at least not until they had discussed all this. Or her brother and sister, either. "Let's exchange phone numbers so we can talk sometime before any of us come for a visit, okay?"

"No," Oren said. "You need to stay out of each other's lives."

But Richard said, "Good idea." He reached into his pocket as Madison reached into her purse, and they pulled out their cell phones. "What's yours?"

Madison told him, and he entered the digits into his phone. In moments, her phone rang, and she captured his number, adding his name as a contact: *Wesley.* That was all. Not *Richard Foster.*

Not *Dad.*

Then it was time for her to go. She considered just saying bye, waving over her shoulder and leaving quickly. But maybe she should buy a book here. Right. On what? What to do when your dead father reappears?

Or how often to get in touch with your dead father?

Or— Enough. She'd certainly tell Bryce and Jillian what had happened. Probably their mother, too.

Would Alec have any interest?

She certainly hadn't been thinking a lot about him today, and she doubted he'd care much about what she'd been going through.

Another reason that maybe she should end…

No reason to think about that now.

"Okay," she finally said, noting that Oren, too, was standing, although he hadn't approached them. He was frowning, though. "I'm on my way home now. Nice meeting you, Wesley." She could have bitten her tongue after that, but on the other hand, her words had come out with the sarcastic tone she'd intended.

He didn't seem to care. In fact, he came up to her again and took her hands in his. "I can't begin to tell you how glad I am to see you again, Madison. And yes, please, let's keep in touch."

"Like I said," Oren interrupted again, "stay out of each other's lives. Look, you can both use me to communicate with the other. That'll be safer."

Maybe so, but Madison felt certain her father would start calling her daily. *Sure.*

"Time to leave." She waved over her shoulder and headed to the front door.

She was glad that Oren accompanied her to the door. He'd apparently locked it before, and she didn't want to struggle with it.

As she anticipated, he pulled in front of her and turned the switch that unlocked it and turned the *Closed* sign back around. Before he opened it, though, he turned back to Wesley.

"Okay, I know you're going to do whatever you want. Well, I'll be back here soon. And you already have my number."

"Right," Madison's father said, and he waved at both of them.

Madison hurried through the door. There were a few people waiting outside for the store to open again, and they used the opportunity to pop in.

Madison maneuvered around them, heading down the sidewalk to where she had parked her car.

To her surprise, Oren stayed at her side.

"Look, Madison," he said to her, "I know this had to be difficult. I think we need to talk about the situation, including more about why Wesley remains in witness protection, at least sort of. And why I don't think you should stay in touch. And, well, here's what we'll do. I'll drive you home right now to Grave Gulch, in your car."

"Really?" As ridiculous as it sounded, Madison appreciated the idea. She didn't particularly want to be alone right now. She needed someone to talk to. And this man, as difficult as he'd come across, well, she really wanted to talk to him about what he knew. And what he didn't know. She assumed he wanted to accompany her to make sure she actually left town and ended up a distance from the man he was protecting. But—

"How will you get back here?" she asked, assuming he wouldn't want her to drive him back. "Isn't this where you live?"

"No," he said. "I sometimes work here, but my headquarters is in Grand Rapids."

Which made it sound even worse. "Then, how will you get back there?"

"I've been working with some trainees who need new assignments. I'll have one bring my car from here to Grave Gulch and another come pick that trainee up and take him back home. And don't argue with me about it. That's what's going to happen."

Madison had already learned that arguing with Oren didn't get her very far. And this time, she liked what he was proposing.

Still, she made herself sound irritated as she responded, "Well, okay then, I guess. You can drive me home, Marshal."

"Yes," he said. "I can, and I will."

Chapter 4

Madison's car was a small white sedan—appropriate for a kindergarten teacher, Oren thought. She'd parked it around the corner, in front of a small candy shop.

They didn't talk much as they walked there, although when they first passed the bridal shop Madison had mentioned, Oren's mind swam with questions. Who was she marrying? When? She apparently hadn't gone inside either last week or this week, so she hadn't found the dress she wanted there—not yet, at least. But maybe she was looking other places, too. Maybe she had already found her perfect dress elsewhere.

And why did the idea of this lovely but difficult woman getting married annoy the heck out of him?

"Here we are," Madison soon said and took a key fob from her purse. She aimed it toward the car and pushed a button. Oren heard the doors unlock.

He headed first to the passenger's side, where he

pulled the door open for her and stood there, his brief-case in his hand. He'd gotten it from his car before going toward Madison's vehicle.

Madison had headed toward the driver's side, per-haps by habit—or maybe to irritate him. He'd already told her he would be driving, after all.

Partly for her safety. Her mind was surely in turmoil after all that had occurred that afternoon. Not to men-tion that she might be in danger now, having met and talked with Wesley Windham.

And him? Well, he wanted to spend additional time with her. Just to learn more about the situation con-cerning her father, he assured himself. It wasn't appro-priate for him to feel attracted to her, even though he did. After today, it wouldn't matter. He might see her again, but infrequently. And hopefully not just the two of them together.

If they were together, he'd quiz her more about her family and her missing father. Not that she'd have much new to say about Wes. But she might be able to supply more background that could be useful to Oren and the US Marshals Service. Or not. They already had a lot of information about Wes and the situation that led to his being in protective custody, and Oren had reviewed the files in depth after taking this assignment over from an-other marshal who had recently retired. Some of those files were even on the computer that he had with him, though not all of them. As far as he'd been able to tell, not much had gone on with Wes recently. He'd been under their protection for a lot of years, after all.

And Wes had contacted him because he'd seen some-one following him—Madison. Were there any other people to be concerned about now? The threats were deemed minimal, but he still remained under their protection.

"Ready to get in?" Oren asked, still holding the passenger door for her.

"Oh, that's right," she said after standing a few moments staring at him. "This is something new," she said. "I don't think anyone else has ever driven my car since I got it, except mechanics when I've brought it in for some minor work."

"Well," Oren said, "in case you're worried, I'm not only a marshal, I'm also a damn good driver."

Madison laughed as she slid inside. "You'd better be."

His turn to laugh, although he grew serious again as he got into the driver's seat.

"Do you know where we're going?" Madison asked as he carefully pulled onto the street. There was some traffic around them, but not much. Kendall was fairly quiet, even on a Saturday.

So was Grave Gulch, a couple of hours away. Oren might live in Grand Rapids, but he had good reason to visit the small city of Grave Gulch as often as he could, thanks to family ties.

His parents also lived in Grand Rapids. He was close to his mom. His dad, too, very unlike Madison's situation. He could only imagine what she felt like now. But his sister lived in Grave Gulch, like Madison, and he hoped to see her soon.

He didn't need to focus on their destination as much now as on the woman in the car with him, who had already gone through some pretty emotional moments this day.

"Well, I do know how to get to Grave Gulch," he

replied to Madison. "You'll have to direct me to your place once we're there."

To her home, he assumed. Not to the school, since this was Saturday. But that would be that. Maybe they could share a meal at a nearby restaurant before he left, hopefully at his sister Olivia's deli, while he waited for his ride home…or not.

But if he was honest with himself, he realized that wasn't the only reason. Though she wouldn't be wrong to despise him for what he'd done—tried to keep her far from the man who'd actually turned out to be her father—Oren was coming to like Madison. Maybe too much.

But he admired her attitude. Her gumption in ignoring what she had promised him, a marshal, an officer of the law, to drive out of town fast when he'd first agreed to release her from his irregularly achieved custody. And she'd dealt with the fact he'd arrested her in the first place and ignored it afterward… Well, yeah. That was admirable, even if it was irritating and potentially dangerous.

Anyway, he was interested in seeing where she lived, would remember it, might even drive by it now and then to check on her well-being when he was in town, but that would be it.

After all, she was hardly likely to do anything to endanger Oren's charge, Wes—yes, he could still think of him as Wesley and not Richard after their last conversations with the guy—who just happened to be her father.

Her father. She was being so quiet now. Thinking about that? Overthinking?

"Hey," Oren said, partly to start a conversation, and partly because he really wanted her response to what he was going to ask. "I can imagine what a shock all of this has been for you. And—"

"No," she said. "I bet you can't imagine it. Not really."

"Then, tell me."

Maybe he couldn't completely relate to her situation, but he had worked with many people in WITSEC—witness protection—and had learned a lot about them and how they felt about missing their families if they were relocated or even had to fake their deaths. But he was coming to care about Madison and would be glad to hear more about what she was thinking. They had just stopped at a traffic light before getting onto the highway toward Grave Gulch. He turned briefly to look at her and was somewhat surprised she was looking at him.

"I'm not sure that's a good idea," she said. "I don't know anything about you or your family, but…well, okay. Here's some of it. I grew up a Colton, as I mentioned, which is a large family with lots of branches, in Grave Gulch and elsewhere. But we were a bit different from most of the rest. Colton is our mother's last name. Our father—Wesley, now—never married her, as I also mentioned, although I guess you could say they were engaged."

The light had changed. Oren drove forward. He noted that Madison grew quiet. Thinking about her own engagement? Oren really wanted to hear about that, but this wasn't the time to ask.

"So what happened?" He had some idea from their earlier discussion with Wes, but he still wanted to hear more from Madison's perspective.

"I was pretty young back then, though I was the oldest of the three of us kids. Twenty-five years ago, when our father supposedly died, I was only five years old.

Bryce was three, and Jillian was two. None of us really knew what was going on then, of course."

"Of course," Oren affirmed. "Not at that age. But—"

"But we learned more as we grew up. Our mom always talked so lovingly about our dad. From what we gathered, he had enlisted in the military but came home on leave as often as he could."

And they obviously didn't care about any embarrassment that might accrue to those kids as they grew up. Oren didn't get the impression that Madison was upset about her parents not being married, only that their dad had stayed away for so long.

That was definitely different from Oren's experiences growing up, with family around. His parents had been wonderful. Still were. They'd taught him and his fantastic sister all sorts of traditions that they sometimes still engaged in today.

Hearing about Madison's childhood only made him appreciate his own situation even more. And also caused him to vow he'd never abandon his kids if he ever had any of his own.

"So your mom was okay with it?" Oren asked to keep the conversation going. They had reached a four-lane road, still without many cars on it. It would take them most of the way to Grave Gulch. They seemed far from civilization out here, with tall elms, maples and other trees lining the highway, nearly leafless this late in the year.

"That's what she told us later. She said they always planned to marry but had decided to wait till our dad finally left the military, which she said he'd intended to do right around the time...the time she was notified that he'd been killed in action. She'd believed it, of course. So did his parents, apparently, who were sent what were supposedly his remains and had them buried. They stayed in touch with her for a short while, but they made it clear to my mom and her parents that they didn't believe in having kids out of wedlock. So the only grandparents we saw often as kids were my mother's folks—more Coltons."

He couldn't help wondering what it had been like for Madison, growing up in that family but not really part of her father's family, whoever they were. The Fosters, of course. But—

"Were your dad's family members in Grave Gulch?" Not that it mattered under those circumstances.

"No. They were in a nearby town. And when we were in our teens, we heard they died in a car accident, so my brother, sister and I wouldn't have gotten to know our grandparents on that side very well, anyway."

"What a shame!" Oren exclaimed. What a tough childhood, even if her Colton family did remain close. He was aware of some rather difficult situations relating to the Coltons in Grave Gulch during the last few months or so, though. For one thing, the former police chief had been a Colton but had resigned because of some things that had gone wrong in the department, and that hadn't been all.

But did her father know his family was gone? Wasn't that a good reason to get in touch with his kids? Oren knew he'd be tempted to break his protection to do so... but Richard Foster?

Apparently not.

Madison could understand Oren's interest in her family, even now. They got into the news a lot, partly because of tragic occurrences in Grave Gulch. Some of it related to apparent corruption in the police department beginning when her cousin Melissa had been police chief, and even more. And then there'd been things that happened in the past, when her father supposedly died—and instead wound up in witness protection. The somewhat sordid situation helped to explain some things in the life of the man Oren now protected. Nothing in the news, or what her mother had been told, explained why her father had stayed away after the convict who'd threatened him and his family had died. But Wesley had provided his own absurd story about that.

Definitely absurd. But she forced herself to tamp down any anger as it began to rise inside her. What good would it do?

Still… Would she be able to forgive him for avoiding them for so long?

Well, Madison didn't want to think about any of that right now. She was also done talking about it for the moment. Except…

"There's a lot I don't understand yet about my father and what happened to him and why he didn't contact us. And right now one of the things that make me curious about it is…you. Why are you marshals still protecting him after all these years?"

Madison didn't look at Oren's face as she asked the question, and that felt difficult. She found the marshal too worthy of her stares. She rarely saw such good-looking guys, not at the school where she worked, the neighborhood where she lived or elsewhere. His strikingly masculine features enhanced his dark facial hair… Oh, yeah.

And her fiancé? Well, he wasn't bad-looking, but he wasn't that good-looking, either. *Ordinary* was the word that came to her mind when she searched for one.

Still, he was a respected third-grade teacher with a

normal family. Maybe that was a reason she had been attracted to him. But that wasn't a good reason to stay with him, with nothing else.

And right now she didn't want to search for anything related to Alec.

She drew her gaze from Oren and watched the road ahead.

Sure, she had driven the opposite direction earlier, but she hadn't focused on the roadway except to the extent needed for safe driving.

Today, her mind had been focused on her motivation for making this trip: finding the man whose appearance had kick-started the chaos in her mind.

"Well," Oren said, "we're still protecting your dad for the same reasons we were when the marshals all those years ago recruited him to testify in the case against that gunrunner Amaltin, although there hasn't been much going on with Wesley or his long-ago case for most of those years. But once we take on an assignment, our service stays on it, or returns to it, anytime the situation requires it."

"And my learning my father is alive presented one of those situations?" Madison asked.

"Well, we knew who he was, of course, and the Marshals Service changed his identity for his protection. But the fact you suspected, and now know, that makes our focus on his case necessary again."

Madison felt her body tense up. "But you don't need to protect him from me. I might be angry with him, but I'd never hurt him."

She saw Oren glance toward her, then return his attention to the road. Didn't he believe that?

Fortunately, he apparently did. "I figured that. Now that I've met you and gotten to speak with you, I'll be able to tell my superiors that I don't think you present a danger to our subject, even though he let us know you were following him. But…your knowing about him and potentially accidentally referring to it could become a reason he could be located again. There's always a possibility you could unintentionally endanger him."

Ouch, Madison thought. Well, she'd be careful—but Oren continued before she could reassure him. "Apparently the people who worked on the matter long ago did buy into your dad's concerns that the gunrunner he outed and helped to send to prison had associates. Some of those associates might still be around even now. And though it's unlikely they even know your father is alive, or have an interest in going after him now, it never hurts to play things safe."

"Got it," Madison said, which wasn't exactly true. On the other hand, if she was in her father's position, she might feel relieved that help was always over her shoulder.

After all, someday she might need to be protected from something in her life coming to the attention of bad guys who wanted revenge… She almost laughed aloud at that ridiculous idea.

But it obviously wasn't ridiculous to her father. Or to the Marshals Service.

Okay, she really had been thinking too much about all this.

She liked this man, despite having just met him— and despite the fact he'd arrested her.

Though, it still seemed a bit strange that he was driving her home and she was enjoying it.

They would be alone together in this car for at least another hour and a half. She'd been doing most of the talking so far.

It was his turn.

"So," she said, "tell me a little about you. I gather you live in Grand Rapids."

"I do now, thanks to my job, and I really like that city. It's where I grew up."

He looked a few years older than Madison, so even if they had grown up in the same place, they wouldn't necessarily have met in school or somewhere else.

"Is your family still there?" Madison asked.

"Yes. My parents still work there, too. But my sister is now in Grave Gulch. And now I visit her as often as I can. We're Jewish, and Olivia opened Bubbe's Deli there. She named it in honor of our late grandmother."

"Really?" She'd passed Bubbe's Deli, she was sure, but she didn't think she'd ever eaten there.

But the idea of this great-looking guy Oren having a sister in her town, one who owned a restaurant… Madison wanted to know more.

"Where is the deli located?" she asked. "And what does your sister serve there?"

"It's downtown and called Bubbe's Deli because *bubbe* means *grandmother* in Yiddish, and our grandmother—who's no longer with us, unfortunately—introduced us to some wonderful Jewish classics. My sister Olivia now has a lot of them on her menu."

Oren was smiling broadly, clearly proud of his sister and grandmother and their heritage. Madison smiled back. She loved her family but hadn't learned anything that special, at least in terms of cooking, from them.

Family loyalty, though? Yes, she had learned about that while growing up, thanks to things that had occurred in other branches of the Coltons. There'd been an unsolved murder case way back that had caused a number of family members to go into law enforcement, partly to protect each other.

Then there was her father…

Madison glanced at a road sign ahead of them. They seemed to be making good progress toward Grave Gulch. Traffic wasn't too bad, and she figured all the cars traveled at the somewhat generous speed limit or better.

She realized that her time with this man would soon be over. That was a good thing. Wasn't it?

Somehow, she didn't think so. Despite how they had met and their interaction with her father—well, she liked Oren.

And once he dropped her off at her house and his ride arrived, they were unlikely to see each other again, or at least not much…unless he decided to show up each time Madison decided to visit her father.

If she ever did again.

Although, she figured she would at least go to Kendall with company, to introduce her brother and sister to Wes and to possibly observe their mother's reaction on seeing him again.

But for now, time to return to the conversation they'd been having.

"Okay," she said. "I've got a feeling a visit to Bubbe's Deli is in my future. Tell me more specifically some of the food your sister serves there."

"Well, it's kind of standard deli stuff, including knishes, matzo ball soup, corned beef and pastrami sandwiches on rye bread and more."

"Sounds good! Only, well, I've never had matzo ball soup. What is that?"

"Great stuff. Chicken broth and large matzo balls, which are dumplings mostly made out of matzo—

unleavened bread that's typically used at the Jewish holiday Passover. The texture and seasoning are excellent. One of my faves at my sister's restaurant."

"It really does sound good. I'll have to give it a try." She was serious, only it might feel odd to visit this marshal's family restaurant. Would she introduce herself to his sister? Probably not. Why should she?

But sampling the food there did have some appeal, and if she ever saw Oren again she could talk to him about that—and less about her father. Maybe.

"Good idea," Oren said. He didn't look at her now as he spoke but into the sideview mirror. "Maybe we can go there tonight."

Wow! She hadn't meant her discussion of the place and its food as a hint, but the idea of going there not just to check it out but with Oren along sounded great.

"Maybe so," she said, hoping it worked out.

But why did Oren keep looking into the mirror that way? Madison turned and saw some cars behind them, but everything seemed okay.

Didn't it?

Chapter 5

What the hell was going on? A black SUV seemed to keep approaching them, then falling back in their lane… and then speeding around those other cars and nearly catching up again. But not quite.

Oren probably hadn't noticed when it began. He was mostly keeping his eyes on the road in front of them, then glancing over toward Madison as much as seemed safe while they talked.

Maybe he was imagining things. Could be the driver was just trying to speed a bit, then changing his mind.

But each time he seemed to change his mind when he reached their car. There were other vehicles ahead of them, so the driver could have approached the ones in front, then fallen back. But that wasn't happening.

At age thirty-seven, Oren had been in law enforcement over a dozen years. He had learned a lot—and he could tell something here definitely wasn't right. Should he speed up to get far ahead of that driver? But this car, though it drove well, wasn't exactly built for speed. That was one reason he'd stayed in the right lane.

Should he slow down? No. That would make it too easy for that other driver to reach them, if that was what was going on. While that tactic would definitely suss out whether they were his target, they might get hit or forced off the road.

And even though he was armed, Oren wouldn't attempt to use his weapon with Madison in the car unless it became absolutely necessary.

"What's going on?" Madison demanded. "What's with your driving, Oren? Are we okay?"

"Yeah," he said, hoping that wasn't too much of a lie. "Just hang on."

As Oren pondered more how to handle this, he noticed an exit just ahead with a short road leading uphill to some service stations. Maybe that was what he should do: wait till the other car was near them, then veer suddenly onto that roadway, at an angle, and fast enough that the other car couldn't follow.

He realized then that Madison had stopped talking, too. He didn't want to attempt to voice his concern, but he did want to warn her that things were about to change.

"Need to get off this highway for a minute" was all he said as they approached the exit, going a little more than the speed limit. He hoped they appeared to be heading forward beyond it—but instead of passing the exit he yanked the steering wheel to the right, and the car headed up the exit ramp.

"What's going on?" Madison cried out again. Out of the corner of his eye, he could see her gripping her seat with both hands, but he didn't have time to tell her.

Though Oren had hoped otherwise, the other vehicle veered toward them rather than staying in its lane, then exited up the ramp, too. Oren heard the squeal of tires on pavement as drivers behind them stomped on their brakes.

What was *with* that guy? Why was he driving that way?

Despite the exit only having one designated lane, the other car, now speeding, pulled up beside them, then slammed sideways.

Oren felt the impact on his side, which pushed him the other way and dug his seatbelt into him, juddering his ribs.

"No!" Madison screamed.

Oren swore and kept his hands on the steering wheel as he regained balance. An accident? No way. He needed to take control of the whole situation.

Of the other driver.

Only, as Oren turned to look at the guy, he saw that the jerk, now right beside them, had a rifle pointed toward them. For an instant, Oren stared straight at him. He seemed young. Did he appear familiar? There was something about his eyes that did somehow, though Oren couldn't figure out who he was thinking of. Dark eyes. Intense. Furious. And, yes, familiar.

Hell, that didn't matter. So what if he'd met their would-be murderer before if they wound up dead?

As Oren quickly accelerated and jerked the steering wheel, the guy took a shot at them, the sound exploding. Thanks to Oren's maneuvering, though, he missed hitting Madison's sedan—or either of its occupants. But that wasn't enough. Oren had to respond, but his weapon was too small to be of much use, especially against a rifle and while they were moving. He ignored the panic that rose within him and yelled at Madison to stay down.

One good thing about that ramming was that it had partially turned Madison's car so it was sideways on the exit road; their pursuer was aimed up the hill. Oren couldn't quite see its license number, but the plate was Michigan blue and white, and had a *B* and a *7* on it.

Now, instead of stopping or veering to speed up the hill, Oren turned the steering wheel again so they were aimed back down the hill they had just come up.

That gave them some advantage over the other driver, who couldn't turn his fast enough.

Oren sped back down the road, going the wrong way. Fortunately, no other cars on the highway had followed them up this ramp. Oren accelerated as they reached the highway again and entered the road at the exit, turning so they were headed back into the flow of traffic.

Oren glanced at Madison to make sure she was all right and still hunkered down. Fortunately, she looked okay.

He looked in the side-view and rearview mirrors. He glimpsed the other car—maybe attempting to follow them but not successfully, far behind them, thank heavens.

Oren didn't know what that was all about. Something to do with Madison meeting her father? But why? He intended to find out. Without stopping or playing into that weapon-toting lunatic's hand. Which meant calling 9-1-1 was out of the question. If they stopped to talk to the local cops who responded, their attacker might find them more easily—even if Oren had armed authorities attempting to help him.

Still speeding, weaving his way around the cars that had wound up ahead of him, he called his office in

Grand Rapids. Deputy Marshal Jon Lettier answered. "What's up, Oren?" he asked. Nice guy, but this wasn't the time for pleasant conversation.

"Some bad stuff," Oren replied and briefly related what had happened, including a description of the car that had hit them and where they were. He also explained why he hadn't called 9-1-1. "But I'd like you to contact the state police to see if anyone reported seeing the supposed accident out here on the highway—any onlookers from other cars, or even our attacker reporting the damage to his vehicle. Have them send a patrol to check out the area, too, and hopefully find the other guy. Also, please call Wes Windham to make sure he's okay, in case this has something to do with him. There's something strange going on here."

"Got it," Jon said. "You okay?"

"Yeah, at least for now. I'm leaving this area, though, so give the authorities you talk with my number. I'll provide them with a description of the other car, but I wasn't able to make out a license number, just part of it."

"Okay, I'll let the state police know what happened. The Grave Gulch PD, too—that's where you're heading, isn't it? I'm sure they'll check into things but I'll tell them not to stop you. And you stay in touch with me. You hear?"

"I hear you," Oren acknowledged. Would he keep Jon informed about everything? Or the local authorities? Not likely, unless that driver was immediately found and apprehended.

He doubted that would happen. Things were happening too quickly. Were too strange.

And the fact he had been able to see the driver and perhaps recognize him? Or at least get an idea…

"Thanks," he said, finishing the conversation. "Talk to you soon." He pressed the button to hang up.

"Okay, Oren." Madison spoke demandingly from beside him. He could tell from her hoarse tone that she'd been crying. Maybe still was. "I didn't want to interrupt while you were talking to, well, whoever it was on the phone, but what happened? Do you know what that was about?"

Oren had an urge to put his arms around her and hug her to soothe her, but of course he didn't. "Not really, but—"

"I know it may be far-fetched, but could it be related to my dad, and the fact that I found him here, and... Well, I don't know."

"Neither do I," Oren said. "But it does seem ridiculously coincidental that this occurred on the day you just happened to trail and find Richard Foster." A thought struck him now about why the guy with the gun had possibly looked familiar. He would have to check whenever they had an opportunity to stop and he could use his laptop.

He surely didn't really resemble the pictures Oren had seen of Louis Amaltin. But what if Oren's impulse had been correct and the shooter had been a relative?

"Unless, of course," Madison continued, "you're being attacked as a marshal. Are you involved in some other dangerous case now? Could they have been after you?"

To soothe her a little, Oren responded, "Could be." But that was a lie. None of the other matters he was currently working on had struck him as particularly dangerous: tracking down assets seized by a federal criminal by illegal activity, working out a new identity for a woman about to go into witness protection...

Sure, there could be perilous aspects to both of those situations, but nothing had seemed especially stressful.

"Then, what are you doing? Shouldn't you stay involved in whatever cases you're working on and just leave me alone?"

He glanced over toward her. Her face appeared pale; she looked highly distressed.

"I'm doing exactly what I should be doing. I'm not going to leave you till I'm sure everything around you is okay."

Her shoulders appeared to relax a little. "Thank you," she said softly.

Fortunately, there were no surprises during the rest of the drive. Oh, Oren did see a fleet of three bright blue Michigan State Police cars, lights flashing, heading in the opposite direction across the highway: a good thing. They were probably the result of Jon's call. Maybe, if their attacker was still behind them, he'd exit more quickly, or at least act as a normal driver with the state police around—assuming his car hadn't been damaged enough to make it conspicuous.

Oren glanced often at the other vehicles around them and their drivers, but no one appeared to be checking him out, as some might if they'd seen the incident.

All seemed okay as they reached the outskirts of Grave Gulch.

"Are you going to take me right home?" Madison's voice sounded hoarse. Was she nervous about being left alone soon?

She should be, Oren thought. "Not yet," he said. "I need to make a stop first."

Which was true. He'd come up with an idea where to go for now to park and get into his briefcase and check out the file he was now itching to see. Fortunately, he knew Grave Gulch well enough to know where one of its main parking lots was located, near the shopping district in the center of downtown. The lot was three stories high and fairly long, and a lot of workers at the local businesses, as well as their customers, parked there.

Right now, Oren just needed a place to keep watch over his surroundings while he did what he needed to, and he grabbed the ticket from the machine as he entered, which made the automatic gate in front of him rise.

He would keep Madison with him in the car, of course, observing their environment closely.

"What are we doing here?" Madison asked. Her voice sounded stronger now, which Oren considered a good thing. But was she going to argue with him?

"I just need to look at something in my files without being out in the open where we can be seen easily. It won't take long."

"But—"

"When I'm done, I'll check again with my contacts, and if all seems all right we'll head for my sister's deli for dinner. Okay?"

"Maybe, but should I call one of my relatives in law enforcement to come here to help?"

Interesting possibility, Oren thought, but it might just make them more obvious. "Not at the moment," he said. "Maybe later. But we should be fine in this garage."

"I—I guess so," she said, sounding uncertain. "But how long is this going to take?"

"Not long," he promised. He backed into a space in an area that wasn't particularly crowded so he could watch the parked cars and the ones that passed by, as well as the people in or walking around them. He soon got out and examined the damage to the side of the car. Not pretty, but not too bad, either.

Madison joined him, touched it and sighed. "Fortunately, I have insurance," she said.

"Good. But please don't report it till we've had some opportunity to try to find the guy who did it."

"I'll wait for a little while, but not long." She got back in the car.

He opened the rear door on the driver's side so he could pull out his briefcase, sitting on the back seat since the steering wheel wouldn't give him as much space to use his laptop,

An idea had come to him about who their attacker resembled. Was it feasible? Heck, he'd seen something similar today as Madison recognized the man who was her father twenty-five years later. Maybe that had led to him coming up with this totally ludicrous idea.

But what if it was real?

Just in case, he was looking up the information he had on that gunrunner, Louis Amaltin, against whom Wes—Richard then—had testified. Oren hadn't known Foster twenty-five years ago, of course, but at least some of the files the Marshals Service kept were quite broad and intense, including photographs of all parties involved. And he had studied them in depth when he had taken over Wes's protection in Kendall.

He found what he was looking for. It amazed him—but it shouldn't have.

"Can't you tell me anything about what you're doing?" Madison was leaning through the gap between the front seats, staring at him. Her brows were knit over her green eyes, and she looked as worried now as she had several times earlier today.

Should he? Maybe. She should know at least part of

this, and he would have to find a way to keep her safe since, if he was right, this did involve her.

"Okay," he said. "How would you like to hear something really ironic?"

She seemed to stiffen, yet she managed a small smile. "More ironic than finding my father alive after all these years?"

"In a way, yes, since I'll need to dig in even harder to make sure he stays that way."

"What is it?" she demanded. She appeared so frightened again that Oren had an urge to return to the front of the car and take her into his arms, hold her protectively tight.

As if that would also take care of her father.

"Well, that gunrunner he testified against all those years ago—"

"Who's dead, right?"

"Right. He was a married man back then when he was captured and incarcerated. Louis Amaltin had a young son, who perhaps looks like him now. I don't know that for certain, of course, but the man who ran into us before and shot at us—"

"You're not going to say he looks like Amaltin before he died and could be his son, are you? And he somehow tracked my father down, despite his being in witness protection, learned I was his daughter and tried to hurt me? Boy, you're right. That would be ironic." She shook her head, and her red hair bobbed gently around her face. "Especially after all the recognition from the past that's already gone on today."

"Exactly. That is what I was going to say. But that's not all."

The slight amusement in her expression seemed to

melt back into fear, as maybe it should. "Tell me," she said.

Once again, he wished he was holding her tightly to him, in protection…and, ridiculously, because he was beginning to like this brave woman a lot.

"Well, consider some more irony. But it's also an explanation why that guy came after us, assuming I'm right and he's Amaltin's son."

"Please tell me," she urged again.

Oren did reach out, and Madison thrust her hands between the seats.

He took them into his own and said, "Would you believe that today is the twentieth anniversary of when Amaltin was killed in prison?"

Among other duties as a kindergarten teacher, Madison helped her students begin to read.

But she didn't attempt to teach them literary techniques at that age—like irony.

Yet, as she and Oren had talked, so much of what had gone on today struck her as the opposite of normal, everyday living. Discovering a dead father was alive. Apparently reminding that man enough of her mother decades ago that he recognized she was his daughter after all these years. And now this: the son of the person her father had helped to put in prison where he'd died, chose an anniversary of that death to find and try to kill the witness's daughter…

Weird. Yes, ironic. And it all made her worry about what would come next, since a lot of it involved deaths or assumed deaths. And the man who had wanted to kill her and apparently Oren, too, was still on the loose.

How had he found where she was? And why had he come after her and not her father?

Unless… "Oren, is my father okay?" she said, turning to him in the back seat.

"You're sharing my thoughts," he said. "I'm going to hang out with you, of course, but I've got a call to make before we head to dinner."

She didn't know who he spoke with a minute later, but she figured it was someone else from the marshals' office. He told whoever it was that he had already called the office and requested that someone be sent to Kendall to keep an eye on Wes Windham until his return. Now, he wanted to be sure that person was on the way— or, preferably, already there. "I'm in Grave Gulch," he continued, "and want to do more work here. I'll be out here at least until tomorrow, so I'd like whoever's now on the assignment to contact me… Right. Yes… What's that? Who… Call me back."

He hung up. Then stared straight ahead.

"Is something wrong?" Madison asked. "I mean more than we've already experienced, and—"

"I don't know." Oren's voice was sharp. "I think so, but… Well, something's going on, and they're apparently just learning about it in my office. They'll let me know more soon." He looked over at her. "So, are you ready for dinner?"

Chapter 6

So what was going on now? Oren worried about the hubbub at the office for the entire drive from the parking lot to Bubbe's Deli. Something was going on. Jon had made that clear before hanging up. Oren needed to learn more.

Oren also needed to learn more about Amaltin's possible son apparently having found Madison. How?

The deli was only a few blocks away. Oren liked the way downtown was set up, with long four-lane main streets of a mile or more organized in a grid. Lots of retail places one or two stories high, as well as taller buildings containing other kinds of businesses and even the Grave Gulch Police Department were located in the center of town.

He liked the town well enough to consider moving here to be nearer his sister—but this wasn't where his job was. Plus, their parents were in Grand Rapids.

It had been a couple of weeks since Oren had last visited, which was why he paid attention—a little—to what he was seeing of the town.

And he paid attention to his passenger. Despite what they'd gone through on this road trip, she now seemed more relaxed than she had since he'd met her. Pretty lady. Worth watching, especially when she didn't appear so stressed.

But too involved in things she only partly understood.

Mostly, though, as he drove his mind buzzed around the phone conversation he'd just had with Jon—a much more intriguing and potentially upsetting conversation than the others they'd recently had. Maybe it wouldn't seem so bad if it had been completed. But the part that had occurred had definitely stirred up Oren's mind. Still did. Especially because Jon had ended their conversation by saying a couple of other calls were coming in then that he had to deal with. Sounded like bad stuff, he'd added, and hinted it might involve Oren's assignment. But Jon didn't have enough information to fill Oren in yet. He'd promised to call as soon as he could. Oren certainly hoped so.

"I think I'm finally zeroing in on where the deli is," Madison said from beside him. Her tone sounded excited, happy—totally different from what Oren was feeling. "The thing is, I've seen it, maybe even noticed it, but it's close to some of my family's favorite restaurants that we've been frequenting for years. When I'm out for meals it's usually with other people I'm close to, and around here, where the food is generally good and I'm used to it, I rarely try to suggest something different."

What restaurant does your fiancé like best? was

the question that stomped through Oren's mind, but he didn't ask.

He didn't care.

Did he?

Certainly not now. There were too many other things on his mind that were more important.

"There!" Madison exclaimed, pointing through the windshield. "Right?"

"That's right," Oren said, and in fact they were only a few storefronts away from Olivia's place now. Which was fine.

But when was he going to get the rest of his phone call?

He came here frequently enough that he knew where to park despite the area along the curb being full: in the lot behind the deli. He drove around back and up the short driveway. A couple of empty spaces were marked *Staff*, and he pulled into one of them.

"Are you a staff member?" Madison asked.

"Close enough. My sister isn't going to disown me for parking here. She never has before. And we won't be here very long."

"Of course. Quick dinner. That's all." The somewhat-sad expression on Madison's face almost made Oren smile. Did she want to stay with him longer? He definitely wanted to see more of her. To protect her, that was all.

Or was he just trying to fool himself?

Whatever. He faced the steering wheel as he pushed the button to turn the engine off. "Okay," he said. "Let's go in." Although he usually told Olivia in advance when he was coming to town and visiting the deli, Oren hadn't today—not surprising, considering all that had happened.

They could have gone in through the back door from the parking lot, but Oren had an urge to give Madison the best view of the place, and that would mean entering from the door to the sidewalk at the front. There was a narrow walkway between the deli's building and the Italian restaurant next door, and that was the way he led Madison—him in front, just in case the dangerous sleazebag who'd come after them earlier that day was waiting for them. Highly unlikely for many reasons. If he was still around, how could he guess where they were heading? But Oren wasn't taking any chances that he could avoid.

The deli had a second floor, which Olivia used for her office. Oren wondered if one of the places Madison frequented with her family and friends was the Italian restaurant, but he didn't ask. He wanted to take her hand to lead her along the narrow walkway but decided that wouldn't be appropriate. The paving was flat, and she was unlikely to stumble, anyway. Plus, if she did, she could reach out to one of the buildings to steady herself.

The area was busy. It was nearing six o'clock, a popular dinner time, although the deli tended to be crowded for another hour, then would wind down as the evening wore on till it closed at nine o'clock. Oren had often stayed around late enough to check that out. Then he would sometimes stay overnight in Olivia's spare bedroom in her house nearby. The drive home to Grand Rapids took a couple of hours.

For now, he just stood at the window, looking into the front area where the electronic cash register sat on a counter to the left, along with a credit-card reader and some candy for sale in the glass case below.

Across from it was the takeout area where specialized deli food was prepared to go: warm slices of corned beef, roast beef and pastrami sold by the pound, rye bread, knishes, gefilte fish and more.

Or people could order full sandwiches and matzo ball soup to go. Delicious stuff, as far as Oren was concerned. He often took some with him when he returned to Grand Rapids. But he always enjoyed eating here, at one of the deli's many tables, and sometimes with Olivia sitting down to keep him company.

From out here, he couldn't show any of that to Madison. He led her inside. "Just so you know," he said, "this place has some great Jewish-style food, but it's not kosher. We appreciate our heritage, of course."

"I can't wait to try some," Madison said, which made Oren feel good. She certainly had the right attitude. He preceded her inside.

Olivia was there at the cash register. She trusted some staff members enough to handle customers' payments, but she seemed to enjoy handling that herself when she could—and getting the opportunity both to thank people who were leaving and to greet those who were coming in.

Olivia had big blue eyes and untamed black hair, complemented by her round earrings.

He gestured for Madison to join him at the counter so he could introduce them. He couldn't help noticing his sister's curious expression as she looked from him to Madison.

"Good evening," he said. "Madison, this is my sister, Olivia. She owns this special place, and you're about to get one heck of a good dinner."

"Hi, Olivia," Madison said, stepping up to the counter. She waved slightly as she smiled.

As Olivia smiled back, though more tentatively, Oren

said, "And Olivia, this is Madison. She's helping me on a case."

That was brief and ambivalent enough to get Olivia wondering, Oren knew, but it was all he felt comfortable saying right now about the situation.

"Nice to meet you, Madison," Olivia said, then turned again toward Oren. "Go ahead and take one of your favorite booths at the back," she said.

"Fine," he responded. "Hope you'll come sit down with us for a while."

"Maybe a little later," Olivia said. "And I hope you enjoy your meal." She was looking at Madison again, her expression still curious, but Oren put his arm around Madison's shoulders and gently led her down the restaurant's main aisle toward the conglomeration of tables and booths he liked best.

They were soon seated, and at Madison's request Oren made some suggestions about what to order. He wasn't surprised that she chose a bowl of matzo ball soup. They'd talked about it earlier, and he'd expressed how much he enjoyed the delicious taste of this delight that Madison had never eaten before.

He ordered some, too, but just a cup, which meant a smaller matzo ball, and a pastrami sandwich. Their server was Sally, a delightful woman who'd waited on Oren many times before, and she promised to bring them both some water right away.

As she left, Oren's phone rang. "Sorry," he said to Madison, pulling his phone from his pocket. Seeing Jon's name displayed, he knew he had to talk. He pressed the button to answer. "Hi, Jon," he said.

"You ready to hear some awful stuff?" the deputy asked him.

"Lay it on me," Oren growled.

* * *

Madison wished she knew what was going on.

Oh, she'd known Oren was expecting a phone call. He'd seemed frustrated before when his last conversation had ended abruptly and he had indicated it would continue sometime later. And he wasn't happy that it wasn't immediately.

Well, the time had apparently come.

He didn't look at her, just at the table. The waitress brought their water, and Oren grabbed his glass and took a swig as he listened. Madison figured he wished it was something stronger. Did they serve alcohol here, at the deli? Should she order him some?

"So where is she now?" Oren was asking. He scowled unreservedly—although the difficult expression did nothing to change how handsome the guy was. He glanced up at Madison briefly with angry blue eyes but looked away quickly, as if he didn't really want her to know his mood.

But Madison wanted to know what was being said on the other side of the conversation. She leaned forward on her pale red seat at the booth near the deli's back wall.

"At least she's still alive," Oren continued. "Right?"

The question shocked Madison. Who was *she*? What had happened to her? Or was Oren referring to Madison herself?

At least the answer must have been positive, since Oren said, "Fine. I'm not far from that hospital now. I'll head right there."

Hospital? That added to Madison's desire to learn more and made it clear he wasn't referring to her, although the reference to a hospital suggested *she* was still alive.

Whoever he spoke with must have responded negatively. "Okay. Glad you guys are already on it, of course, and I don't want to stress her out even more. But I want to hear everything that's learned from her as soon as possible. Got it?"

Apparently that person did get it, since the conversation soon ended, just as Sally placed their meals on the table in front of them. Good timing, Madison thought. Or not.

She wanted to hear everything that was on Oren's mind now.

But the guy was apparently not only a good federal marshal, he was a good actor, too. He put the phone down on the table beside him and looked up at the server, appearing pleased and relaxed. Or at least that was how Madison read him. "Thanks, Sally," he said. "It all looks delicious, as usual."

"I'll tell your sister you said so," said Sally. Her grin reflected amusement, and she looked fond of the guy she'd just served. It appeared genuine, not just because he was her boss's brother.

"Yeah, you do that," Oren said.

Sally winked, then walked away.

"She seems nice," Madison said, hoping to begin a conversation with Oren. "Now, tell me what was going on in that phone call."

"Yeah," he said. "I will. But not here and not now." He leaned across the table toward her. "I'm not just going to drive you home later," he said. "And I hope your sofa is comfortable."

"What!" The word came out a lot louder and sharper than Madison intended. But she also suspected what Oren now planned.

He wanted to stay the night with her, in her condo.

Good thing Alec didn't live with her. But there were a lot of reasons for that. What was going on?

Nothing positive. That was for certain.

Although the idea of being with this appealing but difficult man overnight somehow got Madison's juices flowing. Bad idea.

She wanted to reach across the table and strangle the marshal when he moved his gaze away from her and pulled his cup of soup closer to him on the laminated-wood tabletop.

Instead, she said, "What makes you think I'd welcome you at my place? Maybe your sister would let you stay with her. And—"

"Does your fiancé live with you?"

"No, but—"

"Okay, all the more reason for me to join you. And, if you want to hear what my conversation was about, you need to let me hang out with you at your place, at least for tonight. In fact, even if you don't want to hear, you're going to let me stay there. Things are going on, and you appear to be right in the middle of them. I need to—"

Before he could finish, his sister joined them. Olivia wore a short silvery dress that Madison admired. She approached Oren's side of the booth and gestured with her hands for him to move over.

He grinned at her and obeyed, leaving Madison disgruntled and wanting to shout at the man. Tell him to stop playing games with her.

Tell her now what was really happening.

But he'd already implied at least some of it. Was she in danger somehow? She certainly believed so, after they'd been rammed and shot at.

How else might she be in the middle of what was

going on, a subject of his earlier, clearly complicated conversation?

"Hey, bro," Olivia said, then turned her head. "And hey, Madison. Have you ever eaten here before? In any case, what do you think of our matzo ball soup? Have you eaten it other places? Do you make it at home?"

Madison had the impression that Oren's sister wasn't just asking about her opinion of the soup, here or elsewhere. She might have been attempting to get a little info on Madison's background.

Madison didn't want to get into it. Yes, she was a Colton, but maybe no one would recognize her, since she wasn't in law enforcement, and she certainly didn't want to bring up the connection.

Olivia's arrival at their table, and her questions, did manage to divert Madison's attention, at least a bit.

"This is my first time here," she said, smiling at Olivia. The Margulieses shared good family genes, Madison thought. "And I really don't frequent delis like this anywhere, although that might change after this meal. I might even try cooking my own, as you suggested. I'd heard good things about matzo ball soup before, but nothing I heard is anything like the real thing. It's wonderful!" Madison knew she was laying it on a bit thick. She didn't *need* to impress Olivia or try to make Oren's sister like her. But she had, in fact, tasted the soup and some small bites of matzo ball, and she'd really enjoyed it.

"So glad to hear that," Olivia said. Then she turned back toward Oren. "Good to see you," she said, "but I wasn't expecting you." Did Oren usually tell her when he wanted dinner at her deli? "Can you tell me what brought you here?"

"Nope," Oren replied, his voice a lot lighter than it

had been before when he was talking to Madison about the phone call with contents he'd refused to reveal.

"Then, tell me at least, is it good stuff—" Olivia shot a quick glance toward Madison "—or marshal stuff?"

"I'll let you guess," Oren said. Madison figured that answer told Olivia what she wanted to know. If it had been *good stuff*, surely Oren would have told her. And what kind of good stuff? Was she asking if Oren and Madison were on a date?

What did she feel about that? Madison couldn't help thinking about Alec. Maybe if she'd already broken off their engagement… Well, did she really want to go on a date with Oren? But they had other reasons, scary ones, to be together right now.

"Got it." Olivia then turned her head, scanning around them. The place was crowded. And people who'd been sitting at a booth near them were standing now, looking toward the front of the place—maybe ready to pay and leave.

She figured that was what Olivia thought, too. Oren's sister stood. "Got to leave you here now, but let me know if there's anything I can do for you, okay?" She looked first at Madison, but her gaze landed on her brother.

Was she inviting him to stay longer? Maybe even spend the night at her house? Or was Madison reading too much into her words?

"Sounds good," Oren said. "See you again in a bit."

Olivia slipped away, preceding her customers down the walkway toward the front of the restaurant.

"Hope you weren't just trying to say nice things to my sister," Oren said. "Do you really like the soup?" He'd finished his cup and had just taken a bite of his sandwich.

"Definitely." Madison spooned off another piece of matzo ball.

"Good," he said. "We should finish up as quickly as we can, though. It's getting late, and I want to go to your house soon."

"Sure," Madison said. The bit of matzo ball seemed to stick in her throat, and she swallowed hard.

She had the impression that Oren wanted to get her away from other people, to the privacy of her home, as fast as possible. Most likely because of that phone call.

Well, good. At this point, she wanted to get out of here, too. Go somewhere that Oren would be willing to talk to her.

Reveal all.

What was going on?

Chapter 7

The drive to Madison's place didn't take long—a good thing, Oren thought. She lived in the better part of town—not surprising since she was a Colton, despite not being a member of what he believed to be the most affluent branch of the family.

As she gave directions, she told him they wouldn't pass the grade school where she taught kindergarten, though it was nearby. It was in Grave Gulch West, the more affluent area of town, but she didn't think that made a difference in how well her kids learned.

Oren appreciated her position on that.

"Fortunately, most of my students have families that are thrilled when their kids do well in classes, even starting as young as kindergarten. And it's always a delight when I get a student struggling with learning issues who I can help to point in a better direction."

Oren liked the sound of that, too, and the sweet sound of Madison's enthusiastic voice.

He also liked that they were talking about something other than the phone conversation that hung between them like a ticking metronome holding explosives.

He nevertheless kept looking around for that car that had hit them before—and observing all others, too, in case the fiendish, dangerous driver had obtained another one. And if so, maybe even stolen it, judging by the kind of person he seemed to be.

Which Oren knew even more about after his most recent conversation with Jon—that he would soon be discussing with Madison. Like it or not. But he had to, for her safety. He'd notify the cops soon about what was going on—even sooner, if he saw anything worrisome.

"Make a right turn here," Madison said from beside him. They were already in a nice residential area. One side of the street held small but attractive homes. There were larger buildings on the other side that Oren assumed were apartments or perhaps condominiums.

He followed Madison's directions, and they soon pulled into a driveway on an adjacent street. Madison told him to continue till its end in a nearly full parking lot.

"I take it you live here," Oren said as he parked in the spot Madison indicated was hers. The structure was three stories high and appeared to be made out of an attractive shadow-gray limestone, with balconies for each unit.

"That's right. Second floor. It's got a view onto the street, and it's also easy to walk up the stairs, although there is a small elevator in the building that mostly the people on the third floor use."

And it was in fact easy, both to get into the building—

although fortunately, Madison did need to use a key so it wasn't open to the public—and to walk up the flight of wooden steps covered with black, designer stair treads to help prevent people from falling, Oren assumed. But he was disappointed to see no security cameras.

They soon reached the second floor and once more she used a key to open the door to the hallway. Good. There was at least some security here.

Just in case— "Do you own your unit?" Oren asked as he followed her. "And does anyone else like a manager have a key?"

"Yes, I own my unit. We all do. And no one has a key other than us and whoever we give one to. We do have a condo association that takes care of the essentials like landscaping, cleaning the common areas and all that. And in case you're asking about security, too, yes, we pay for a security company to patrol the area sometimes."

Oren had to laugh. "Was I that obvious?"

"What do you think?" Madison countered.

She had the last unit down the hall, on the left. Oren figured there were ten units on this floor, five on each side.

They were soon inside Madison's place, and she closed the door behind him. He wasn't at all surprised that it was well decorated, with attractive multicolor area rugs on the wooden floor and furniture in the living room in complementary colors of lavender, beige and deep pink.

"Nice," he said, as she led him into the kitchen. Also nice, with a tile floor and silvery appliances, as well as a square wooden table with four matching chairs.

Okay. Good. He was paying attention to other things besides what was on his mind. *Madison.*

Till just then, at least. "So, let's talk," Madison said after placing her purse on a stool near the stove. "Have a seat. Oh, and I gather that what you have to say isn't pretty, so would you like a beer?"

He looked into her sparkling green eyes. She seemed amused. Well, that was a good thing for now.

He doubted she'd feel the same way once they'd talked.

"That sounds good," he said, "if you'll join me."

"Of course." She pulled two bottles out of the stainless-steel refrigerator: a nice, dark amber beer from a popular high-end brewer. She also got a couple of beer steins from an upper cabinet near her sink and pulled a bottle opener from a drawer. She soon handed Oren a full glass, then waved toward the table. "Have a seat," she said. "And I'm going to take a swig first to get myself warmed up for what you're going to say."

Oren wanted to laugh, but he couldn't. "Good idea." He pulled a chair from the end of the table and sat down. She sat across from him, and they both drank a little beer. It was cold, and as tasty as Oren had anticipated.

"So tell me," Madison said.

Oren realized he had been delaying not only to protect her but to protect himself from relaying to her the current circumstances that were even more miserable than he had anticipated—even after their attack on the way here and his assumption about who the guy who'd come after them was.

No, after *her*. That guy had vengeance in mind, and Oren had to assume that Madison was his target.

But not his only one.

"Okay," Oren finally said. "Here's what I was told by someone else in my office. And it's pretty ugly. After discussion with some other law-enforcement agencies, including around here, they've learned that someone bribed a newly hired records clerk in my office to grab some files and give them to him. Turned out the clerk looked over those files herself, and after she told him a little about the contents, the guy said she should meet him here in Grave Gulch with them to get paid off."

"And does that guy happen to be the one who ran into us and aimed his rifle at us, the son of that gunrunner?"

Oren hadn't been attempting to hide anything from Madison, but he appreciated her intelligence in latching right on to what he hadn't yet said. "Yeah, his name is Darius Amaltin. His father's name was Louis."

"And the connection to us—whatever he was looking for in those files—did that happen to be my father?"

"Exactly. Darius hadn't been able to figure out before where Richard Foster was or how to find him. But those files had at least some of what he needed."

Madison took another swig of her beer but continued to look Oren straight in the eye. Those green eyes of hers could drive him to distraction if he let them. But he wouldn't.

"Our father had been safe before thanks to you and your witness protection," she said. "I appreciate that even more now. But why did Darius want the clerk to meet him here?"

"I gather she told him something, but not everything, about the Grave Gulch connection she saw in the files. He'd already hinted he didn't want to pick up or pay for the files in Grand Rapids or be anywhere near our Marshals Service offices, considering what he had in mind," Oren told her.

"So what did he have in mind?" Madison asked. "Nothing good, I'm sure."

"Absolutely not," Oren said. "You see, that foolish

clerk has been in the hospital here in town for a few days. Will be there a while longer before she's arrested for what she did, but at least she's recuperating."

"Recuperating?" Madison's voice was raspy.

"Yeah." Oren didn't particularly like his own angry tone, so he cooled it a bit as he continued. "Darius met her in a motel room in Grave Gulch to pay her off and get the files—or just to get the files. Once the clerk turned over what she'd brought, he shot her in the head—didn't pay her, of course—and fled with them."

"Shot her in the head?" Madison had paled, and her long fingers now cupped her face as if she otherwise couldn't hold up her own head. "And she survived? Thank heavens. But—"

"Yes, and though she's now still hospitalized, she's able to tell her story. Beyond what the clerk—her name is Nita—had told him to get him here, Darius learned enough in those files not to directly find the man in protective custody he was after but to become aware the man had had several kids here in Grave Gulch, and not just one—and he's been watching all of you, I gather, for at least a few days. He didn't mention any other relatives of yours, at least, like your mother. But your brother and sister are in this town, too, right?"

Madison nodded, and he saw tears in her eyes. She clearly feared not only for herself but also for her siblings. "Bryce and Jillian are both around here, at least now, so Darius can probably find them, too. Bryce is an FBI agent. And Jillian is a relatively new crime-scene investigator for the Grave Gulch PD. Our mother lives here as well. This is a good place for Darius to accomplish at least part of his horrible goal—hurting our father by doing something to us before…before killing him, I guess. Isn't that it? I'd imagine Darius didn't know where he was before. But why did he zero in on me? How would he have known…? By following me—well, I may have led him to our father." Her head fell forward, so she seemed to be staring at the table, and Oren had an urge to go over to her and give her a hug.

Bad idea, of course, so he sat still. "For one thing, a schoolteacher would probably be easier for him to get to than an FBI agent and a member of the local police force. Plus, you were apparently the first one to leave town. After Darius checked you all out and didn't see any of you hanging out with your father, and neither did he recognize anyone here in town as being Richard Foster, he must have decided to follow any of you who left town in case you were about to visit your dad—like when you went to Kendall, at least the second time. And who did you see there? The exact person Darius was after."

Madison drew in her breath. She was clearly crying, even as she took another long swig of beer. "Then, I did lead Darius to him." She seemed to choke on the words as she looked at Oren. "Is my dad still okay?"

"I'm sure he is, at least for now," he answered.

"That's good, at least. But I'm so sorry. If only I'd known… I'm glad in a way that he did come after me instead of my father, but why did he do that to me—and you, too, unfortunately?"

"My guess is that you're right," Oren said, "and he wanted to kill you or one of your siblings or your mother, or maybe even all of you, so your father would suffer pain like what he might have been feeling all this time since his own father was killed in prison. I'd imagine, now that Darius has disappeared again, that he is still after you, and maybe Bryce and Jillian, too, and possibly your mother. And assuming I'm right, after he's done with all of you, he'll go after your father. But I learned some good news on that front in my call. Your dad's been moved into a safe house in Kendall now." He couldn't help it. "Mind if I grab another beer? And would you like one, too?"

"It's fine if you take one. And yes, please, bring me one as well. And—well, how did your fellow marshals in your office learn all this?"

Oren stuck his head in the refrigerator and soon returned to the table with the two bottles that he'd already taken the caps off. He poured one first into Madison's nearly empty stein, then filled his own.

"Well, after the clerk, Nita, disappeared, the deputies checking into her situation discovered some files were gone. She didn't have any family in Grand Rapids, so there was no way of checking into her more that way. But they got in contact with me because the missing files involved a case I recently took over when the former marshal on the case retired."

"My father, in witness protection," Madison piped up immediately.

"Exactly. And I'd already noticed in those files, when I'd gone through them, that the twentieth anniversary of Louis Amaltin's death in prison was coming up. The idea of my having the case on such an important anniversary was sort of interesting to me, but I hardly thought that date meant anything. The gunrunner's death in prison. A shame, but so what? Only, what if the son wanted to get his hands on the witness who helped to convict his father—and his family—partly because of the anniversary?"

"What had Darius been doing all this time—waiting for this anniversary to start killing people? Or had he done bad stuff before?"

"I don't know for sure," Oren said. "I was told a little bit about him in my phone conversation about the injured clerk. Apparently Darius had skirmishes with the law before and had seemed very determined, to the officers involved, to accomplish whatever he'd begun. And there were some indications that he'd mentioned being furious because of the death of his father."

"This is all so strange," Madison said, shaking her head so her red hair swished gently around her face. Oren had an even stranger urge now, after his thought about hugging her, to go close and gently sweep that hair back and stroke it with his hands...

No way. Sure, she was beautiful, and he didn't have anyone in his life now. Didn't want one. Relationships never worked out for him. He'd tried enough in the past.

One woman he'd been interested in had also wanted to become a marshal—and she'd dumped him for one of his superior officers, which seemed even more inappropriate.

Then there was the lovely accountant who neglected to tell him she'd been married before and had a child. He wouldn't necessarily have minded the kid—only the fact she'd tried to hide it from him.

There was also another woman who just seemed very nice and sweet and sexy—but they had just grown tired of one another. Otherwise, he dated, spent the night with some women, but didn't find any he wanted to get closer to.

And Madison? Well, nothing could come of any attraction to her. She was part of the important case he was now handling.

He forced his mind back to where it should be. "Yeah," he said, "the entire case is strange, and where it stands now... Well, my job now is to protect people, you included. I want to meet with your law-enforcement relatives and the local chief of police tomorrow at the police station, if that's possible, and talk to you about how to deal with the situation, including regarding your mother."

"Oh, good," Madison said. "I'm worried about all of us, and Mom in particular. And how she'll be when she learns… Well, I'll be glad to discuss what to do."

Oren nodded, understanding her concern, of course. He continued. "I gather, from the research I've done and records I've looked at, that the interim chief right now is Brett Shea. With your sister Jillian's connection with the local police, and yours with her and your brother, I want your help to try to set up that meeting. Okay?"

Oren was surprised at the sudden dubious look that marred Madison's beautiful face. "I'll call Jillian, and Bryce, too, of course. I'm fairly sure I can get them to meet with us, and hopefully Jillian will be able to arrange for Brett to join us. Not my mom yet, though, till the rest of us have talked first. And I'll ask Jillian to set it up at the station tomorrow—unless the interim chief says otherwise. I've got cousins who work there, too. But there have been a lot of demonstrations at the station recently, thanks to some things that have been going on in the department, one person's actions in particular, and—"

"I've heard about that," Oren said. "A forensic scientist who was part of the force doing some pretty nasty things, right?"

"Right. And there is serial killer Len Davison on the loose, too. And—well, it's getting late. Let me start my calls, and we'll see what we can arrange."

"Fine. And I've already seen what a nice couch you

have there in your living room. It looks comfortable enough for me to spend the night right there."

"As if I had a choice," Madison said, but her beautiful red eyebrows were raised apparently not just in skepticism, but in amusement, too. "And I do have a spare bedroom, so if you have to stay, you could use that."

"You're right," Oren said in a light voice in return. "You don't have a choice." Unless, of course, she wanted him to hang out in her bedroom with her… No. That wasn't going to happen, even though the very thought made his body start to react. And she was *engaged*.

Inappropriate. And even the thought of what they could do together might distract him from what he really needed to do here.

"And thanks for offering me the spare bedroom," he continued, "but I'll sleep on the couch."

He didn't mention why he had to stay, or why he chose the couch, but he was certain that Madison knew. He was going to protect her. And hanging out in an extra bedroom might mean he wouldn't hear if there were any problems in the night.

For now, he'd hang out with her till her bedtime. And before that, he wanted to participate in any of the calls she made to her siblings, too, to make sure, even though members of his department had already been in touch to warn them as well.

Chapter 8

This was all so frightening. And it had been that way from even before she had met the man who had in fact turned out to be her father.

No, at least some of it had started at the time the man who was now with her, who said he still intended to protect her, had arrested her for jaywalking. *Jaywalking.*

That thought should have made Madison want to laugh again. Instead, considering all that had happened since, and all that could happen in the future, whether or not Oren was with her... Well, she almost wanted to cry.

But she wouldn't. She would stay strong. She would act perfectly normal as she spoke with her sister and brother so she could help to protect them. And they could all protect their mother.

She hoped. It crossed her mind that if she'd been closer to Alec, maybe he could have helped her deal with her difficult situation. But she didn't even want to tell him about it. Right now, she had an urge to call Grace, not because she was a cop but just to have someone else to talk to about all this absurdity. Even more appropriate, maybe, because Grace had been with her when she had first seen the man who had in fact turned out to be her father, though Madison had pretended to laugh it off then. But Grace would be a good one to talk to now, since she had gone through some rough stuff recently—as well as finding the right man in her life.

Madison wouldn't call her now, though. Nor would she phone her mother. She and her siblings would need to discuss letting Mom know what was going on, and taking care of her, when they met.

"Okay," she said to Oren now. "Let's do it. I'll call my sister, Jillian, first about setting up the meeting at the police station and getting the interim chief to join us."

"Let's see how it goes," Oren said. "If there's a problem, maybe I can help as a member of the federal Marshals Service."

"Wow." Madison managed a smile. "If there is a problem, maybe I can temporarily join the local county sheriff's department. It may be the only law-enforcement arm around here that we don't already have represented."

Oren laughed, then said, "Okay, I agree—with your starting the calls, not becoming a sheriff's deputy." He grew serious immediately. "Just so you know, it's fine for you to warn your sister and brother about the potential danger they face, but they've already been told some of it. They were called by one of our deputies, who gave them no details but told them they were potentially being stalked by someone who intended to harm them and others in their family, so they should be very cautious. That may not be unusual for Coltons, but at least they were forewarned."

"That's good, I guess," Madison mused. "I was going to call to warn them, but since they've already had a heads-up, and they're both in law enforcement, they'll know how to protect themselves. But it'll be a whole lot better for them—and me—once we've discussed it in more detail tomorrow and they know what's going on."

"That's what I figure, too," Oren said. Madison liked the way he looked her straight in the eye and nodded. "You'll all come out of this just fine, if I have anything to say about it."

"Or do about it," Madison responded with an attempt at a smile. "I already have the impression you're all about action."

"Exactly."

"But as I've already indicated, I'm also concerned about our mother. Do you know if Darius is after her, too?"

"He mentioned only you and your siblings when he stole the files and shot Nita, so hopefully not. But we can't be certain, of course."

Madison ended that part of their conversation by putting her phone on the table in front of her and swiping the screen on. She pressed the phone icon, looked under recent calls and pushed Jillian's name.

Then she put it on Speaker. She doubted this conversation would contain anything personal, and it might help to have Oren join in.

"Hi, Madison? Are you okay?" Jillian answered right away. "I had the strangest, even scariest, conversation before with a deputy marshal and wanted to discuss it with you tonight, but I was told to wait till around now to call you, if I intended to. And you can be sure I'm not happy about it. In fact, I nearly called you, anyway."

Why would the deputy Oren mentioned tell her that? Madison glanced across the table at him, but he shrugged as if he was puzzled, too.

"Have you talked to Bryce?" Madison asked. Would their brother have been told the same thing?

"Yes. He asked me to set it up as a conference call when I did get in touch with you. Should we add him to this conversation?"

Madison looked at Oren, who nodded.

"That sounds fine," Madison said. "And just so you know, I have someone with me now who'll also be participating. His name is Oren Margulies, and he's with the US Marshals Service."

"Hello, Jillian," Oren said before Jillian could question anything. But Madison, knowing her sister, figured there was a lot going through her mind.

They soon had Bryce on the line, too. Like Jillian, he seemed irritated he'd been told that not only could his life be in danger but also that he'd get more information tomorrow.

But Madison was glad that the result of this chat was to confirm that her siblings did know something was going on and were taking care of themselves. And that they'd all get together tomorrow to discuss it in a meeting at the police station. That was confirmed, too, after Jillian left the call to get in touch with Grave Gulch Interim Police Chief Brett Shea. The plan was to get together at nine in the morning.

"Do you know what's going on, Madison?" Bryce asked while they waited for Jillian to return.

"Kind of," she replied. "And I've already agreed to wait to discuss it till tomorrow, so don't try to get me talking about it now, except to tell you to be careful and stay safe tonight." She glanced at Oren, who had just finished his second stein of beer. He nodded his agreement with her, and she rolled her eyes.

Jillian soon returned to the call. "It's all set," she said. "We'll meet at the station at nine."

But— "With all those demonstrations, will we be able to get in?" Madison asked.

"Not sure there'll be any tomorrow, but I've been able to enter the building, even during the worst of them," Jillian said. "From what I gather, now that our cousin Melissa is no longer the acting police chief, things are calming down a bit. But give me a call if the front entrance seems blocked, and I'll let you in through one of the rear doors."

"Got it," Madison said. They soon said their good-byes and hung up.

And there they were, she and Oren. Alone in her condo that night. Together, yet not together.

She was much too attracted to the guy. She knew that. But it could largely be because he'd been protecting her. Never mind that he'd arrested her earlier.

He rose across the table from her. She had an urge to join him and give him a good-night kiss—maybe one that could lead to something a lot more fun.

But that wasn't going to happen, she chided herself. How could she even think such a thing? Sure, she might be questioning her relationship with Alec, but they were still engaged.

But that was the point. She might not even consider kissing Oren if all was right between Alec and her…

She stood up, too. "You may be sleeping on the sofa, but you might as well be comfortable. I'll show you where my extra pillows, sheets and blankets are, and you can grab whatever you like. Towels, too, so you can use the bathroom out here." Fortunately, although it was more of a powder room, it contained a small shower.

"Sounds good," he said, and she first walked to the refrigerator, where she got him a bottle of water.

Then she showed him where everything else was. "I assume we should get up tomorrow morning around seven thirty or so, since it's Sunday, not a workday. I'll set my alarm. I have the fixings for breakfast, so we can eat right here. And—"

"And thanks for all this." Oren held the water bottle in his left hand as he drew closer to her in the kitchen. "And don't tell me to sleep well. I'll sleep as much as I can, but I'm used to this kind of thing, believe me. The slightest noise will wake me up."

She understood he was attempting to make her feel at ease, allow her to sleep that night, and she appreciated it. She appreciated *him*.

"Thanks," she said and realized her voice was hoarse.

Oren was right in front of her. He put the water down on the table, and before she could get sensible and retreat to her room, he moved toward her, and she was in his arms.

His body was hard against her—and so was the particular part of him below that made all lingering vestiges of sensibleness in her fly away. She held him close, and in moments they were engaged in a kiss.

His touch was hot, strong, enticing, and she enjoyed the feel of his rough facial hair against her face. She had an urge to pull back just long enough to tug him down the hall and into the bedroom.

But fortunately, one of them still remained sane: him. He pulled back and looked down at her with his sexy blue eyes.

"Good night, Madison," he said hoarsely. "Sleep well. There's nothing to worry about tonight. I'll make sure of it."

Nothing but her sanity, Madison thought as she wished him good-night, too, and headed to her room.

As she got ready for bed, she kept reliving that kiss in her mind, over and over, her body reacting even without Oren's presence.

It didn't seem right that she'd gotten so close to the man who was protecting her—and yet also it felt very right.

And when she finally got beneath the lacy beige coverlet on her queen-size bed, she realized that despite all she had gone through that day and her current worries about the man who wanted to kill her family, she was falling asleep and appreciated the presence of the dedicated—and handsome—marshal who she'd no doubt would do as he'd promised and keep her safe.

And only when she was nearly asleep did she realize she'd come home but hadn't yet called her fiancé.

Well, she'd get in touch with Alec tomorrow. After she'd had her important meeting with her siblings, Oren and the cops.

And do what she needed to do—finally break up with her fiancé.

Oren woke several times that night, as he'd programmed himself to do. He pulled off the sheet he'd thrown over himself on the sofa and walked around, taking his phone off the charger he always kept with him and using it as a flashlight.

He listened at the front door. He looked out windows. He walked down the hall, pushed open the door slightly and peered into Madison's room, ignoring his impulse to do more.

He'd already done enough. That kiss was uncalled for...no matter how much he had enjoyed it. He was here as a professional, guarding her.

And she was engaged. Well, at least all appeared to remain fine in her home.

And Oren wondered where the hell Darius Amaltin was and hoped all Madison's family members were also safe.

He woke on his own around seven thirty, as planned, and heard Madison stirring. He showered and got dressed, and as he exited the bathroom he found her in the kitchen cooking breakfast: a cheese omelet and toast plus coffee. "Hope it's okay," she told him, and it was a lot more than okay.

She'd made breakfast for him, as if he'd spent the night for something beyond her protection. They'd shared a kiss. He would just have to keep in mind even more that he was here on an assignment. Nothing more.

At least they didn't spend much time eating that excellent meal. He knew Grave Gulch well enough to get to the police station without directions, but that didn't keep him from glancing toward Madison often. She'd dressed in an outfit he assumed she also taught in, a pretty, pale green dress and brown shoes with low heels. Professional enough for a meeting at the police station.

And him? Well, he hadn't picked up the change of clothes he kept in his car before they'd left, or dropped in at his sister's house to pick up clothes he kept there, so he still wore the same gray sports coat, shirt and slacks he'd had on yesterday. He'd slept in his underwear— and fortunately hadn't seen Madison all night, to tempt him to take them off.

Up till now, they'd mostly just talked about nothing, like what a nice day it was for autumn in Grave Gulch. But as they neared the station, Madison said, "I gathered from what you said yesterday that you're aware of the protests that have been going on around here."

"Olivia has kept me informed. I understand they're partly about recent police misconduct."

"It's more than just that. Some people are protesting the supposed corruption of the local police department since a forensic scientist there, Randall Bowe, had apparently been creating or destroying evidence, maybe thanks to bribes, so sometimes even murderers have gotten off scot-free. And there's Len Davison, and some people have accused my cousin Grace of an unjustified shooting, even though she's been cleared. The public's not happy about that. Me, neither. Anyway, better go slow here." Madison leaned toward the windshield. "I know Jillian said the protests seem to have stopped now that our cousin Melissa is no longer in charge of the police department, but we should still be careful."

"Oh, that's right. The rookie cop who was accused of inappropriately shooting was a Colton, and so was the former police chief, right? And you're a Colton, too. Will the protesters come back if they know you're here?" He kept his tone light. He was joking, after all.

"Let's hope not," Madison said dryly. "Besides, Melissa and Grace aren't the only Coltons on the police force. There are a lot of them—certainly not including me. But the idea of so many Coltons appears to rattle a lot of people. And some have blamed Melissa for the misconduct of that forensic scientist."

"Any idea why so many Coltons got into law enforcement?" Oren couldn't help asking.

"I understand it was because a family member was

killed in a still unsolved murder years ago—Amanda Colton, who was then married to my uncle Geoff. It prompted a lot of the family to spend their lives seeking justice, even if they couldn't achieve it for Amanda."

"Interesting," Oren said.

They had reached the station, no slowed vehicles or protesters in sight, and Oren pointed that out to Madison. "Thank heavens," she said.

Oren pulled into a parking lot near the front of the station, telling Madison to remain in the car till he came around for her. But would someone with a goal of killing people visit a police station with that in mind?

Besides, Darius didn't know about this upcoming meeting—did he?

Oren soon opened Madison's door and watched as she pivoted, admiring her lovely legs as she exited the vehicle. "Thanks," she said.

Oren continued to look around, including at the station. It was a nice building, one story, made out of stone and clearly antique. Quite a few people were heading into or out of the station but not congregating as if in a protest. A good thing.

He resisted the urge to take Madison's hand to lead her to the door. Instead, he followed her. She soon had her phone at her ear, and he assumed she was calling her sister to let her know they'd arrived so she could meet them and take them to wherever the meeting was to be.

"Great," she soon said. "We'll be there in a minute."

Madison had visited the lobby of the Grave Gulch Police Department a few times, mostly to meet Jillian for dinner after both had finished with their jobs for the day. Jillian's ending time varied more than Madison's, since the obligations of a crime-scene investigator could change at any minute, whereas a kindergarten teacher generally had a more predictable schedule, including any after-school meetings with her students and their parents, plus her preparations for the next day. And occasionally, Grace joined them.

Madison therefore knew what the greeting area of the police station looked like and usually appreciated this delightful building that had been constructed way back in the 1850s—when she wasn't about to have a meeting about the danger to her family.

Behind the gated front desk were other desks for some of the department's employees.

At the moment, a group of three people she assumed were civilians stood at the front desk. She also saw a few uniformed cops in the greeting room and others inside the open enclosure. She tried eavesdropping after she heard one of those nearby say the word *protesters*. Best she could discern, they were relieved that whoever the protesters had been, they weren't around any longer, though they still hung out sometimes at other places nearby, like around city hall and the courthouse. "They're still demanding justice for that missing forensic scientist Randall Bowe's crimes," one of them said.

"No big surprise," said another.

But Madison couldn't listen any more. That wasn't why she was here. She wondered where their meeting would be held and wished Jillian had let her know. She turned toward Oren, ready to ask if he'd ever been here before, but she saw Bryce walk through the door they'd entered from. She grinned. "Hi, bro!"

FBI agent Bryce was dressed professionally for the meeting at the police station, in a black suit, beige shirt and red tie. "Hi, sis." He gave her a hug.

Madison always considered Bryce a nice-looking

guy. Now, under the circumstances, she found herself pulling back and staring, comparing him in her mind with the man she'd discovered was their father Richard Foster, now known as Wesley Windham. Bryce gave her a puzzled frown as she continued to regard him. Same shape of eyes beneath shaggy brows. A high forehead. Dark lashes. Lips that were a bit narrow. Fair skin. A somewhat-pointed chin. Ears that hugged his head.

She knew her mind was repeating all she had thought about when she'd viewed Wes in person and in the not-so-great photo she'd taken of him last week. But yes, her brother did look a lot like their dad, though with darker hair and eyes, of course.

Bryce pulled away. "What's going on, Madison?"

"Something amazing," she replied, "and scary." She then noticed Oren just behind Bryce, watching them. "For now, though—" she motioned for Oren to join them "—Bryce, I'd like you to meet Marshal Oren Margulies. Oren, this is my brother, Bryce. It's thanks to him…" She let her voice taper off. She'd no doubt Oren would know what she meant.

"Hi, Bryce." Oren had joined them and now held his hand out to the agent, who shook it.

"Hello, Oren." But then Bryce looked back to Madison. "So tell me what's going on."

"Not out here," she said, and, fortunately, that was when Jillian hurried from a door behind the reception area toward them.

Jillian's hair was light brown and a lot longer than Madison's. And though Madison was reasonably slim, Jillian was even more slender. Madison admired her, though she refused to be jealous of her younger sister. Jillian was twenty-seven.

"Hi, all of you!" she exclaimed as she reached them.

She looked from Madison to Bryce, then toward Oren, obviously realizing that, whoever he was, he was part of this group. "Come with me. Chief Shea is meeting us in one of the conference rooms."

Motioning for them to follow, Jillian led them first to the front desk, where she spoke to the uniformed officer in charge. After they showed their IDs, the gate was unlocked, and Jillian led them to one of the original wooden doors, which she opened, and then she waved for them to go inside. "I'll let the chief know we're all here—right?" She glanced again at Oren, then looked at Madison.

"Fine. This is Oren. I'll explain when Chief Shea gets here." Madison joined Bryce and Oren as they sat down at the long wooden table at the center of the room. "So you're a fed," Bryce said to Oren. "What do you do in your job?"

"A lot." Oren grinned as he glanced toward Madison, who'd taken a chair beside him. "Protecting people, arresting people—"

That made Madison laugh—and feel glad she could find her arrest humorous now.

"I think Oren will be the one who'll talk most here," Madison said. "He's got the background. I'm just a newcomer to the situation, and in a way so are Jillian and you."

"But—" Bryce interrupted.

He was interrupted, too, as Jillian came in with Brett Shea.

"Okay, all of you," the interim chief said. "What the hell is going on?"

Chapter 9

Nice introduction, Oren thought. But the man who approached and clearly thought himself in charge glared at the three siblings, then stopped his gaze on Oren. And yes, he was in charge, in this location and under these circumstances.

Interim Chief Shea was maybe early thirties, five or six years younger than Oren. He looked fairly rugged, though, as if he'd seen some pretty nasty things in his life in law enforcement. He was tall, with reddish hair and blue eyes he didn't move from Oren. He of course wore a uniform with a badge, nameplate and lots of stripes, as well as the obligatory belt with tools and a gun.

"What's going on, Jillian?" Brett said. "You told me there's a dangerous situation in town but didn't tell me anything about it. Who'll explain, so we can figure out how best to handle it?"

"That would be me," Oren told him smoothly. "I'm Oren Margulies of the US Marshals Service. Of the three members of the Colton family who are here, the one who knows most about what's going on is Madison, and she's in the most danger."

"Really?" Jillian bent down near Madison's chair to give her a hug. Her hair brushed her sister's shoulder. "Please tell us more about what's happening," she said, looking at Oren, "and how we can keep Madison, and ourselves, safe."

"He's about to do that," Madison said in a soft and somewhat-confident voice that made Oren want to hug her, too. Of course he didn't, but he managed to smile at her while her sister sat back down. But then Madison said, "Just let me start off, though. It's something my brother and sister and I never imagined." She looked at Bryce first, then Jillian. "Our father is alive."

"What!" Jillian rose again.

"Okay," Bryce said through gritted teeth. His fists were clenched on the wooden table. "Get this story started." He looked at Oren, who could only imagine what emotions must be rushing through both of Madison's siblings.

"I should probably have invited Grace to be here, too, since she was with me when…when I first saw him. I'll make sure she hears about it."

Madison described what Oren already knew. She first told them about seeing someone who looked much too familiar on her first visit to Kendall—familiar enough that she returned. She didn't mention what had brought her to that town in the first place—looking for a wedding gown—which Oren found interesting. It even gave him a little zing of pleasure that she wasn't talking about that part of her personal life, even to her family.

She then described how she met the man, without mentioning Oren's arresting her to keep her away, which he appreciated since it wouldn't help with what they were attempting to accomplish. "He recognized me, too, kind of," Madison said with tears in her eyes. "He thought I looked like our mother, but with my age and red hair he knew it was me. And when we talked... Oh, yes, he's our father."

"Then, why hasn't he been in touch with us all these years?" Bryce demanded. "I don't see much reason to have anything to do with him after he deserted us and Mom."

"I'd better let Oren explain, including why we're in danger." Madison looked at him with her watery green eyes. Oren's urge to hug her increased, but of course he stayed where he was. He had a story to tell.

And Oren wanted to make that story as concise as possible but also wanted to ensure that the siblings and interim police chief had enough detail to understand. He explained how he'd been put in charge of a man in protective custody of the Marshals Service when his predecessor retired. The subject's name was Wesley Windham—formerly Richard Foster.

Without stopping at the gasps and exclamations of Jillian and Bryce, he looked at Brett. "Richard Foster was the father of these three."

He went on to explain how Foster had been in the military and had witnessed a murder on his final trip home. He'd helped to identify the killer and been recruited to testify at his murder trial. The perp, Louis Amaltin, had been sentenced to prison. He'd threatened Foster with revenge, thanks to his cohorts who were still free, so that was why Foster/Windham was put into protective custody and now lived in Kendall, Michigan.

"I think he decided to stay far away from all of you for your protection, which is required due to the danger I'm about to describe," Oren said. Bryce and Jillian appeared skeptical, which he understood. He explained that Amaltin had been murdered in prison, but of course all his colleagues still posed a threat, so Wes Windham remained in protective custody.

Was that a solid reason for him never to contact his family? Oren hadn't been too sure of it before, but after what had just gone on with Madison and him and the attack they'd endured, he now figured it had been a good decision for Wes's sake.

"Amaltin had been married and had a kid," Oren continued. "Amaltin's murder occurred exactly twenty years ago now, and his son, Darius Amaltin, apparently wants revenge on Wes by killing his family first, then maybe coming after him. He attacked Madison already." At her siblings' respective additional gasps, he explained what had happened on the road driving to Grave Gulch, letting them know he'd stayed with Madison to keep her safe. "And I can't help believing that he'll probably come after one or both of you, too, followed by Wes, although he fortunately hasn't mentioned your mother."

"Is that miserable jerk here in town?" asked Brett. Of course the local police chief would want to know that.

"Don't know for sure. But he's been here and knew how to find Madison as a result of bribery and attempted murder." He described how the foolish bribed clerk had been found.

"That's horrible," Jillian exclaimed. "And oh, Madison, I'm so glad you're okay. Bryce and I have been trained in ways to keep us safe, and we can always call on our colleagues for backup. But… Well, we also need to figure out the best way to inform, and protect, Mom." She turned toward Oren. "I know you'll be concerned about our father, since he's your assignment. But, please, can you continue to help keep Madison safe?"

Oren nodded. "I have colleagues in Kendall protecting your dad," he said. "For now, Madison is my assignment. I already figured she's in the most danger of you siblings, since you two have law-enforcement backgrounds and he's seen her. Madison may get tired of seeing me around, but for now, at least, she's stuck with me." He realized that might sound too personal, so he added, "Good thing she's got a comfortable sofa that I tested last night while also doing rounds. And I'll be working on ways to get Darius captured while Madison's in safe environments. I'll have to check on security at the school where she teaches, of course."

"What about when she's with her fiancé?" Jillian asked. "He's just a teacher, too. Darius might use him as a tool to get to Madison."

"No," Madison said softly. "I've been worried about Alec, of course. I think this might be a good time to break off our engagement. He doesn't need to be involved."

"At least for now," Bryce agreed.

Oren was interested that Madison didn't respond to Bryce's remark. Maybe she did just want to protect the guy.

Or maybe she actually wanted to end the engagement for personal reasons. He tried not to feel too happy about that possibility. It was none of his business.

"I'm not thrilled that all this is going on in my town," Brett said, "but we'll stay in close touch."

"Sounds good," Oren said.

"Thanks for letting me know," Brett responded.

"Us, too," Jillian said. Her head was cocked as she looked at her sister, and that long hair of hers dangled down one side. She was attractive, too. She didn't wear a ring, so maybe she was available, unlike engaged Madison.

But he really didn't care about Jillian's marital status. Of course, he didn't know Madison well, either. But something about her really attracted him.

Yeah, his interest in her continued to grow. That was highly inappropriate. Besides, he'd had those three go-nowhere relationships in the past that had soured him on anything more than casual dating. He now knew that attempting to settle down with one woman wasn't for him. But Madison was in danger. She had already been recognized and attacked. He would do his job and safeguard her—and nothing else. He knew better than to cross the professional line.

He turned to their FBI-agent brother. "So Bryce," he said. "You're a fed, too. Anything you can do to help your family?"

"I'll notify my superiors, of course. Have them check on those Amaltins and their background, see if there's anything we can do to add to the search and investigation. Do my best to protect my family, too."

"Sounds good." Oren rose from his chair. Being in the police station had to be good and safe. But he'd accomplished what he needed to here, so it was time for Madison and him to leave. Although she might want to spend more time with her family. If so, he'd have them nail down where they were going and what they were planning to do. And otherwise? "So Madison," he said, "what would you like to do now?"

Like, are you ready to go into witness protection till the cops bring in the guy who wants to kill you?

He wouldn't ask that now, though, in front of her family.

"I'm fine with heading home now," she responded.

But Oren shot a glance at Brett and found the interim chief was looking at him.

"There's something else I want to talk to you about first, Margulies," Brett said. "You, too, Bryce. Please come to my office. We can leave Madison and Jillian in this room. They'll be safe here, inside the station, but the thing I need to discuss right now doesn't concern them."

Really? What could it be? Oren shot a glance at Madison, and though her eyes widened in obvious surprise, she said, "That's fine. Jillian and I can catch up a little more. We haven't been spending a lot of time together lately."

So it was apparently settled. Curious about what Brett intended to talk about, Oren pushed his chair back under the table as the other men in the room did the same thing.

"Thanks," Brett said to none of them in particular. "Gentlemen, please follow me."

Madison couldn't help wondering what it was that the interim police chief wanted to discuss with the marshal and the FBI agent. Cop stuff. Or law-enforcement stuff.

Something he didn't want to talk to his own employee, Jillian, about.

For now, Madison watched the three men leave the conference room.

"I wonder what that's about." Jillian moved so she

was sitting beside Madison in the chair Oren had just vacated.

"So do I," Madison responded. "Maybe Bryce will tell us about it later." Or Oren would tell her—maybe.

"Guess that'll depend on what it is, and whether the chief says it's okay to mention it. If it was, he might as well have just talked about it here while we were all in the same room together."

"You're right." Madison smiled. "In any case, it's good to see you. What's going on in the world of crime-scene investigation?"

She liked how Jillian grinned, her eyes sparkling. "Nothing much that's new, although a rookie like me certainly learns a lot daily." She laughed. "And let me suggest again that you get into some kind of law enforcement like our brother and me."

"Oh, I'm just fine as a kindergarten teacher. I like working with kids, seeing their progress and all."

And I want to have kids someday, too, Madison thought. That was one reason she'd gotten engaged to Alec. Still…

It was as if Jillian read her mind. "So I guess you'd better do whatever's necessary to warn Alec about what's going on, too. I gather you didn't find the ideal wedding dress on your trips to Kendall. But finding our father instead? Wow!"

"Wow, indeed," Madison agreed. "And I didn't spend much time—" *no time at all, in fact* "—checking out dresses in that shop I told you about. And now, I'll really be worried about Alec. As I've said, maybe I should end things with him. I could let the world know so that horrible Darius person will leave him alone." She paused. "I think it's time to break up with Alec anyway, for lots of reasons." That all sounded a bit hollow. She knew it.

But Jillian probably wouldn't accuse her of insincerity about Alec or anything else. She'd undoubtedly support whatever Madison decided.

"I've wondered about that," Jillian said. Interesting. Was it that obvious?

"But with Bryce and you and Mom," Madison continued, "I'm afraid I can't do anything like that to keep you safe. We'll have to figure something out. Your being in law enforcement doesn't mean that miserable man can't hurt you. And our father..."

"Amazing that you actually met him. We'll have to go to Kendall with you someday soon. You'll have to introduce all of us."

"That's what I'm hoping," Madison said, "as long as we're all protected from that dangerous creep Darius."

As she hopefully was, thanks to Oren.

Oren followed the other men from the conference room into the large, enclosed entry area. There were a bunch of other people around there, mostly uniformed cops, and he also heard voices from beyond the reception divider. He figured this place was always busy.

Brett led them through the ornate door at the far left corner, then closed it behind them. "Please have a seat." He walked around them and sat in a large chair at the desk that must be his.

"So what can we do for you, Brett?" Bryce asked.

"Well, I mostly want to bring another fed, Oren, up to date on that situation you're aware of, Bryce, and I'll update you, too, since there've been some recent changes. Very recent. Like, ten minutes before our meeting in the conference room."

Interesting, Oren thought. He felt oddly proud that he was going to be given whatever information Brett was about to relate. Sure, he was a fed, but his marshal status didn't put him in charge of much besides the assignments he was given.

So what was this about?

First thing, Brett asked, "Are you aware, Oren, of the demonstrations that have been going on around this station, as well as other landmarks in this town, like city hall?"

"Yes, somewhat. Madison talked about them on our way here. I guess she talked to Jillian about them, too, who told her things seemed to have calmed down, at least right here."

"True." Brett sat back in his chair, locking his fingers behind his head. "And do you know what they were about?"

"I think she said the main cause was that a forensic scientist who worked for the police department was purposely modifying some evidence and how it was evaluated. The community is angry and worried about both the evidence tampering and the inmate releases, plus a recent surge in citywide crime." Most likely justifiably, Oren thought, but he didn't say so.

"Exactly," Brett said. "We've been trying to chase the scientist down and bring him in, but good old Randall Bowe has been hiding. Even our best resources haven't located him yet."

Oren nodded, wondering where this was going. He glanced beside him toward Bryce, who was nodding. "I'm not sure what the Marshals Service can do to help," Brett continued, "but I figure your knowing what's going on can't hurt, and if I think of any specifics I need from either of your agencies, I'll be sure to let you know."

"Thanks," Oren said, although that depended on what Brett was talking about and what he'd need.

Brett started describing how the situation had changed a short time ago. Turned out he had gotten a phone call just before the meeting from Baldwin Bowe, the brother of Randall and a ghost bounty hunter, who used mercenary tactics to find people. Baldwin had told Brett that Randall had finally answered the burner-phone number he'd given to Melissa. The cops had supplied that information to Baldwin.

Baldwin had apparently told Brett that the phone conversation had been weird and difficult. According to Baldwin, Randall had ranted in his ear for two minutes or more, talking about everything from how their parents had always liked Baldwin better, and how their dad was a cheating louse, and that everything was everyone else's fault, not his.

"Baldwin told me he'd asked Randall where he was," Brett said, "and tried to get his brother to meet with him, but Randall hung up on him. Baldwin said he's going to try to figure out where Randall might be hiding, and if he can help catch him, he will. But in the meantime, he's after another fugitive in his bounty-hunter capacity, so he won't have a lot of time to chase his brother at the moment." Brett paused. "So if either of you has any suggestions about how to track Randall down now, let me know. I'll have our techs look into tracking the location of that burner phone, of course, but my suspicion is that Randall will stay far away from it now, at least for a while."

"Good guess," Oren said. "Anyhow, nothing comes to mind at the moment, but I appreciate your letting me in on this, and I'll ponder what might be advisable to do next. I'll run it by some appropriate people in my department and let you know if they've any suggestions."

"That's what I hoped," Brett said. "Glad I briefed you on this. We need to find that guy before anyone else is injured or killed as a result of him—and also to prevent our department from looking any worse for keeping him on staff as long as we did."

Chapter 10

The meeting of the men was apparently over. Or at least that was what Madison figured when first Bryce, then Oren trooped back into the conference room. In a moment Brett joined them with a black Labrador retriever beside him on a leash, who looked at the people in the room and sniffed the floor. Cute, Madison thought. She'd heard that the interim police chief had been a K-9 officer, and now she believed it.

They all sat back down, with Oren beside her again after Jillian moved across the table once more.

"Everything okay?" Madison asked. Did their meeting have to do with the Amaltins? She hadn't thought so, but were Jillian and she being protected from whatever it was, for some reason?

"Fine," Oren said, nodding his head toward Brett, who was glancing around the table. And then he said softly, "I'll tell you about it later."

Which made Madison feel a little better. At least she'd learn about whatever it was that drove Brett to talk to the two feds around here, even if it was the person who was putting her in the most danger.

If so, she most certainly wanted to know what was going on.

"Okay," Brett said, once more taking charge. He leaned across the table in Madison's direction. "I'll notify some of my subordinates about what's going on and let them know to keep an eye out for anything in town that indicates Darius Amaltin has paid us a visit. I don't really want to find out, and I doubt any of you do, either."

Maybe one person here—*me*, Madison thought.

"But not everyone needs to know the details," Brett continued, "unless there is some indication of further criminal activity."

"Sounds fine to me," Oren said from beside her. "But all you Coltons had better be careful and keep an eye out for your own safety, too—yours and your mother's." He looked from Jillian to Bryce and then back to Madison. With her, he winked as he nodded. She interpreted that to mean he was going to be keeping an eye out for her safety, as he'd already promised. Which she appreciated, of course.

But she intended to be damn careful, too. And to observe the world, and their surroundings, deeply enough to try to keep Oren safe as well. Darius had undoubtedly seen Oren driving her car, even if he didn't know who the marshal was then. But he could have learned more since.

All five of them stood and walked toward the door. "You're going to keep in touch with us, aren't you, Madison?" Bryce asked, only it seemed more like a demand than a question.

"Of course. And I expect the same from you, too." She looked from her brother to her sister and then looked again at Brett as well as the dog by his side. She resisted going over to pet it, since she understood police dogs generally needed to be left alone except by their human partners. "I'm hoping this includes you, that you'll let us know if the Grave Gulch PD learns anything about that Darius, like where he's staying and what he's planning next."

"To the extent it's necessary to protect any or all of you, absolutely." Brett's blue eyes were narrowed, his lips tight in a positive grimace as if he was making a vow by his words.

And maybe he was. But that didn't mean that Madison and her siblings or their mother or Oren would remain safe from Darius's wrath.

"Maybe we should meet here and talk again soon," Jillian said. Madison wondered whether a rookie CSI could set up this kind of meeting that included the interim chief and others.

Brett said, "Maybe so. Let's see how things go, and we can coordinate something in a few days if it makes sense."

Oren nodded, and since he apparently believed it made sense, so did she.

Especially if it kept all of them safe from what Darius had attempted to do to Oren and her on the drive here, or from anything else.

"Ember, come," Brett said to the dog, and the black Lab stayed at his side as they left the room.

As the meeting broke up, the three siblings also committed to get together again soon, though nothing definite was decided there, either. And soon, Madison and Oren were walking back to her car outside.

Madison could practically feel the tension in the marshal beside her as he kept watch around them.

Well, she might not have the law-enforcement background, but she was used to watching her surroundings, too…mostly to make sure kindergartners weren't getting into trouble. But now she likewise kept an eye on her surroundings, including the police station and everyone she saw while she was inside, and everyone on the street and sidewalk.

Would she recognize Darius Amaltin if she saw him? She hadn't gotten a good look at him when he'd shot at them, and if the police had found his picture on his driver's license or in their system, she hadn't seen it yet. But most likely he'd be watching them, so she kept her eyes open for anyone who seemed to be observing others around them—or, most especially, them.

Fortunately, nothing. She hoped she wasn't missing anything obvious, but at least Oren's degree of stress didn't appear overwhelming, although he was definitely observant. But that wasn't all that was on her mind. Portions of her conversations with her siblings came back to her. The timing might not be perfect, but she had things she needed to do.

Like call—

Her cell phone rang in her pocket. She guessed who it might be, mostly because she'd just been thinking about calling Alec.

She glanced toward Oren, who had a curious look on his face just as they reached her car.

Oren opened the passenger door for her, and she slid in, then answered the call. "Hi, Alec," she said, attempting to sound cheerful.

She wasn't about to tell him what was going on with her. But she did want to…to make things right between them. Right, in the way she had just been pondering and had sort of discussed with Jillian. This wasn't a great time to do it, though. And she didn't want to do it on the phone.

Especially when Oren slid into the seat beside her.

"Hi, Madison," said Alec. "What's going on? I haven't heard from you. Did you buy that dress you were so excited about? Are we one step closer to the wedding?"

Of course she had told her fiancé about her trip— no, *trips*—to Kendall and talked about the boutique. Otherwise, they might have seen each other on one or both of those Saturdays.

"Um…no. It wasn't quite right." *Because I've decided I don't want to marry you, no matter what I wear*, she thought. A small twinge of guilt shot through her but she shrugged it off. Alec would be better finding someone he loved and who loved him too.

"Okay. I get it. But I want to see you. Can we get together for dinner tonight?"

"Dinner? Tonight?" she said aloud so Oren could hear, even though it shouldn't be his business. But her going somewhere without him *was* his business right now. "I don't…" She happened to be looking around again, mostly so she didn't meet Oren's eyes. An idea came to her. "Could I call you right back? I have a thought about getting together, but I need a couple of minutes."

"Okay," Alec said, though he sounded miffed. "Call me right back, then." And he hung up.

Madison turned to Oren. "I do…I do want to get together with my fiancé tonight." She left it at that for the moment just to see his reaction. He knew she was engaged. She had a sense that he had more in mind than just protecting her.

"Okay," he said, and he sounded totally neutral about it. Was she wrong? He hadn't done anything to signal any more interest in her, but she'd felt it, anyway.

Or was that wishful thinking by a woman doubting her feelings about her fiancé? Whatever it was, she needed to be fair to Alec.

"Here's what I have in mind. See that coffee shop?" She pointed to the coffee shop across from the police station. It was an ideal place to meet Alec, a place they could talk at one of the side tables and still be near the protection of the police station.

"Yeah," Oren said. "Are you having a craving for coffee?" He said it as if he didn't believe in the possibility, so Madison decided to play with him.

Craving? The word caused her to react. Coffee craving? Yes. But surely…she couldn't have one for Oren, too.

She made her voice soft, maybe a little husky. "Oh, yes. A definite craving. One I can't ignore."

"Then, let's go get you a cup." Okay. Oren wasn't buying into it. "I wouldn't mind some, either, though I don't need it."

Madison laughed. No more games. Not right now. "Neither do I, really. But…" She grew quiet. "As you no doubt figured, that was my fiancé on the phone. He wants to get together with me tonight. We haven't really seen each other much lately except at school, and what I want to talk to him about can't be said there." She looked at Oren pleadingly. "We mentioned having dinner together, but instead I'd rather go right across from the police station, so we'd be safe, and grab coffee that I can leave with if the conversation is as bad as I fear—"

"I get it," Oren said. "Yeah, call him back. I'm fine with your setting up a date with the guy right there and right now."

In fact, Oren liked the idea more than he should.

He wasn't certain what she'd been up to while they talked about coffee, but he chose not to go there.

More importantly, she was going to dump that guy, end her engagement. Or at least that was what Oren gathered.

Of course, he could be wrong. She might decide to fling herself into his arms and profess love forever.

But at least in a coffee shop there couldn't be much physical about it.

He definitely didn't want his imagination to take over.

If she did dump the guy, all the better. Oren would have no responsibility, real or assumed, to protect the man she otherwise might have married. And if word got out to the world that they were no longer an item, Darius would likely have no reason to threaten the ex-fiancé. *Alec*, was it?

Oren thought of the kiss he'd shared with Madison, as he'd started to do a lot. But no way was that a harbinger of things to come. After his prior relationships with women that had all fizzled… Well. He particularly thought of Anabel, the woman who'd wanted to also become a marshal. He'd thought at first she might be the one…but she hadn't been. So—no more dating. Not now, at least.

He would remain Madison's protector. That was his job, so he'd have to be near her. A lot…

Madison called Alec back. Oren checked some things on his own phone as she talked, since he didn't really need to eavesdrop.

Madison ended her call, then looked at Oren. "Alec will be here in about ten minutes. I want to go into the coffee shop and pick out as private a table as possible. Would you like to help?"

"Private and safe," he stressed. "Yes, I'll be happy to help make that decision."

He walked beside her toward the coffee shop. That involved crossing a street, which they approached about halfway between traffic lights. "Care to jaywalk?" Madison asked him, grinning.

"Hey, like I said, I'm in law enforcement. I have to follow the law—unless I'm after someone who's breaking it."

"Then, how about if *I* jaywalk again?"

He wanted to laugh and thought about how Madison made him smile a lot. Much more than any other woman… Well, so what?

And in fact, it wasn't a big deal. But the light changed, and cars drove down the street both ways. Not a good time to jaywalk. "I think we'd better go to the corner and obey the light," he told her.

"Guess so. You win, Marshal." She was the one to laugh.

Once inside, he helped Madison choose a table in a corner toward the back, in an area that didn't appear particularly popular. He took a table for himself even farther down that row so he could watch Madison and her date—he hated to think of this meeting that way, but the guy was her fiancé, after all—and also the front of the place and its wide window.

Madison sat down also facing the front, which meant

her back would be toward Oren. That would be fine. It would give Oren more opportunity both to watch for unwelcome people—one in particular—entering the place, and also see the expressions on Madison's guy's face as she told him whatever she intended to tell him at their meeting.

To leave her alone was what Oren assumed. But that could change, of course. Alec could convince her he was the world's gift to women, particularly her, and get her to change her mind.

As much as Oren despised that idea. It even made him grit his teeth now as he left Madison at her table and headed toward his own.

Unlike a lot of chain eateries, this one had servers who came to the tables to take orders. Oren had noticed that as soon as they entered, so he felt comfortable maintaining his place there. A young lady in long, skinny pants and a bright shirt came over almost immediately, and he requested a large black coffee. No food. He figured that, if all went as he hoped, he'd have dinner with Madison later, probably stopping for takeout on their way back to her place.

The person they were waiting for was just entering the shop. Oren assumed the guy walking through the door was Alec, since as soon as the waitress left her table, Madison half rose and waved in that direction.

The guy, who had a mustache and glasses, smiled and waved back, and soon Alec had joined her, with a small hug and kiss.

Then Madison and Alec began their conversation.

Oren wished he could hear it, but he studied Alec's face, hoping to be able to figure out what was being said. But he'd also thought of a couple of things to talk to Brett about, so he made a quick call to the police captain as he watched.

And tried not to think too hard about the conversation he was observing and the lovely woman who'd initiated it—nor his own somewhat inappropriate hope that Madison was, in fact, ending her engagement.

"Hi, Madison!" Alec said enthusiastically as he joined her at the table.

He gave her a hug before sitting down, and she sort of hugged back. At least his kiss was brief and not heated at all. Alec didn't hesitate at all in ordering his rich, fancy latte. Madison asked for a large decaf.

When the server was gone, Alec continued. "So tell me what's going on. I understand you didn't find the perfect wedding dress on your trips to Kendall. Have you found one someplace else? Where? Or if you haven't, where are you looking next?"

Madison made herself smile as Alec spoke so enthusiastically. He looked like the teacher he was: short, medium-brown hair that had begun to recede at his forehead and a matching mustache. His glasses were large and black-rimmed. When he smiled, he revealed perfect teeth that he'd told Madison were the result of a lot of dental work while he was in college.

Heck, he was a good guy. An okay-looking guy.

But essentially, he was just fine. Although he wasn't nearly as handsome as Oren, that was irrelevant. And he certainly didn't kiss as wonderfully as Oren. But that wasn't why she was going to talk to him now. Even if the other stuff hadn't been going on in her life, ending their relationship just seemed the most appropriate thing.

"Well, I haven't…" Madison began in response to his questions and managed to say she'd checked the internet for other ideas, which she had. A couple weeks ago. She was glad when the server placed their drinks on the table in front of them. "That was fast," she said, then thanked her.

Madison watched as Alec immediately tasted his latte, seeming to savor it as he moved his lips and tongue around the disposable cup. She resisted shuddering as she watched his disgusting action. "Thanks," he then told the server. "Tastes great."

Good. She figured he'd send it back and demand another, otherwise. It wouldn't be the first time. He seemed to feel more masculine and in charge if he sent food back after it was served, which Madison found rude.

When the server left, Alec leaned over the table toward Madison. "So tell me what's next." He smiled broadly.

Madison took a sip of her decaf. Okay, she knew what she was going to do. What she had to do. But how much should she tell him?

Nothing beyond the most necessary, she figured.

"Alec, there's something I need to tell you."

The smile on his face disappeared, and his brown brows lowered behind the frame of his glasses. "That sounds serious," he said and took another sip of his drink as if it had been spiked with alcohol, which he loved.

"It is," she said, staring down at her coffee. But that wasn't right. She needed to look at him as she said this, and so she did, looking right into his pale brown eyes. They appeared curious. And worried. She took a deep breath and continued. "Alec, I'm really, really sorry. But I'm ending our engagement. I don't want to marry you."

His expression shifted, reflecting surprise. His eyes

moistened, though no tears fell. Fortunately, he didn't stand or holler at her, either. He just sat there, looking at her.

What was he thinking?

"I understand, Madison," he finally said, his voice soft. "I think that's for the best. I don't think marrying each other would be good for either of us."

Really? Madison tried hard not to breathe a huge sigh of relief or yell out a *yay!*

"I'm so glad you understand" was what she said, then wondered a bit at the pang of sorrow that went through her. He wanted out of it, too? That was good, but still…

What he said next made her feel even worse. "The thing is, you know I like you a lot. A whole lot. You're pretty and sexy and sweet. Nice. A smart teacher. But… Well, I really don't love you, Madison, and I don't think you love me, either."

Shock somehow shot through her. He didn't love her, either? He'd never given any indication…

And yet *she* was the one breaking things off. She hardly imagined she'd feel any hurt, yet somehow she did.

Not a lot, though. Ecstatic love forevermore was hardly the reason she'd entered into an engagement with him. But she wanted kids someday, and Alec had seemed like he'd be a good dad.

Not that she would tell him that now. She wouldn't even mention the fact that her life was in danger and that, by booting him out of her life, she could be eliminating that danger from his.

"No," she said in response. "I'm really sorry, Alec, but I don't love you, either. You're really a nice man, and I like you. I admire you and your teaching, but still…" She removed her engagement ring and handed it to him.

"Okay, then." He rose, stuck the ring in his shirt pocket and picked up his latte. "We're in agreement. A good thing. We'll see each other in school, of course, but that'll be it."

"Right," Madison said, a little surprised at the new pang of regret that ran through her—but didn't last long. She was free!

Except for all the dangers around her. And her need to be near another man who was a whole lot more attractive to her, someone she didn't dare get close to, even assuming he had any other kind of interest in her.

"So, see you tomorrow, friend," Alec said as he started away, aiming a small wave at her.

"See you tomorrow, friend," she said in return, then watched her ex-fiancé leave the coffee shop.

She was free! She felt relieved but also guilty as the thought of her kiss with Oren zipped through her mind, even though it really had nothing to do with her breakup with Alec, except maybe in her own mind.

Well, she apparently hadn't hurt Alec's feelings, and that was a good thing. But she was surprised at her own pang of sorrow suddenly being alone and not having a current chance at a wedding and kids and...

She vowed to thrust it aside. Quickly.

Chapter 11

Interesting, Oren thought, taking a sip of his cooling coffee.

As that guy Alec left, Oren had been able to hear their last words to one another. They'd called each other *friend*.

Which indicated that Alec had been okay with Madison dumping him. That made Oren want to smile. It was therefore unlikely the guy would give Madison a hard time later.

Oren hadn't been able to eavesdrop on what was being said at Madison's table, of course, thanks to the distance as well as the place growing busier and therefore noisier. But though he'd been prepared to pop over and try to cool any arguments down, there hadn't seemed to be any, and Madison had handed back her engagement ring.

An unwelcome thought went through Oren's head as

he watched Madison watch the man leave. How would he react if Madison and he became an item and she dumped him?

Not that they would get together that way. But if they did, he felt sure his reaction, if she ever tried walking away, would be anything but calm and friendly.

Not that he'd ever hurt her. But his attitude would undoubtedly be furious and hurt and—

Fortunately, before he could overthink this nonsense any further, Madison turned at the other table and looked at him.

"I'm done here," she said just loud enough that he could hear her over the noise of other nearby patrons.

"Okay." He stood. Reaching her side, he said, "I'm going to get my cup topped up. Would you like more?"

"Yes, please." She handed him her cup.

She was so calm. So quiet. He wondered what she really was thinking. Even though she was the one to end that relationship, was she sorry about what she'd done now?

He took their cups to the counter, and the smiling barista filled up both of them. After he returned to the table and handed Madison's back to her, he sat down across from her and said, "How about if we pick up some dinner on the way back to your place?"

The expression she leveled at him seemed contemplative. Surely it was no surprise that he intended to stay with her again that night. "That sounds fine," she said. "I just wish I didn't have to impose on you that way."

"It's no imposition," he assured her. "It's part of my job." He realized how unfriendly that sounded and added, "Besides, I'm happy to do it to keep you safe."

"Thank you." Her voice sounded a bit hoarse, and

she cleared her throat. "And maybe I can help to keep you safe, too."

He laughed. "Of course." He liked her attitude—even though he doubted there was much she could do to help him that way.

She certainly couldn't do anything to keep his heart safe when she was the one who was endangering it… *Forget that.* Thinking about having some kind of real relationship with her made him feel warm and fuzzy—and mad at himself for even considering it.

They soon left the place and walked to her car. Oren scouted their surroundings but saw nothing and no one that worried him. He helped Madison inside the car once more. After he got into the driver's seat, they discussed where to pick up their food and decided on a pizza place halfway between where they were and Madison's condo.

Once they reached the restaurant they had to wait about ten minutes, but after that it was straight on to Madison's. Still, nothing on the way got Oren overly concerned, though he remained watchful.

Soon, they were sitting at her kitchen table. They'd already had their coffee, of course, but she again offered Oren beer or wine, which he declined that night.

"I don't know what you have in mind for tomorrow," Madison said as she served pizza from the box, "but I need to get up early and head to my school. Tomorrow's a kindergarten day for me." She grinned, and he returned it, glad that she appeared relaxed and far from depressed after what she'd just gone through.

"I guess it's a school day for me, too, then," Oren said, also smiling, as he ate his first slice. For the next few minutes, as they both ate, Madison described generally what a school day was like for her: when she reported to her classroom, when her students began arriving, what she anticipated working on with them tomorrow, how their recess generally was handled.

Her workday sounded interesting, certainly different from his. He appreciated how she must be around those kids. Sounded so sweet...

Oren had already intended to hang out in the area and walk through the school as often as made sense. He'd arrive with Madison and get her to introduce him to the principal so his presence wouldn't be a problem, although he'd want her to be discreet about describing why she needed a lawman with her for now. He'd ponder that and suggest before they got there what she should say.

And of course he would be outside observing when Madison took her students out to the playground for recess.

He felt sure he'd enjoy watching her, seeing what she did. He regretted it wasn't appropriate for him to join them.

After they were done eating, Madison excused herself. "I'll hang out in the living room now, but after our earlier discussions I want to call Jillian and tell her about how things went between Alec and me. You can eavesdrop if you wish. But I think it's only fair to say my sister really liked the idea of me ending things with Alec, how well it worked out. Although..."

"Although?" Oren prompted. Was there something else she'd spoken with Alec about? Some other issue that they hadn't resolved?

Something else he needed to protect her from?

"Although," she finally continued, her red brows raised and her mouth somewhat pursed, "our mother loved the idea that I was engaged. She was helping to plan the wedding. She liked Alec well enough, too. She's not going to be happy, and I want to talk to my sister about how best to let our mom know that it's over."

Well, Oren thought, he might feel good about Madison's ending her engagement, but maybe not everyone would feel the same way. Hopefully, whatever her mother said wouldn't make Madison rethink what she'd done.

Madison sat on her comfortable lavender living room couch, her coffee cup on the end table beside her despite it being cool and nearly empty. But she didn't care. She was talking to her sister, her cell phone at her ear, and the conversation was emotional.

Admittedly a lot more emotional than her discussion with Alec had been.

She knew Oren sat on one of the fluffy beige armchairs across from her, but she mostly watched her lap as she talked.

She felt warm, protected, happy with him watching over her the way he was. Maybe that wasn't a good thing—but it was the way things were at the moment.

"I thought you'd be talking ecstatically," Jillian was saying. "You did tell Alec that you no longer wanted to marry him, didn't you?"

"Yes. And I didn't mention any possible danger but explained the truth, that I just didn't think it would work out." Madison paused, then said, "Which was actually fine, since he said he didn't love me, either. And I have to admit that hurt my feelings, even though it was the best response he could have given me. And I didn't need to tell him the real reason I'd gotten engaged to him was just to have someone there so I could have kids someday."

Jillian laughed, and out of the corner of her eye Madison noticed Oren stand. By the time she looked at him, he'd turned his back on her and approached the window a few feet behind his chair. He probably was checking the front yard to make sure no one was there who shouldn't be, but Madison wished she could have seen his face at her admission to Jillian. Would he have laughed, too? He couldn't possibly care about how Alec felt, let alone how she felt.

But she was surprised at how much she cared about what he was thinking.

But then her conversation with Jillian grew even more emotional, as it shifted from her dumping Alec, with his happy consent, to the fact that Madison now had to tell their mother. No more Alec, whom their mom had liked.

No more wedding, though the idea of having one had made Verity Colton ecstatic.

"Let's get together with Mom for dinner tomorrow," Jillian suggested. "We can have a delightful girls' night out, then let her know about…about Dad. And more, including the danger she could be in, too, and that she's also being watched by cops. Okay?"

"Sure," Madison said. "That's a great idea. And you'll be there, too, so that may take at least some of her emotionalism off me regarding Alec."

"Or not. But at least I'll be able to try to act as a buffer."

"Thank you, thank you, thank you," Madison told her sister.

"And I'll even call Mom to set it up. How about six o'clock? That's a good time for dinner."

"Six is fine with me." Madison noticed Oren's head move from side to side as he apparently continued to scan the yard. Was that really a good idea? She didn't have the living room brightly lit, but there was some light behind him that would give away the fact someone was looking out the window. If Darius was there, Oren could be in danger.

Time for her to protect him?

"And I have a good idea where to eat tomorrow," she told Jillian as she rose and approached Oren. Drawing up to him, she bumped him slightly with her shoulder, and he aimed an irritated, and maybe quizzical, glare toward her that surprisingly set her pulse racing. She waved for him to follow her away from the window, which he did. "My new friend Oren introduced me to one really nice restaurant here in town that we haven't frequented, Bubbe's Deli."

"Your *new friend*?" Jillian asked. "You mean that marshal who's protecting you?"

"Exactly," Madison said, watching that very marshal's expression change to bemused. Or maybe *amused*. "We went there for dinner, and I really liked the place. It would probably be good to introduce Mom to it, too. And it's arranged well, so we can get a booth in the back where it's quiet, and we can have an emotional, and maybe even loud, conversation without, hopefully, bothering other customers."

She didn't mention how much she'd liked the food and meeting Olivia—and that she was now wondering whether the rest of his family was so warm and caring. Maybe she'd find out one of these days.

"Sounds good to me," Jillian said. "I'll call Mom now and tell her what we're doing, though not the reason, of course. If there's a problem, I'll let you know. Otherwise, let's touch base tomorrow to finalize plans."

"Great," Madison said. They exchanged a few more sisterly comments, then ended the call.

As she pushed the button to hang up, Oren said, "Really?"

"Yes," she said. "Why not?"

"Why not, indeed? Now, I think I'll take another walk around this place outside, then get ready for bed."

Madison felt her insides plummet. "Do you really need to do that? If Darius is out there—"

"I'll be careful. And I'm sure you're aware I'm armed. I want to make as sure as possible that he's not going to attempt to get in here tonight."

Madison sighed. "I understand, but—"

"No *but*s." He gave her a glare that dared her to contradict him again. She wouldn't. But she'd be damn worried. "I'll be back in soon," he continued. "I'm sleeping on your sofa again, in case you had any questions about that."

"Nope," she said. "You know you're welcome to choose the guest bedroom, but I figured you, my brave marshal protector, would choose the same accommodations as last night." Not her bedroom, unfortunately... but she didn't want to distract him while he was watching over her. And she figured that she'd be prepared to call the GGPD if anything appeared to go wrong.

"Exactly," he said. "And we can say good-night here and now so I won't have to bother you when I come back inside."

"Fine."

They were standing at the side of her living room, much farther from the window, which made Madison feel relieved—for the moment. But Oren was going outside. He'd likely be even more in danger there than while standing at the window—or maybe not. In either case, Madison was worried for him, and not just because he was her protector. And she was the one Darius seemed to be after.

She liked Oren, appropriate or not. She didn't want to see him hurt. Period.

But she knew she wouldn't be able to convince him to stay inside. Sure, it was his job. But she gathered that bravery was who he was.

She had an urge to throw herself into his arms for a good-night kiss.

Instead, she figured she would indeed get ready for bed—but she would listen for his return. Maybe glance out the windows often herself—carefully, of course. And then, if all went well, that would be the best time for a relieved kiss goodnight.

First, though, she called Grace, who'd been the first to hint that Madison should dump Alec. Unsurprisingly, Grace was delighted.

Plus, she mentioned that she hoped Madison would find her true love someday soon—as she recently had, with Camden Kingsley.

Sounds good, Madison thought. *Someday. Maybe.*

And she ignored the image of Oren that passed through her mind.

"Hey, we need to get together again one of these days," Grace said. "Maybe even get some more Coltons to join us."

"Sounds good," Madison said but didn't want to plan anything right now.

Especially not with Oren outside looking for the man who wanted to kill her.

Where the hell was the guy now? Not that Oren wanted to run into Darius here, in this nice residential community, when it was late and fairly quiet except for the sounds of a TV or radio now and then. And dark, although the condos here had outside lights both on the buildings and on poles, mostly somewhat dim.

The air was cool and humid. Maybe some rain, or even snow, was in the forecast.

Walking slowly and carefully, remaining attentive, Oren stayed in the shadows as much as he could, in the lawn areas in front of and behind the buildings. He ducked in and out of the parking areas, too—although they were lit.

No sign of him. No sign anyone but Oren was out here creeping around.

Could it really be as safe as it felt? Most likely not. Darius had surely done his research. He undoubtedly knew where Madison lived. He hadn't shown up here last night, either. But Oren had no doubt the murderous son had something else in mind around here.

Did he now intend to kill only the man he blamed for his father's death? Maybe he'd dashed back to Kendall.

If so, other deputies were in charge there, taking care once more of Wes, in protective custody.

And here? If Darius's original plan still filled his mind, Madison's siblings could be on the guy's radar, too. Of course, they knew it now. And they were both in law enforcement, so hopefully they'd be damned careful and also be watching.

And their mother? The woman the former Richard Foster had apparently promised to marry all those years ago—after having three kids by him?

Darius probably knew about that, too, since he'd apparently done his homework about the family and followed, then attacked, Madison.

Well, Brett knew about it, too. And Brett had promised some police protection for Verity Colton, which Oren assumed would include patrol cars passing frequently through the neighborhood where she lived.

The mom they would probably have dinner with at Bubbe's tomorrow evening—an idea that made Oren shake his head. Too many connections between his family and Madison's that way—though he doubted Darius would go after any Margulies because of it. Unless, of course, he decided to kill Oren to get him out of the way so he could get to Madison.

Not going to happen.

And it appeared that nothing was going to happen tonight, or at least not now. Oren decided it was time to return to Madison's condo.

Which he did, still carefully, still watching everywhere around him.

He'd borrowed Madison's key to come out here, and now he used it to get back into the building. Once inside, he listened. Some voices emanated from the nearest unit, a man and woman, too soft for him to hear what they were saying, but they sounded calm. He kept listening nonetheless as he headed up the stairs. He could no longer hear those voices once he reached the top, and he heard nothing else.

He walked around the second-floor hallway, both looking at the rows of doors and listening. Still nothing seemed out of line, although he again heard what sounded like TV shows through a couple of them.

Soon, he used the key to reenter Madison's place. Her hallway lights were lit, but he didn't hear or see her.

He did knock on her door, though. "I'm back, Madison," he called.

"Everything okay?" she responded.

"Seems that way. Everything okay here?"

Her door opened, and she entered the hallway—wearing silky gray pajamas that shouldn't look sexy but did.

"I think so," she said, blinking. He saw that the light inside her bedroom was dim, so the brighter hallway illumination probably bothered her eyes. "Just remember I need to get up around six thirty tomorrow." She frowned at him as if making sure he understood how important that was.

Of course he remembered it. He'd probably be awake anyway, but just in case he'd set his phone's clock. "I will," he said. "Good night."

"Good night." Before he could react, she took a step toward him and kissed him very quickly on the lips, then turned and headed back into her bedroom, shutting the door behind her.

Leaving him much too sexually charged for such a minimal encounter. But of course, nothing would come of that.

Yet he felt caring. Too caring. Wanting to at least give her a good-night hug, too.

Silently, he wished her a good night's sleep, though he'd of course get up often to make certain all remained okay.

When that alarm went off the next morning, Oren was already awake. Maybe that wasn't surprising, since he'd gotten up at least five times during the night. Checking out the unit.

Checking on Madison, in her bedroom. He seldom heard her breathing deeply. Was she as awake as he?

He'd refrained from doing as he wished: talking to her. Going inside. Giving her an even better good-night kiss. And maybe more…

Nope. He was a marshal on duty. That was all, no matter what his instincts goaded him to do.

He'd probably get tired during the day, but at least they'd be around a lot of people at the school.

Not only would he have Madison introduce him to the principal and whatever security they had around there, he'd request that the principal get whatever passes he needed to patrol the school grounds.

He wouldn't get into detail, of course, but he'd let any security folks know there was a chance Madison might have an issue. Nothing major, he'd indicate. Otherwise, if it sounded bad, they might wonder why she'd even come to school that day and potentially put kids in danger.

Which in a way was a good question. But they didn't really know if or when she was in danger, where Darius might be, or what, if anything, he had in mind.

Now, Oren did as he had yesterday morning: rose, showered, got dressed. He'd run his clothes through Madison's washing machine before heading to bed last night, draping himself in a bath towel before it was all done.

Maybe today his car would arrive, and it contained a change of clothes. Or maybe he'd be able to drop by Olivia's to pick up a change of clothing he kept there. He'd be seeing his sister that evening, after all.

She'd understand he was just doing his duty by hanging out with Madison. Protecting her. Despite his undeniable attraction to her.

Chapter 12

Everything started out well that Monday at school. Madison got there when she wanted to, early in the morning—after Oren and she both grabbed a quick breakfast of cereal and coffee at her house, then left when she said it was time. Oren acted like she was in charge for a change, which she was. Even so, he was clearly the marshal who protected her, and she appreciated it. She appreciated *him*—for that reason and maybe too many others, like his kindness, his willingness to hang out with her even on her workday, his sexiness… but she hardly even knew him.

As she expected, he also observed everything around them as they headed to the school.

Of course she looked around, too. Even though she didn't have his law-enforcement assessment skills, she considered herself fairly intuitive. She'd recognized her father, hadn't she?

Fortunately, she didn't see anything—anyone—noteworthy here now, either.

She'd gotten tired of Oren being her chauffeur, so that morning she insisted on driving them to their destination—it was her car, after all—and parked in her usual area behind the school.

"Nice," Oren said as he looked at the building before they walked inside. Madison had to agree. Like other notable buildings in Grave Gulch, this school had been here for a while and had been well designed many decades ago. It wasn't especially fancy, but it was two stories high, and there was attractive concrete scrollwork decorating the outsides of the windows on the brick building.

Her kindergarten classroom was on the first floor, which worked well since her young students didn't generally have to use the stairs. Madison led Oren there first thing so she could lock her purse in her desk and check the laptop she left there to confirm her lesson plans for the day. Nothing stressful, but a lot that kids could learn while having fun. That was her primary intention.

Meanwhile, Oren walked around the room, surveilling it, she assumed, including looking out windows along the far wall from different angles.

And she watched his many angles. Who knew that his intense observation for her protection would seem so sexy?

Okay. Enough of that.

Although being on the first floor was good for the kids, Madison wondered if she should be worried about it for her own safety that day. It would be easier for someone from outside to see in and get inside and...

And nothing. Today would be fine.

"Are you ready to introduce me to the principal?" Oren said as she looked up from her laptop.

"Sure." She led him down the hall, saying hi to other teachers she saw who were just arriving.

Including Alec, who seemed nice and friendly—and relieved? Or was she just reading that into his happily brief greeting?

Alec also shot Oren a curious look.

She laughed internally. Oren was the current guy in her life—but not for the reasons Alec might be thinking.

If only… Forget that.

She led Oren to the far end of the hall on the first floor, where the school's offices were located. They entered the outer room. The principal's assistant wasn't there yet, so Madison knocked on the door behind the desk that led into the principal's office.

Madison expected Principal Nelson to call out and ask who was there. Instead, the door opened, and the principal looked out.

"Good morning, Madison," she said. "Something on your mind?" She looked toward Oren, who remained behind Madison.

"Yes. I'd like to introduce you to Marshal Margulies of the US Marshals Service—" she gestured toward Oren "—and let you know why he's here."

Principal Mae Nelson aimed a curious stare in his direction, then gestured for them to join her inside.

It was a nice-sized office, with a desk in the middle and file cabinets along the side, all organized and neat, which Madison always considered representative of who Principal Nelson was.

Mae, an African American woman in her forties, was pretty, with long wavy black hair with some gray in it pulled back in a braid down the back of her neck.

And she was one smart, excellent administrator.

"Okay," Principal Nelson said. "Sit down and tell me what's going on."

Before she could speak, Oren said, "I'm just here as a precaution today, Principal Nelson. There are some issues going on in another town that might remotely affect Ms. Colton here, so I'm just keeping an eye on her to be sure there are no problems in Grave Gulch. And I most certainly won't allow anything to happen here at an elementary school. So far, there's just been a rumored consequence of something that went on long ago that had to do with Ms. Colton's family, so we're just being extra cautious. I've followed up with GGPD, and they recommended I tail Madison for now. I asked Madison to introduce me to you so you'd know why this strange guy who's definitely not a kindergartner will be hanging out around the school, including in her classroom."

Madison watched as Oren pulled his badge from his pocket and showed it to the principal, who studied it for a few moments.

Madison was glad to see Principal Nelson smile. "No, I wouldn't consider you a kindergartner, Marshal." But the smile morphed into a frown. "Can you guarantee that nothing will go on here, that no students are in danger?"

"I don't generally like the word *guarantee*," Oren said. "And I have no reason to think this person will target any students. But I can guarantee I'll do my damnedest to protect everyone here, and I'll have the ear of the local cops if anything goes wrong—which it shouldn't."

The principal rose and folded her arms in front of her. "What is this really about?" she demanded.

"A case we thought was pretty well closed ages ago,

but since it isn't completely closed I can't discuss it, other than to request that you be careful and let me know if anything around here appears different from usual. Okay?"

"Yes, it's okay," Principal Nelson said. She accepted Oren's business card, then aimed her concentrated gaze toward Madison. "And you'll let me know if anything goes wrong." It wasn't a question.

"Of course," Madison agreed.

"Would whatever this is stay away from here if Madison also stayed away from here?" Principal Nelson asked Oren.

"We couldn't be certain," he said. "But my being here keeping an eye on things should help."

"I hope so."

Madison's classroom was still empty when she and Oren returned to it, but this was near the time that students began to arrive. Almost immediately, Cora, a classroom aide, popped in and said good morning. Madison was glad to see her. The aides provided whatever help was needed fast, ran errands and accompanied young kids who needed to use the restroom.

Today, in particular, Madison wouldn't have wanted to send any of her students on their own.

"Hi, Madison," Cora said.

"Hi, Cora." Madison turned slightly. "I'd like to introduce you to Marshal Oren Margulies. Nothing to worry about but he's watching over the school for the moment because of a potential security issue." Her assistant knew about the Coltons and their involvement with law enforcement. She also knew to keep any curiosity to herself. Madison might tell her more later but didn't need to now.

Dressed in a smock over her shirt and slacks, Cora

was youthful and energetic and full of smiles for the kids. Madison thought about warning Cora to keep watch around the school since the aide would be wandering around a lot. She started to tell Oren about the aides, but kids began entering before she had a chance to get his opinion whether she should have given Cora a heads-up about watching for anything different at the school. She figured she could always ask Oren to accompany Cora or any others when they escorted the kids. But then he'd be leaving her alone...

Better that he ensured the kids were okay.

The kids each greeted her with "Hi, Ms. Colton." They all removed backpacks when they reached their assigned seats, chairs with desk arms. The backpacks went underneath after they took out a notebook and set of crayons.

All fifteen of them were soon there. Time for lessons to begin, including learning more letters by reading and printing, and counting the items in pictures in some books. Plus biology discussions about various animals.

Madison kept an eye on Oren when he was in the room, but he left often. Had he seen anyone he shouldn't? But he gave no indication of it.

She was so glad to have him there—for her protection, and everyone else's. She knew she was lowering her eyes and smiling too much when he happened to look at her.

She got a brief chance to talk with him during recess, which occurred about an hour and a half into the class. "Don't stay out here too long," he told her as they stood at the side of the playground where Madison and Cora kept an eye on the kids playing on swings and slides. "Limit your recess time as much as you're able. Not sure, but I thought I saw…you know. In the distance, walking away fast. Still…"

Really? He'd possibly seen Darius? She hustled the class back inside not long after that—and hoped that everyone, including her and Oren, would remain safe. At least there it was easier to keep an eye on everyone.

Everything went fine that day, including lunch. She was glad when the class was over and the kids either went home or into school childcare. She remained in her classroom, making notes about all that had occurred and plans for tomorrow. She also called Jillian, leaving a message at first. Her sister soon called her back.

"Of course I didn't say why," she said to Madison, "but Mom is delighted with the idea of meeting for dinner tonight. Bryce will be joining us, too."

"Great!" Madison really was glad she'd be able to get together with her family, though she didn't look forward to telling her mother what she had to about her engagement, let alone the possible danger. "Are we all just meeting there?"

"I'm picking her up, but Bryce and you—and Oren, I assume—can get there on your own."

"See you then," Madison said. She knew it would feel somewhat odd to have Oren there at a family dinner, but his presence was definitely needed.

She would feel just as glad to have him there as she'd liked having him around all day.

Okay. He might have been mistaken, looking so hard for Darius that he believed he'd seen him in the distance when he hadn't.

But in any case, Oren intended to be damn careful, keep watching even more.

The figure he'd seen had been across the street from

the fenced playground, standing behind a parked car. He'd appeared to be looking toward the school and the students—and Oren. But he hadn't remained there after leveling a glare in the marshal's direction.

Oren didn't believe he had imagined it. He was hardly an imaginative person. Still, he'd been carefully attempting to scrutinize their surroundings in case Darius was around, and maybe he'd seen characteristics in that guy that actually weren't there. It could have just been a local resident, or even a parent, glancing at the school for no inappropriate reason.

He kept up his inspection of the area for the rest of Madison's school day, also watching when any of her students left her presence. He accompanied the aide often when she walked a kid to the nearby restroom.

He sort of enjoyed himself. He hadn't thought it would be fun to hear the enthusiastic, high voices of kindergarteners as they got excited when Madison praised them for achieving something, like reading a word or counting some pictures.

He'd thought now and then about having kids of his own. Rather liked the idea. But so far all the relationships he'd begun had gone bad so he couldn't count on it.

He definitely wasn't going to ponder what it would be like to marry Madison and have kids with her. Sure, this kindergarten teacher would be a good mom.

And right now, he was also uneasy.

Not just because he thought he might have seen Darius around here, in this environment where peace should reign, but also because he hadn't been able to verify it.

Or even go look for his target.

Darius, or whoever he'd seen, had been too far away

and had quickly disappeared from his vision. Too quickly. Going after him would have been futile.

Staying here, keeping a protective eye on Madison and everyone around her made more sense.

But that uneasiness...

He was glad when her school day drew to an end, several hours after her students had gone. She'd had a couple of meetings with other teachers, touched base with Principal Nelson once more and spent time on her computer, evaluating kids and planning lessons for the rest of the week. Or that's what she'd told him.

But finally, around five fifteen, she stood up from her desk in the classroom and started walking toward him. Oren had just taken his most recent patrol around both the interior and the exterior of the school.

Now Madison said, "I'm going to close things down in about five minutes. Are you about ready to leave?"

"Sure," he said. And was he ever.

He knew that Madison had made arrangements to have her sister show up at Bubbe's with their mother and meet their brother there around six o'clock. Oren recognized he might find it enjoyable to watch those Coltons together over dinner. The family and its closeness were well-known.

His sister would be there, too, so he'd also have someone around.

Meanwhile, he had taken time now and then to contact his colleagues in Kendall and at the home office in Grand Rapids.

The deputies now assigned to Kendall had assured him all was peaceful there. Nothing new in Wes's existence for the moment. Of course, he was only working in the bookstore part-time now that he was back in full-time protective custody.

"Okay," Madison said, "let's go."

"Am I driving this time?" Oren asked as they shut the door of her classroom behind them. "I know the way to Bubbe's best."

"I'm sure I can find it." Madison looked up at him as they walked, the expression on her pretty face confident. And he had no doubt that she could, too. "And I'm driving. I don't want my family seeing me riding in my own car with someone else behind the wheel—especially now, when part of the reason for this get-together is to let my mom know Alec's out of my life."

When they started out, Oren, as passenger, noticed Madison drove a longer way to get to the deli than he would have, and he told her so. Her expression from the driver's seat seemed more amused than sorry for the error. And it wasn't an error, as it turned out.

"I know. But I'm taking a slightly longer way to avoid passing by the school where my mother teaches. I just want to meet them there, not trade waves on the way."

"Got it." Oren wasn't surprised. Madison knew her way around Grave Gulch. "I'll just be quiet and let you drive."

"No need to be quiet," Madison responded, and for the short distance to the deli they did talk, mostly about her school and teaching—and Oren continued to enjoy being in Madison's presence and just talking with her.

When they arrived, Oren told Madison to park in the employee's space they'd taken last time.

Olivia would be glad to see him, he figured, as well as happy to get to serve their party of five that night.

Oren just hoped it would be a pleasant, quiet meal, despite the fact that Madison was going to tell her mother she was no longer an engaged woman.

How would Verity Colton react to that?

And to the fact that Madison had seen her father, if she hadn't already told her mother—and he didn't think she had.

And the potential resulting danger.

How would Madison's mother take the news?

This could wind up being a very interesting evening.

Maybe even more than he imagined, since, after Madison shut off the car, she scanned the parking lot. "Don't see them here, but they could have parked anywhere," she said.

And before Oren could agree, she maneuvered over the console between them and planted a quick but much-too-enticing kiss on his lips. "Wish me luck," she said without explaining why she thought she would need it. And then she got out of the car.

Chapter 13

Okay, so why had she done that? Madison didn't even look at Oren as they walked around the restaurant to the front. She'd kissed him. And enjoyed it. And regretted it—sort of. They weren't in that kind of relationship. Although it had been one hot, enjoyable kiss... What was he thinking now?

And her? Well, she did it to kind of boost her courage. Not that she wasn't happy to be getting together with her family. She loved them. But she figured her mom wasn't going to be thrilled about no longer having the fun of planning a wedding and would have no hesitation about letting Madison know.

And Madison would have to mention having seen, and talked to, her dad. What would her mom think about that? How would she react?

Oren would be there with her. Protecting her, though not from her mother. And not being a love interest the way Alec had been. Of course, her siblings knew Oren's role in her life, but she'd also have to explain it to her mom. Even more important, she had to warn her to be careful.

But surely Darius, now that he'd started after Madison, wouldn't try to include other family members in his horrible plot, except the main focus of his anger, her father.

Would he?

She certainly hoped not.

They'd reached the end of the walkway between the two restaurants, and now Oren gently held her back as he scrutinized the street and sidewalk. His hand was on her arm. If she turned, maybe she could stand straight against him and—

No. She didn't want to distract him, no matter how much she enjoyed his touch.

"Okay," he soon said. "Let's go in."

Oren had told Madison he'd already called his sister and she was reserving a table in a back corner. Madison's family should therefore have a good place to get together and talk—and eat some of the food Madison had enjoyed so much when she was there before with him.

Madison saw Jillian walking toward them along the sidewalk, and with her was their mother. Madison dashed forward, arms out to give her mom a big hug.

"Madison!" Verity Colton exclaimed. "So glad to see you, dear." Her mother hugged her back, then pulled away and looked her up and down.

Madison was still in the dress she'd worn to school that day and figured her second-grade-teacher mother was, too. Mom's was a navy blue that went well with her short, platinum blonde hair. Madison studied her mom's features, thinking how she'd often been told that they resembled each other—most recently, of course, by her father. Madison didn't always see it, but their lips, noses and cheeks were similar shapes, and even their eyebrows arched somewhat alike. But Madison's hair was red, of course, and she wore it long, unlike her mother's almost pixie cut.

Did they actually look much alike? Well, it didn't really matter. They must resemble each other well enough for her dad to recognize her after all these years...

"So how are you doing?" her mom asked. "I know Bryce is joining us too, but I don't see Alec. Is he coming?" Mom's gaze had left Madison and was now aimed straight at Oren.

"Let's go inside and get our table," Madison said, not wanting to attempt to explain anything now, out here, and without a glass of wine in front of her.

Jillian broke into the conversation. "Good idea." Then she leaned toward Madison and added more softly, "Everything okay?"

"Hope so," Madison replied, but she knew that her attempt at a smile didn't get very far.

Her mother stopped and looked at Oren. "Hello," she said, her tone cool. "I'm Verity Colton, Madison's mother, and Jillian's, too."

"I know. Nice to meet you. I'm Oren Margulies. My sister owns this deli, and she's saving a table for us."

That was enough explanation for now, Madison thought. But it was time for her to get this going. She hurried to Oren's side, careful not to even brush against him slightly. "Mom, Jillian, come on." And she led even Oren into the restaurant.

"Hi, Madison. Welcome," greeted Olivia. "And you

too, bro. Your favorite large table in the back is all yours this evening."

"Thanks, sis," Oren said.

"Yes, thanks so much, Olivia," Madison echoed her appreciation, then added, "We're expecting one more person this evening, Bryce Colton. He should be here soon."

"Like now," said a familiar voice from behind Madison. She turned to see her brother—right behind her. They exchanged hugs. "And hi to you, too, Marshal," he said to Oren, who shot him a smile and a lopsided salute which he returned.

Made sense, Madison thought. It felt natural, having Oren the marshal there, with her FBI agent brother.

In moments, Oren led them all through the deli's middle aisle toward the back, where there was an empty table for six in the corner, which they wouldn't completely fill. The tables around it were mostly occupied, and a hum of conversations filled the air.

So did an aroma of delicious food. Madison thought she caught the slightly spicy scent of warm corned beef.

Madison ordered matzo ball soup, of course, as well as coleslaw. Some of the others also chose soup, but mostly sandwiches were on their radar, including corned beef and pastrami, either on rye or challah. Madison didn't pay a lot of attention to who ordered what, except she did notice, and wasn't surprised, that Oren chose corned beef on rye. It was a choice that tasted good, and Oren undoubtedly ate it here a lot.

Once they ordered, their mom stood and raised her wineglass. "Time for a toast, everyone. You all have a new baby cousin." Her gaze lit on Madison, who figured that was a not-so-subtle hint that her mother hoped she'd have similar news soon. Verity explained, though, that her brother Frank had become a grandfather. His son, Travis, had welcomed his first child, Hope, with his fiancée Tatiana.

Madison was glad to toast baby Hope, but figured that news might make it a little more difficult to relay her own news to her mother. Madison was buddies with her cousin Travis. She was happy for him…and maybe even a little jealous. Maybe someday Travis would hear that Madison had had a baby, too. At least Madison could hope so.

She couldn't help a quick glance at Oren. Unlikely that they'd ever get into a relationship like that, but the idea somehow felt good to Madison, especially now that Alec was no longer part of her life. Interesting, though, that Travis's fiancée, Tatiana Davison, was his co-CEO at the company he'd started, Colton Plastics. And maybe even more interesting was that she was the daughter of serial killer Len Davison.

Their dinner went well, fortunately. Madison, sipping on her red wine, figured she would wait till they were nearly done to address the issues she needed to with her mother. That way, they could enjoy themselves for the longest time possible.

Her soup was, of course, as delicious as the last bowl she'd had here—and she did partake in some challah on the side, as well as her tasty coleslaw. Her siblings and mother appeared to enjoy their food, too, as well as the company.

Although the camaraderie didn't include Oren much. Oh, sure, he mostly sat with them and occasionally even caught Madison's eyes as he then scanned the room with his own, making it clear to her that just because he sat with them didn't mean he wasn't watching out for her safety. And for her family's.

Her mother glanced at Oren a lot, as if wondering who this man who'd joined them for dinner was and why he kept looking around. Plus, he occasionally rose, excused himself and walked away, potentially giving the impression he was off to the restroom, but Madison knew better.

And even when he just sat there and ate, he appeared alert and uneasy, which didn't help Madison's state of mind. Maybe this wasn't the best place to have the conversation that would inevitably start soon.

But it did make sense for her to be with her two siblings when she had the discussion with their mother.

They understood. They'd back her up.

And hopefully her mom, who wouldn't be thrilled, would understand.

As they ate, most of the conversation centered around their mother's day at school.

Once they'd all finished their meals, they still had drinks on the table, and Madison sipped more of her tart red wine as she looked at her mom, who was across the table from her. She, too, held her wineglass, and she looked away from Jillian to Madison, who sat beside her sister. And yes, Oren was once more on her other side—for her protection, of course, though she wasn't about to tell her mother that right now, though she'd have to eventually.

She didn't have to explain to her law-enforcement siblings, who knew the facts.

"This has been a fun evening, but I think it would be more fun if Alec was with us so we could discuss even more of the wedding plans than we can without him. But I haven't heard anything from you lately about where things stand, even whether you found a dress on your out-of-town shopping expeditions." She paused. "Did you?" Her glance darted quickly to Oren at Madison's other side, then back.

Madison resisted the urge to put her wine down and hold Jillian's hand for reassurance. Or, even more enticingly, Oren's. But neither would be appropriate.

Instead, she waited a moment before responding, allowing her ears to take in the sounds of some of the conversations around them, all sounding upbeat, at least from a distance.

She, likewise, attempted to sound happy. "Alec and I decided to call off the wedding, Mom." She made herself smile a bit.

But Mom's blue eyes grew huge. "What?" she exclaimed, so loudly that Madison cringed and glanced around at the nearest tables. Sure enough, some patrons there were staring at them.

Madison shrugged as nonchalantly as she could. "We talked about it, Mom. Both Alec and I agreed that we really weren't cut out for each other. Yes, we like each other a lot—he's a nice guy—but more as friends than a man and woman in love or planning a future together. In fact, we agreed that we really don't love each other, so it would be better for us to end our engagement. Maybe that way we could each even find someone else more suited to us." Madison felt an urge to glance at Oren but stopped herself. That might give him, or the others at the table, the impression that she considered him possibly more suitable for her.

Well, why did she have that urge to look at him? Surely *that* idea wasn't really in her mind…

Although… Well, this wasn't the time to consider it, but in the brief period she'd known Oren, she found him a lot more suitable for a potential long-term—forever—relationship. She knew she could count on him. That he would take care of her, to the extent she needed taking care of.

But, heck, that was his job. That was all.

Although…well, Madison had to admit to herself that she was a lot more sexually attracted to this man who happened to be in her life than she'd ever been to Alec. And she liked the idea that Oren was so close to Olivia.

Bryce and Jillian seemed fine that Madison had broken things off with Alec. Would her siblings be okay if she ever entered into a relationship with Oren?

Didn't matter. That wasn't going to happen.

"I…I don't understand, honey," her mother said, her expression appearing…well, anguished. "I know you care for one another, or you wouldn't have gotten engaged in the first place. And there's nothing standing between you, preventing you from getting married. Did you have an argument? You need to contact Alec again, fix the situation, get your plans back together."

There were tears in her mom's eyes and that made Madison mist up as well, but not for the same reason. She believed she understood what was really on her mother's mind. "I'm so sorry, Mom, but that's not going to happen. We're through. But this situation—my situation—isn't at all like what you went through with Dad. He had reasons to leave…" At least at first. And soon Madison was going to have to fill her mother in on that part of the current situation as well.

First, though, she needed to convince her mother that her breakup with Alec was for the best.

"Yes. Yes, he did," Mom said, now looking down at the table in front of her. "But Alec isn't in the military. And that's why, if there's nothing in the way, you should just move forward as you planned. Get married. Continue with the rest of your life…"

Madison glanced at Jillian, then at Bryce. Both appeared utterly sympathetic, but neither jumped in to help her.

She was the first of all of them to even get engaged. Of course, she was the oldest. But the situation just wasn't right.

And her mother couldn't expect her to move forward with the wrong man, no matter what had happened in her own life.

Madison suspected that her mom wanted her children each to find someone and marry quickly so they'd never have to go through what she did with their dad—having the man she loved die before they'd ever gotten married. Or at least that was what she'd believed.

At least things at the table had quieted down, so no one else appeared to look their way. And Olivia had joined them. Oren handed his sister a credit card, which Madison really appreciated. Of course she would pay him back, but at least they would all be able to leave as soon as it seemed appropriate.

And Madison added generosity to the list of things she liked about Oren.

Now? Well, she really wanted to talk more with her mother, find a way to prevent her from stewing over what had happened.

"I can understand why you're upset, Mom, but I really am continuing with the rest of my life just the way I should."

"It's *not* the way you should." Her mom's voice was raised again, once more drawing attention to the table. She stood all of a sudden and pushed back, almost knocking over her chair, making Madison cringe. "Excuse me. I need to— Where's the restroom?"

She didn't wait for an answer. She turned her back on them and hurried away.

"I'll go with her," Madison told the others, but just then her phone pinged, which made her hesitate.

"I'll go take care of her," Jillian said, rising and hurrying after their mother.

Madison checked her phone, although she planned on following them as fast as she could.

Until she saw the message from an unknown sender.

How nice that you have the whole family here together. Time for me to make sure all of you are gone so the man who killed my father will suffer even more. See you around, in the deli—maybe the bathroom. Who knows? But you will all see me soon.

Oren had been watching Madison with sympathy while she engaged in that anticipated disagreement with her mother. But not watching too closely. Out in the open like this, he wanted to keep an eye on their surroundings.

But when Verity dashed away, Oren rose, figuring Madison would follow her mother. Jillian joined her, but Madison had stopped. Looked at her phone.

A text, Oren figured. And judging by the horror on Madison's face, it was bad. Real bad.

She'd only gotten as far as the end of the table, and he joined her quickly as the other two women continued walking away. "What is it?" he demanded.

He didn't wait for her to reply. Instead, he carefully grabbed the back of her hand. Her phone was cradled in its palm, and he pulled it toward him. And looked.

And swore.

He let her go gently and pivoted to stare at the rest of the room. Again.

Where was that damn Darius? In the ladies' room? Somewhere else, laughing at them, while he prepared to kill them all?

He needed to know, to protect Madison's family— but Madison came first.

He needed, therefore, to enlist Bryce. No need to yell anything at him, at least. Madison's brother had joined her, too, and stood in front of her.

"What is it?" he asked, his eyes on Oren.

"You need to go get your mother and Jillian. And then…" An idea came to him immediately. "We all need to meet at the Grave Gulch PD right away. I'll call Brett and let him know." At least he now had the interim chief as a contact. And now he might need to become even more.

"A threat?" Bryce questioned but didn't wait for an answer. Instead, he dashed toward the ladies' room.

"What are we going to do?" Madison asked. Her voice was shaky, and so was she.

He knew because he kept one arm around her. His left arm, in case he had to grab his gun from his pocket.

"You heard me. You and I are heading straight for the police department, and your relatives will meet us there. I trust your FBI brother to make it quick. Do you?"

The look in her green eyes revealed terror. "Yes, but—"

"No *but*s," Oren interrupted. "Let's go."

He felt furious. But Oren was most concerned about Madison. Rightly or wrongly, he really liked her. He would protect her—and her family—from Darius, no matter what.

Chapter 14

With Oren in control, they started down the center aisle of the restaurant.

Olivia stood near the front speaking to some customers in a booth. She looked at Oren, then beyond him, where the others followed. "What's going on, bro?"

"Tell you later, but we've got to leave now." Fortunately, the waitress had returned with his credit card and receipt, and he'd added a healthy tip. He'd work things out for partial repayment by the others whenever he was able.

He realized how concerned his sister was, judging by her wide-eyed expression as she looked from Oren to Madison and back. "Is everything okay?" she asked but obviously knew the answer.

"I don't know, but hopefully we'll be taking any trouble with us." He certainly didn't want anything to happen to Olivia, her customers or her restaurant, another good reason to leave fast. He leaned toward her, though. "Keep an eye on things," he said softly, "and if anything looks even a little wrong, call 9-1-1. I'll explain later."

"But—"

Oren had taken Madison's hand again and started hurrying toward the exit once more, not wanting to take time to explain now—or to stay and potentially make things more dangerous at the deli. He stopped just inside the door, keeping Madison right behind him, and again looked around. Of course he might not be able to see one person in the slight crowd outside or in a car driving by, but for now all appeared okay. He looked back into the deli beyond Madison and was glad to see Bryce and the other women not far behind.

And though he hadn't told Bryce much, the FBI agent was doing as Oren did and looking around constantly, hand on his pocket, as he led his relatives out of there.

But as they got outside and those in law enforcement looked around, Verity said, "What the hell is going on here? You're all freaking me out. Is this some kind of game to make me stop pushing Madison? Or—"

"Enough, Mom," Madison said sharply, getting close to her. "There's a lot you don't know about but should. We're—we're all going to the police station right now, and we'll tell you about it. *I'll* tell you about it. It's incredible, and you won't believe it, but it's also really dangerous right now. So just follow Bryce and Jillian, and listen to what they have to say. When we get there, I'll fill you in."

"You'd better." Verity scowled at her older daughter, but at least she listened and started walking again between her two younger children.

"Wow," Madison said to Oren. "She is actually paying attention now."

If he'd thought he had time, Oren would have called a car right away—but they had to leave immediately. He didn't want to drive Madison's, in case Darius had rigged it to explode. But time was important.

Oren did see a police car driving by, with two uniformed cops in the front seat. He stepped onto the street and flagged it down. "Hey, we're on our way to the station because of an urgent matter. Can you drive us there? You can contact Interim Chief Shea to check on us." He gave his name and Madison's. "And if you've another car in the area, please drive those three, also." He gestured to the group behind them. "One of them's with your department."

"I recognize CSI Colton," said the cop in the passenger's seat, staring where Oren pointed. "Yeah, come in, and we'll get another patrol car here in a minute."

"Great." Oren opened the back door and helped Madison in. "I want to ride with you to the station, too," he said to the cop, "but there's something I need to check first. I'm walking around the back of the deli to check Madison's car. Please pull around and pick me up."

"No!" Madison's voice was loud and adamant. "Get in this car, Oren. It's unsafe to even be out there, let alone checking on my car. You know Darius knows what it looks like."

"Exactly," Oren said, and he nodded at the uniformed officer closest to him. "I've had some bomb disposal training as part of my job," he assured Madison, assuming that was at least part of her concern.

"We'll stay in visual contact with him," the same cop said after turning slightly toward Madison, and Oren silently cheered the guy. He probably knew nothing about the situation, but possibly thanks to the mentioned GGPD connections, he trusted them and was willing to protect them.

"Thanks," Oren told the tall, thin, serious guy, whose name tag on his uniform said he was Werther.

The easiest way for Oren to get to the parking lot to check out Madison's car would be to head between the buildings the way he usually did. But that might leave him vulnerable to an attack started from the Italian restaurant next door. Plus, he wouldn't be able to stay in visual contact with the cop car, as Werther had proposed.

Oren was pleased to see another cruiser pull up to the curb, and the others started getting in. He then walked to the far side of the Italian restaurant along the minimally crowded sidewalk, intending to sprint down the driveway beside it to the parking lot in the rear of both eating establishments.

He was glad to see the police car driving slowly beside him, then also turn into the parking lot.

Except—as Oren started to dash down the driveway, with the cop car right behind him, a black SUV tore down it in the other direction. A familiar-looking vehicle, and Oren stared toward the driver.

And found the guy also staring briefly and angrily at him. It was Darius Amaltin, Oren was sure: a young-looking, thin guy with long brown hair and an intense gaze. The guy didn't attack him, most likely because of his police escort. Had he been waiting for Madison to go get her car? Was the text he'd sent intended to get her to leave the deli quickly—and drive away?

Oren was furious at Amaltin. And frightened for Madison. At least she was under police protection now.

And Darius was the one driving away. At the end of the driveway he screeched off to the right.

No way would Oren be able to follow him, and even

the cop car was unlikely to catch up with the suspect, since it would have to turn around first.

Oren had already stopped on the driveway, and now he looked at the two cops in the front seat of the police car. He hurried to Werther's window, and the officer rolled it down. "The driver of the SUV that just left is the source of the danger to us," he blurted. "If you could get someone after him, that would be damn helpful."

"We'll give it a try." Werther frowned as he pulled out his phone.

"Want to get in and let me try to catch up with him?" asked the driver.

"No!" Madison called from the back seat. "Please, no. He may be waiting for Oren to come after him so he can hurt him."

Oren was glad she'd been the one to veto the proposition; no way was he allowing the people guarding Madison to chase down a criminal. It might be possible to catch him, Oren thought, but it was unlikely. He was more concerned that, if the guy was waiting somewhere around here, it would be for Madison.

"We need to get to the station as soon as possible. It would be best if you could get someone else after that car. But—"

"But?" the driver echoed.

"But let me take a quick look at Madison's car." Just in case, Oren thought, and he hurried down the drive into the parking lot.

He quickly reached Madison's vehicle. When he looked back toward her, she was aiming her key fob toward her car.

"No!" Oren shouted, afraid Darius had somehow rigged it… He got down on his knees and looked toward the undercarriage.

Sure enough, he saw a box there with wires that seemed attached to the car.

Damn! If this went off, it might blow up the entire area, including Madison, the cops, Oren himself and even Bubbe's Deli and his sister and everyone there. He was suddenly terrified for all of them.

He rose quickly and returned to the cop car. "Don't even try opening the doors!" he yelled to Madison. "Give one of these officers your key." Then he turned back to Werther. "Better call in a well-equipped investigation team for this one, with people primed to deal with explosives. Have a unit from your station get here to evacuate the area, businesses and all, plus get someone on patrol here right away to make sure no one else gets near the car—or they're liable to get blown to pieces."

As the cops started driving away, Oren called Olivia. "There's a bomb out here," he said.

"Oh, no!" Olivia exclaimed. "I'll get the place and neighboring stores evacuated right away."

Good. Oren knew his sister would do it and do it right. He next called Deputy Kathy Smith, one of the marshals now guarding Wes/Richard in Kendall, to warn them, too, in case Darius had rigged something there to kill his prey—or gotten an ally prepared to do it.

"Thanks," she said. "We'll check things out."

Oren believed her—but he still couldn't relax. Not under these circumstances.

He could only hope that they'd catch Darius now, or at least prevent him from harming anyone.

Madison turned over her car keys to one of the officers in the front—realizing her hand was trembling. All of her was trembling. Hard. She was terrified.

If it wasn't for Oren—

She was glad he had gotten into this cop car, too, after discovering the problem under her car, which she couldn't see but assumed was a bomb since Oren had mentioned getting blown up.

At least he hadn't attempted to remove it—and kill himself by setting it off.

Terrified? No, she was panic-stricken, and trying hard to hide it. Thank heavens she had Oren with her. His presence was highly welcome, and maybe did calm her just a little.

Now they were presumably heading for the police station, where her mother and siblings should already be.

She'd have to explain it all to her mom. Jillian and Bryce already knew. But how would she be able to ensure they all remained safe?

Could the cops do that? Protection wasn't in Jillian's job description at the GGPD. Maybe it was in Bryce's at the FBI, but Madison doubted that. It apparently was in Oren's, at the Marshals Service. He'd helped Madison's father with his current identity. He'd helped Madison with her survival. But—well, he was now probably on Darius's list along with her, and her mother and siblings, according to that text.

And her father.

Madison at least needed to tell her mom about her father soon.

Finally—it seemed like forever, although it was probably only five minutes—they reached the police station.

Were her mother and siblings there yet? Surely they were. She and Oren had been delayed a bit as he'd checked her car and they'd watched Darius drive off and also waited for the next cop car to arrive so no one else could get close to her vehicle.

"Madison. You're here." That was the highly welcome voice of Jillian, who definitely knew her way around the police station. She hurried from behind the gated front desk to where Madison, Oren and their police companions had just entered.

"Yes," Madison said when Jillian reached them. "It was…a bit of an experience. A damn scary one. I'll tell you about it. Are Mom and Bryce here, too?"

"Yes. They're in a conference room. I'll take you there now. We're waiting for Brett to join us so we can discuss what to do next."

"Any idea how long he'll be?" Oren asked.

"He's in the middle of something, but he promised to join us as soon as possible," Jillian said.

"Hey, I think you're okay now," said the cop who had driven them here: Officer Scott, according to his metal ID badge. "We'll be heading off, maybe to see what's going on with that rigged car of yours."

Madison shuddered. She liked her car—but she might never want to drive it again, even if it survived. "Thanks so much. I really appreciate all your help."

"Ditto here," said Oren from beside her, and he reached out to shake the officers' hands.

Madison entered first and saw that her mom and Bryce sat at the long wooden table that took up the center of the room, similar to the last conference room Madison had visited. Her mother immediately stood.

And Jillian was with Madison, who was so relieved her family members were all okay that she felt tears fill her eyes.

Her mom spoke. "I want an explanation, Madison. Both Bryce and Jillian keep telling me that you need to be the one to tell me what's going on. Does this have something to do with your foolish decision not to marry Alec?"

"No, Mom," Madison said. "Well, maybe indirectly since I first saw…" She didn't finish. That was almost humorous, but she didn't think she had any real laughs within her after a near-death experience. "But I think you'd better sit down."

Her mother frowned and shook her head, but she did as Madison said.

Madison also sat, with Jillian and Oren beside her. Their supportive presence made her feel almost cool and human and ready to deal with the emotions her mother was likely to evince once she revealed the story that started all this.

Almost.

Everyone was looking at her. She understood that, but she also wished she had another glass of wine in front of her to relieve some stress.

She began talking anyway. "Mom, I know you're aware that I first went to Kendall to look for a wedding dress a bit over a week ago."

"Yes," her mother responded.

"While I was there, I saw…someone who looked familiar." She shot a gaze toward Bryce, who smiled encouragingly. She saw Oren's hand move on the table, as if he wanted to help boost her mood by holding hers, which of course was utterly inappropriate. Even if he had just saved her life.

"Someone you know?" her mom encouraged.

"Well, yes. As it turned out, you know him, too." Madison paused, then forced herself to continue. "I went back there this week to look for him again, maybe talk to him to see if my imagination was totally out of control…but it wasn't. Mom, it was our father, Richard Foster."

"What!" her mother screamed and stood up. "You're joking. I've told you…I've told all of you that your dear, sweet father… He died years ago in the war."

Jillian rose beside her and placed her hand on their mother's shoulder. "Please, sit down, Mom," she said. "And listen to what Madison has to say. You need to hear it. Our lives—yours included—depend on it." She shot a look at her elder sister.

"But—"

"Please, Mom," Bryce also said. He, too, encouraged their mother to sit down. And, finally, she did. But her expression, the stiffness of her posture, suggested she wouldn't believe a word of what Madison said.

Madison wished she didn't have to believe it—well, all of it—either. She was delighted that their dad was still alive but couldn't completely accept why he'd remained out of their lives, even if it was because of supposed danger after he'd helped put a killer behind bars. And even if his reappearance in their lives had almost just killed Madison herself.

Even though what he'd grimly prophesied was now somewhat coming true.

Her voice hoarse, Madison said, "Dad is in witness protection. He stayed out of our lives, Mom, to keep us safe and to get justice for a murdered man. And as much as I didn't want to believe that when he first told me, what's going on now shows it was the truth."

She started from the beginning, her first trip to Kendall when Grace had come with her. She explained that she'd seen a man who looked a lot like a much-older Bryce. She glanced at her brother, who nodded in encouragement, which she appreciated. She said that her not understanding, not wanting to believe it, made her return the next week to find the fellow again and maybe even talk with him.

She described how she'd seen him, how she'd followed him and how she'd been grabbed and arrested while jaywalking right behind him. This time, she looked at Oren, who raised his black eyebrows and smiled at her.

She couldn't help smiling back again for just a moment, even remembering her first, angry feelings about Oren as he arrested her. She felt a lot different about him now, with his always being there for her. Protecting her.

"Really?" her mother asked.

"Really." Madison explained then who Oren was, how Richard Foster was now under the protection of the Marshals Service, with Oren as his main contact. How he had been under that protection for years, after witnessing a murder and testifying. How Amaltin had died in prison twenty years ago after threatening Richard's life, but Amaltin's son Darius was still threatening him and his family. Shea joined them in the conference room then and took a seat. The chief said nothing, just listened as Madison continued.

Madison described briefly how Oren and she had been forced off the road on their drive here to Grave Gulch—by that son. She then told what had happened when Oren and she left the deli a short while ago—and how Oren had checked out her car and found the explosives. "But it's not just me," she said. "He threatened all of us. He sent me a text message that included my family in his threats. Every one of us needs to be really careful now."

"And go live in a safe house," Brett said, standing,

leaning over the table and looking at each of them in turn. "All of you."

Now, that was something new, Madison thought. She glanced at Oren, who appeared slightly puzzled, too, but he nodded at Brett nonetheless.

"What do you mean?" their mom asked, and Madison was glad. She wanted to know more of what Brett intended, too. She was scared, sure. More for her mom and siblings—and father—than herself. But she'd no intention of making any major changes except being a lot more alert and careful.

And try hard to keep her terror under control. She didn't want to die, but she had to do what she could to help her family.

Brett explained he'd been in touch with Oren's marshal colleagues now in Kendall keeping watch over Wesley Windham. Wesley had also received some texted threats not only against him but against Verity and their children, presumably from Darius.

Plus, the investigators who'd looked at Madison's car found some pretty lethal explosives there, and the officers who'd attempted to find Darius when he'd driven off had had no success.

"It's dangerous out there," Brett finished. "We've done well with safe houses when there've been other people in trouble here in Grave Gulch, and I've got some members of our police force who know what they're doing to help out. Until we get this Darius, we need to keep you safe, and that's the best way. So—got it? All of you Coltons who are here are going to be kind of like Wesley Windham in Kendall. You'll be in a special place under our direct protection, starting immediately."

Good idea, Madison thought...but only for their mother. Maybe Jillian and Bryce, but they were both in law enforcement so a safe house was most likely unnecessary for them.

And her? No way was she going to hide that way.

It would be much better if she stayed at least somewhat visible—and brought Darius into the open to be captured.

She looked straight into Oren's eyes. He was staring at her, too, as if attempting to read her thoughts.

Well, she'd tell him and the rest of them.

And hope they all got it.

Chapter 15

That expression on Madison's face… Not that he could read her mind, but if he had to guess, she was against the idea of a safe house, at least with respect to her.

She confirmed it. "Thanks so much," she said to Brett, looking steadily into the police chief's eyes. "I think it's a wonderful idea—to protect my mother and siblings, if they're willing to stay there for a while. But… Well, I want to do whatever is necessary to capture the man who intends to kill us all. He seems to be mostly after me now, so I don't just want to hide out. Although I do intend to be careful, I need to be around to see if the guy will try to get me so he can be caught. Not that I'm in law enforcement, but if Oren can still help…"

She looked at him with a pleading expression.

Hell, he should say no. Despite his willingness to use all efforts to protect her, he was terrified that wouldn't be enough. He should convince her somehow to head to that safe house and stay far away from any possibility of that jerk Darius finding her.

But if that happened, he'd have no excuse to stay here and protect her. The local PD would have that obligation, which they might meet well. Or not.

As much as he hated to admit it, she was right. If they really wanted to catch the guy, it would be better to have a target who was visible to him. A *well-protected* target.

Before he responded, Bryce spoke. "I understand what you're saying, Madison, but you can't do that. And—"

"I don't like it either, but..." Oren broke in, again staring at her, as if his look would make her change her mind. If it did, he'd just have to live with it.

"Please, Oren," she said. "Or are you going back to take care of our father? You said other marshals are doing that now."

"They are. But the idea of you purposely placing yourself in the crosshairs of that intended killer—"

"With you here to protect me," she said, which he certainly intended if she stayed around.

And as much as he hated admitting it to himself, her trusting him that way made him feel rather proud.

"Look, this is what I think," Bryce said. "If I had a choice, I'd send you to the safe house, Madison. I don't like your making yourself a target by remaining in your usual life, especially when you're right—the guy's apparently after you first. But here's my suggestion. I'll avoid the safe house, too, at least for now. That way, I can help protect you, as Oren does, as well as doing all I can to help find the suspect. And if Jillian goes there, not only will she be safe, but she can help to ensure our mother's safety." He looked at Madison. "Does that work for you?"

She nodded at her brother. "Sounds good."

Oren kept himself from cheering. That certainly worked for him, as long as Madison wasn't going to listen to reason and head to the safe house herself. He'd take care of her, and now he'd also have her brother's help.

Plus, he'd do what he could to make sure her students weren't jeopardized, either.

And she was actually right, he admitted to himself. They were much more likely to find her potentially lethal stalker sooner if Madison stayed in his sights, in her regular life, as much as possible.

"Okay," Brett said, nodding enough for his red hair to shift at his collar. "I'll call a couple of my colleagues here who've put together safe houses before. They've already got at least one location available they've used in the past, and you two, Verity and Jillian, can pick up your essential belongings with those cops with you for protection, then head there tonight. Okay?"

Oren wondered if Jillian would be okay with it. Sure, she was a member of the GGPD, but she did crime-scene investigations, not protection. It was their mother, though, she'd be protecting.

Fortunately, Jillian was fine with it. "I'd really like both of you to join us, Madison and Bryce—especially Madison, since you don't have any kind of law-enforcement background and the guy does seem to be after you now." She looked at her sister but didn't wait for Madison's response. "But I'm willing to go to a safe house for my own protection under these circumstances, and much more so if I can also help take care of our mom." Her gaze moved to land on their mother, who didn't even look at her. But her expression was grim.

Oren figured some of what Jillian said was to placate their mom and make sure she was willing to do as she'd been told: stay in that house for a while. Having one daughter there with her had to make the situation at least a little more palatable.

Even though her other kids would be out in the world, potentially in a lot of danger.

All the more reason for Oren to help protect Madison—and to find the dangerous man threatening them all.

Mostly Madison, which stoked his motivation even more. And continuing to protect Madison on his own? Oh, yeah. Sure, it was his job. But he was beginning to recognize that it was turning into a whole lot more. Yes, he cared for her. And as he considered what he would be up to in the future—well, he was starting to wonder if Madison could remain part of it.

"All right," Verity finally said, standing and shaking her head. "Richard's really alive? And that's the reason for all this?" She looked again at Madison, who nodded, a sympathetic look on her face. "Okay, then. I want to know more. A lot more." She crossed her arms and sat back down. "I know you kids are always concerned about me, and this is a difficult situation. So for now, I'll go to that safe house with you, Jillian— as long as Madison and Bryce promise to be careful. I guess they won't be able to visit us, then leave and come back, since that might give the location away. But please, please, consider changing your minds and joining us. Okay?"

"Oh, Mom, I'm so glad," Madison said, hurrying over to hug her mother. "And I'll keep in touch the best way I can, through the police department. Okay?" She looked up toward Brett, who nodded.

"Sounds good," he said. "You, too, Mr. FBI." His gaze moved to Bryce.

"Yep." Bryce also nodded. "And I'll want to discuss contacts with you—whether Oren and I, and Madison, should keep in touch with you directly or who in your department we should rely on."

"Good idea," agreed Brett. "Once I get all the safe-house details and personnel worked out, we'll talk. In fact, we'll talk more about it tonight."

Though Oren wanted to get Madison somewhere else immediately, there wasn't any place safer than the police station. And it wouldn't hurt to learn more about the safe house.

Brett left the room and soon returned with his K-9, Ember, and a couple of cops, after apparently getting a team together to establish and prepare for running the safe house with Verity and Jillian living there.

The group described the location that would be used, a remote house a distance from downtown Grave Gulch, one with thick walls and lots of other homes around, though not too close, and no woods or anything else to obscure it from the team protecting its inhabitants. Oren gathered that it was owned by the police department, although the deed designated some former cop who'd retired—and still cooperated—as the owner. Oren looked forward to seeing the place, but that might take a while unless Madison changed her mind and decided to stay there with her mother and sister.

The two safe-house specialists Brett introduced them to were armed uniformed officer Daniel Coleman, a K-9 at his side, and Detective Troy Colton. They both regarded everyone in the room with curiosity. They might not be the only ones to provide the planned protection, but at least initially they would be in charge of the location where Verity and Jillian would stay, ensuring they remained out of sight and safe.

Brett then let his safe-house staff know who the others in the room were, not just the two women they'd be taking care of. "For safety's sake, you shouldn't all be in communication with each other much," Brett said after completing the introductions. "We'll get a few burner phones, though, so you can talk now and then on a limited basis."

Finally, it was time to leave. Almost. Oren would need to call the marshals' office in Grand Rapids soon and speak to some of his superior officers. He'd still be protecting Madison, which remained his assignment, but he needed to inform his superiors about the recent events—and learn if they had any additional orders to convey.

Meanwhile, the trainees he'd worked with had driven here to Grave Gulch from Kendall in two cars, one of them Oren's since he'd left it to accompany Madison here in hers. They had both departed in the other car, and Oren's SUV was parked down the street in an indoor parking lot. They'd dropped the keys off at the station after a brief phone discussion with Oren.

Brett now stood with his safe-house folks and Verity and Jillian, as they got better acquainted. Madison and Bryce stood off to the side. Jillian seemed at ease, but their mother appeared anxious. Not surprising. Hopefully, as things progressed, she would relax a bit as people including the two they'd just met attempted to keep her safe.

And Madison? Keeping her safe was definitely Oren's job, his responsibility, his chosen goal—although now he would also have the assistance of Bryce, which was a good thing—now that he was starting to care for her so much. Probably too much. But so what? As he'd been pondering, he wasn't sure what the future would hold, but for once he was wondering if this could turn into some kind of relationship. A real one.

Oren got his car keys from the front desk.

Before they left, Madison said to both Oren and Brett, "I intend to keep my life as much on course as possible—without endangering other people. I want you to know that. I'll go to my school tomorrow but hopefully won't be in my classroom, since I'll want to protect my students. I've given special programs in one of the empty classrooms before, and I'll tell our principal I'll hang out there tomorrow to plan one of those programs. And I'll try to continue to do that till Darius is in custody."

Good idea in some ways, Oren thought. He looked at Brett, though, and said, "I'd imagine our suspect will figure out the potential trap and maybe stay away."

"Which isn't a bad idea, of course." Brett nodded as he considered it. "But tomorrow, at least, I'd like you to do everything you normally do. It's more likely to draw our suspect out. But I'll also have a lot of protection there, including undercover cops who'll look like teachers, others patrolling the streets, in case the guy decides to show up. We will keep everyone there safe, not just Madison. And we'll see then if it makes more sense afterward for you to stay out of your classroom. I'll also run this by the school's administration and security staff."

He didn't allow for any argument. Oren wasn't entirely happy, but of course he would also be there, protecting everyone he could.

And Madison? "As long as you're sure you can take care of everyone," she said.

Oren knew Brett couldn't be certain, but he did say, "We'll certainly do our best."

"We've got to go now, Madison," Oren said. Of course, it wasn't quite that easy, though she did say a hasty goodbye to her family members and promised her mother and sister she'd stay in touch as much as was reasonable.

As an added protection, Brett had an officer drive them to the parking lot where Oren's car was now located so Madison and he wouldn't have to walk along the street in plain view. Fortunately, there weren't many people walking around the area, and still no more demonstrations outside the police station, a good thing.

The cop dropped them off around the corner, and a few minutes later they were on their way to Madison's condo.

"I assume you're still intending to do your regular day of teaching now that Brett told you to."

"Yes." Her tone suggested she expected him to argue about it. They'd stopped at a traffic light, and he looked over at her.

"I can't completely disagree with Brett about it, even though I don't like it. But I'll definitely stay in close touch with Bryce, and even more so with Brett to ensure he actually does have protection around your school and its students, especially yours."

The expression on her lovely face looked anything but convinced. "So we, and the kids, will be safe?"

Oren made the final turn onto Madison's street. "Sure," he said, hoping he wasn't lying. He certainly would do his part, but he knew there were no guarantees that Madison wouldn't be hurt. Which worried him. A lot. "Why else would I hang out with you?"

Madison laughed. "Why else, indeed?"

Soon Oren had parked in the condo's lot, although his navy SUV now occupied a guest space and not one associated with Madison's unit. He wasn't sure what had happened with her car but figured the cops would take care of it till she could start driving again, assuming the explosives had been removed and the car was otherwise okay.

"Wait for me," he ordered as Madison started to open her door.

She stopped and waited and scowled. "I guess this is my life for now," she said.

"Yep, unless you want me to handcuff you and take you to the safe house." Not that he'd really do such a thing, but he figured he was making a point, at least somewhat humorously, with this woman he found really attractive. So attractive he wanted to do a whole lot more than share kisses with her. Like, not only checking the safety of her room, but spending time in it, with her, in bed— No. Forget that. It wasn't humorous…and it also was a bad idea…

"Of course I do." She turned and held her hands, wrists together, out toward him.

He laughed, and she laughed back. But in a moment she grew somber. "I really do appreciate what you're doing, Oren. And I recognize I may need some continued tutoring on what I can and can't do to stay safe. Thank you."

He nodded and exited the car, then removed his changes of clothes from the trunk. Tutoring? Well, she was a teacher, and in some ways he would be educating her on things he felt would keep her safest under these difficult circumstances.

At this moment, at least, he felt she actually would listen to him.

He kept looking around them as he guided Madison out of the car and into her building, then insisted on entering her unit first and looking around.

On the other hand, he thought, as Madison poured them both beer and they sat down in her living room, maybe Darius really had just wanted to scare the family members—while he headed back to Kendall and his real target.

Well, Oren trusted his colleagues who were there and again had Wes in protective custody.

But the only way to be truly certain they were safe was to catch this guy…and he wanted to be the one to do it. To know that Madison would be safe.

How to do it? Well, even considering Brett's help and Bryce's, too, Oren was certain he was in a better position than anyone else, thanks to the woman he was now protecting. Unfortunately. Darius had already threatened her and would undoubtedly come after her again, unless he was no longer in town—and maybe even then, in a while.

They chatted as they drank their beer, mostly about nothing but also including Madison's concerns about a safe house. She rightly assumed that Oren knew quite a bit about them thanks to his work, but she still seemed worried for her family, and no wonder. He was even worried for Olivia, after that bomb threat so close to her restaurant. Still, he tried to comfort Madison with some anecdotes about how people he'd known who'd stayed in safe houses not only survived but were often allowed back to their real lives after those threatening them had been caught.

And despite not wanting to leave her company, he again encouraged her to head for the safe house and stay with her relatives.

Big surprise. She said no. He was secretly glad, though, that they'd be alone.

She also soon reminded him that she needed to get up early tomorrow to go to school.

"And yes," she said, "I understand the risks of staying in my usual life. My biggest concern is that Darius will show up there and hurt someone other than me."

Oren couldn't promise otherwise, but he reminded her that Bryce would be there, too. "What I don't understand is that man's thinking. Yes, he wants revenge on my dad, but what good would it do him to kill anyone now, either him or a family member? Or all of us?"

Oren had no good answer, although he'd worked in law enforcement long enough to know that some suspects just had a desire to do bad things. He stood. "Apparently it's something he's thought about for a long time."

Oren had an urge to end their evening together on a lighter, more humorous note. "Anyway," he said. "it's bedtime. I'll follow you into your bedroom."

She looked at him with a smile that did appear a bit amused, but there was a look in her eyes that suggested more. A lot more. She looked him up and down, stopping for an extra second at the area of him that started to harden immediately when she said, "Oh, I like that idea." Her voice was low and hoarse, which only got him more aroused. And now her eyes connected with his.

Her beautiful, sexy green eyes.

Was she serious?

"And," she continued, "I gather we may be living together for a while, so we might as well not waste any more nights when we're both in my condo."

She sure sounded serious. And he had an urge to grab her hand and lead her into her bedroom. A very strong urge.

But his professionalism fortunately dashed through him suddenly. He had to patrol the area inside and out before he went to bed. And having sex first would be one humongous distraction—one during which Darius Amaltin might well show up at the condo.

Besides, she couldn't really be serious. She'd just ended her engagement, even if she'd never really loved Alec... Oren directed that thought to the part of his body that was telling him otherwise.

Still...

Okay. Enough. Joke or not, he would treat it as such. For his own sake, as well as hers.

"I enjoy the promise of things to come," he said with a sly grin. "Sometime. I'll see you to your bedroom, sure, and look around it to make certain all looks safe. But anything else? Nope. We'll save that for another night."

He winked, then grew somber. "Distractions, even fun ones, are not a good idea in my line of work. So think about what we could be doing as you fall asleep tonight. I will. But I won't allow it to distract me from my protection of you."

Chapter 16

Okay, she'd asked for that dismissal of her invitation. Oren was a marshal, doing his job—not her live-in lover. But as Madison lay alone in her bed that night, she felt her body continue to react to the sexual innuendos she had tossed at Oren earlier. She'd realized she wanted him in a way she'd never wanted Alec. Or any other man, for that matter.

Oren was now lying on her sofa as he had before, probably sleeping. Or not. But he wouldn't be awake for the same reason she was. At least not entirely.

He might be thinking about having sex with her someday—or not. But he was most likely listening for any concerning noises in her condo or the area. Or maybe he was even up and about, checking to make sure everything was in order and Darius wasn't around.

And the idea of going to her bedroom with her other than just to ensure it was safe? That apparently wasn't on his mind, or he must have shoved it far from his consciousness.

Unfortunately. And frustratingly for Madison.

Had she been serious about wanting sex with him? Oh, yes. Too serious. She was much too attracted to the man, for too many reasons, such as his thoughtfulness, his protectiveness, his funniness—and his drop-dead good looks.

But she recognized, despite her discomfort and embarrassment at having even broached the subject, that Oren had done the exact right thing.

Rejected her. Even if she wanted nothing more than to spend the night with him right here, in her bed.

She was glad to awaken the next morning to the sound of her clock radio. She'd actually slept. And she felt herself grow slightly red from the embarrassment that hadn't left her overnight.

Fortunately, Oren didn't mention her inappropriate hints when they met in her kitchen for their quick cereal-and-coffee breakfast. He carried his sports jacket but wore his slacks and a new black T-shirt, which somewhat showed his muscular physique. His dark hair was tousled… Wow. It was a good thing Madison knew she had to head to work.

While they drove to school, a pang shot through Madison as she realized her mother must have taken a leave of absence from her job. She wouldn't be teaching this day, or for a while, most likely.

If only there was something more Madison could do to help her…

Beyond making herself an obvious target to draw Darius out? Surely that was enough.

She didn't mention that to Oren, though. But she did

want his confirmation that her going to school that day was a good idea. They'd talked about it before and now did so again. No matter that she was willing to put herself in danger, and she'd made that clear. She couldn't help being scared, though, and she would do anything to protect the people she loved and otherwise cared about, like her own students—even risk her own life. And Oren would do she same, she felt sure.

Sure, the place would be under surveillance by authorities anyway, but there would likely be more of it with her presence. And the police chief, and maybe Oren, too, believed it was preferable for her to be there with lots of protection around, both uniformed cops and undercover, to keep an eye out for the guy—although Oren would of course be with her no matter where she headed that day or for the foreseeable future.

On their way, Madison noted when Oren slowed the car or turned corners to go around blocks but figured he was checking to see if they were being followed. Apparently not, fortunately, since he kept going and didn't contact Brett or anyone else in the police department.

But the GGPD definitely had a presence nearby. Madison usually didn't pay attention to patrol cars, but she'd have noticed this many in the area before. At least half a dozen drove by in their direction or the opposite way.

If Darius was around here, he'd know he was being sought, which in some ways was a good thing, both for her safety and for that of others at her elementary school.

But that might also keep him away—for now. Or brave and foolish enough to challenge all those out to get him. Madison certainly hoped that wasn't the case, but the little she'd seen and heard of him made her assume it could be.

Once they reached the school, Oren checked the parking area, then accompanied Madison inside. "Good morning," she said to fellow staff members as she passed them in the hallway. She didn't see Alec, but she might later—and here she was again with Oren, whom her ex had seen her with before. Well, Oren wasn't a new romantic interest—which was a shame—and doing his official duty had to come first.

As before, she headed first to her classroom, with her gorgeous, caring, professional bodyguard whom she'd really wanted to have sex with last night…

Okay, she couldn't keep thinking about that. Oren was right to keep things more casual. He even acted completely friendly as she greeted people in the hall, even as he clearly studied them, but of course none was Darius.

They soon reached her classroom, where she was jolted by the appearance of someone she'd never seen in the school previously. Her brother sat in the chair she usually occupied in the front of the room when she faced her students for classes.

"Hi, sis." He looked up from the phone he'd been studying and approached them. "And hi, Oren." He seemed to study Oren's face, and Madison figured her brother was attempting to read the degree of concern there and whether Oren had seen any potential danger on his way in.

"Good to see you," Oren told him. "I assume all appears well here, since you were just sitting there. Anything exciting show up on your phone?"

Bryce laughed. "Nope. Anything exciting last night or on your way here?" Bryce's gaze first on Oren, then her, appeared to attempt to read their minds. *Anything exciting?* Maybe he was searching for more info they had about Darius, but Madison wasn't sure. Was it so obvious that there was at least some degree of attraction between Oren and her? She felt herself turn hot with embarrassment.

"All seems pretty calm since we last saw you," Oren replied, seemingly unbothered.

"Have you talked to Jillian or Mom or anyone at the safe house?" Madison asked. "Is everything okay there?"

"Yes, yes and yes," Bryce said. "I've talked to them all and everything seems fine."

Good, Madison thought. She'd have to speak to them later, too. "Since you were allowed to come in," Madison said, "does anyone know why you're here?"

"I was directed to one of the security guards since I came here so early." At Madison's quizzical look, he added, "I've been in your classroom for over an hour now. Anyway, apparently the guards have been primed to know there's some potential for danger around here. The one I talked to—his name was Bob—seemed fascinated by my FBI ID, but he figured I was related to you since we share a last name. Anyway, he promised to patrol the halls, and he was aware there'd be cops from the PD around, too, mostly in casual dress."

"That all sounds okay," Madison said. "And if you don't mind hanging around here a little longer, I want to go visit our principal and find out what she knows— and possibly fill her in on more."

After she locked her purse in her desk near where Bryce sat down again, she turned to Oren. "Do you want to go talk to Principal Nelson with me? I assume she already knows what's going on, or at least some of it. But I want to make sure she's dealing with it okay."

"Sure," he responded. "I'm fairly sure Chief Shea contacted her himself, but it won't hurt for her to have another contact if she needs it."

"Like you?" Madison asked.

"Like me."

After confirming once more that Bryce would hang out there, Madison led Oren to the end of the hall. Once more, since it was early, Principal Nelson's assistant wasn't in the outer office, so Madison knocked on the inner door.

And as before, the principal opened it nearly immediately. "I was hoping to talk to you this morning," she said to Madison, then shot a quizzical glance again toward Oren. "I've talked to the current chief of police, no less, and he told me some of what's going on, but not everything."

Today, she wore a charcoal dress adorned with a large green pendant. Her hair was pulled back into a clip at the nape of her neck. She waved for Madison and Oren to sit again on the chairs across from her desk. "Okay," she said. "I gather whatever's going on has something to do with you and your family. I considered telling you to go back home today, but Chief Shea indicated it would be better for you to be here, under guard." This time, she stared at Oren. "With you, of course," she continued, "as well as the cops both in uniform and undercover who're around today. It's okay for today, but we'll have to see how things go to decide about what happens next. I can't have law enforcement in my school every day."

"I understand," Madison said. "And my idea is, if

the person who's being sought isn't captured today, I'll teach remotely. That way, my students will be safer."

And if anyone's hurt—or worse—it will only be me.

"Well, that's a possibility." Her boss didn't appear happy about it. "But if things appear too potentially dangerous, I'll have to put you on leave for a while."

Madison wanted to object, but that made sense. She knew she was juggling a bit here, wanting to do her job and protect her family—and herself. She would definitely listen to what her school's principal told her. "Of course," she agreed, though her gaze lowered to her fingers clasped in her lap.

"I agree that we should see how things go today," Oren said, "and maybe for the next few days. For the safety of everyone, we need to get this guy into custody."

Madison glanced at Oren, who wore a determined expression on his face.

"I certainly want to help anyway I can to bring this situation to a conclusion that's safe for your family, Madison—and especially for this school," the principal said. "So let's touch base often, and please keep me informed—" again her dark-eyed, intense gaze landed on Oren "—about how things are progressing. Okay?"

"Okay," Oren agreed.

This conversation over, Madison thanked her boss and led Oren from the principal's office. She took him to the cafeteria, where she got them each a bottle of water. Her throat felt dry, as if she'd been teaching all day—maybe because she was so close to Oren. Or maybe it was simpler than that: her hydration decreased as her nervousness grew.

They headed back to the first floor. Madison chatted about inconsequential things with Oren, partly to calm her uneasiness. There were many people in the halls she didn't recognize. A few were in police uniforms, and those who weren't she assumed included undercover cops.

Fortunately, none looked like Darius. Not that she was certain to recognize him. But she trusted Oren, and he didn't seem to see Darius there, either.

They returned to her classroom. Her students had begun to arrive, and Bryce was talking to them, demonstrating some simple origami by making designs out of construction paper he must have found in her desk. The kids seemed enthralled. And happy. Which made Madison happy, too.

She greeted her students as always and had fun watching Bryce teach some of his skills with folding paper. Then, at her class's normal starting time, she was glad to see that both her bodyguard and her brother moved from the front of the room to the back, where they watched the kids sit down at their table seats after removing their backpacks.

Soon, Madison began her regular classes of reading, printing, spelling and beginning arithmetic. It felt so much like a regular day.

Except that she had two adult men sitting at the back of the room keeping watch over her, looking out the windows along the side of the room a lot, leaving the classroom presumably not only to find the little boys' room but also to patrol the halls and watch for danger. Watch for Darius.

Eventually it was time for recess, which worried Madison. But things went well then, too. It didn't hurt that there were a few people she didn't recognize, both men and women, who most likely were also undercover cops hanging around on the playground. There were even a couple of uniformed cops. Soon, they all returned indoors, and Madison continued her lessons.

And finally, kindergarten was over for the day.

Unlike usual days, though, Madison didn't return to her classroom after they'd gone, to make her typical plans for the next day. Instead, she headed down the hall, with her entourage still protecting her. But while they were near the end of the hallway, Principal Nelson started toward them. "I was just about to come visit you in your classroom," she said. "All of you. Do you two think we're all safe here?"

Oren was the one to answer. "No indication otherwise." And before she could say anything else he added, "My suggestion is that we continue this daily, at least for now—unless we see anything that suggests otherwise. It seems best for all of us."

Did Madison agree? Well, she'd seen no sign that Darius was around that day. No suggestion that anyone in or around the school had been in danger. The idea of going about her daily life felt very welcome, even if she had to keep up the facade that everything was all right.

"All right, then," Principal Nelson said. "We'll continue this tomorrow. But you do promise you'll let me know if anything at all suggests the situation is changing in any bad way, don't you?"

"Of course," Madison said, trading glances with her brother and Oren. Neither said anything to disagree.

They returned to her classroom, where Bryce said goodbye. "It's early enough that I should be able to get on the road and start hunting our quarry, even if he isn't hunting us. My mission right now, while I'm not keeping an eye on you, Madison, is to go after that gunrunner's son and bring Darius down before he can even threaten anyone else. And you—" he faced Oren "—you'll take damn good care of my sister. Got it?"

"Got it," Oren said with a grin.

And what else could Madison do but hug her brother and agree? But of course she said, "That would be wonderful, bro. But please, please stay safe."

"You, too, sis."

Bryce headed out the door.

"So tonight," Oren said. "And us." He looked her straight in the eye in a manner that made her body quiver suddenly with desire. Even though she knew full well that wasn't what he had in mind.

Or even if he did, nothing would come of it.

"Same old, same old." Madison smiled in a way she hoped didn't reveal her inner thoughts.

Chapter 17

First thing as they drove away, though, Oren called Brett, putting his phone on Bluetooth. He wanted to confirm that the police chief also thought things had gone well enough that day at the school.

Which he did. "I talked to Principal Nelson. She called to say you'd left and that you'd spoken with her about having things go the same way tomorrow as today, with the patrols inside and out. I assured her we'd keep an eye on things similarly tomorrow, and she sounded glad. Plus she indicated, Madison, that you were welcome to conduct your classes the same way. At least for now."

"Great!" She sounded as if she truly was pleased. Then she asked Brett if she could call her mother and sister at the safe house. He agreed and gave her the number for the phone they were currently using—a burner phone.

Oren was glad to see Madison so happy. Which kind of surprised him. Or not. He was beginning to like her too much, and he hoped he could contribute to her happiness.

She conducted that conversation with her mother and sister in the car, too, with her phone on Speaker so Oren could hear. Her family members seemed fine, but her mom asked, "Please, even with all this going on, is there some way I can see…your father, Madison?"

Good thing they were at a stop sign, since Madison turned and stared at Oren. Of course. He was the one with the knowledge and connections, even in Kendall. "Assuming he's okay with it, we'll work it out," he said, loud enough for Verity and Jillian to hear.

And in fact, after Madison ended her call to her family, promising to get in touch again soon, Oren parked at the curb and called his boss, explained the situation and got his approval to contact one of the two marshals assigned to protect Wesley Windham.

"It should be fine to take him to their safe house to say hello," his supervisor said, "as long as everyone there remains alert."

"And as long as I don't show up there with our wonderful gunrunner's son's other main target, Madison Colton," Oren added, sending an apologetic glance in her direction.

They talked a little more about logistics. When Oren got off the phone and started driving again, he said to Madison, "It sounds all set. You may want to let your family know that Richard Foster will most likely be visiting them tomorrow, assuming everyone follows through right away—and also assuming he's okay with it."

Which Madison did. And when that call ended, they

were finally at her condo. Once inside, Oren called his sister and arranged for her to send a sandwich for him and matzo ball soup for Madison. The meal arrived in just over half an hour, and Oren went to get it from the delivery person, silently thanking his sister for working so fast.

During dinner, Oren dived into topics of conversation with Madison about kids and origami and why he got into law enforcement: he'd wanted to help after growing tired of seeing on the news that so many bad guys got away.

Madison seemed interested in all he said and got into some topics of her own, including that she'd decided to become a teacher because, growing up, she'd had some really good ones and some really bad ones, and she had wanted to use the good stuff she'd experienced to educate other kids.

Oren liked that, despite how different their careers and backgrounds were, they both aspired to the same goal: helping people.

Soon it was time to start getting ready for bed—with Oren sleeping on the sofa as usual.

Only… That night he felt relieved that all had gone well at Madison's school again that day. Glad to be in her company for the foreseeable future. Glad…well, hell. When she said good-night and started down the hall toward her room, he had to accompany her to check it out.

At her door, she looked at him. Her gorgeous face appeared to assess him again, looking him up and down suggestively with her amazing green eyes. "So," she said, "are you going to come in and check there's no one waiting for me in my room?"

"Of course." He pushed the door open and slid beside her into it, his chest just grazing her arm, but he was definitely aware of the contact.

There, he walked around as he had before, arcing around the queen-size bed that had pillows and a coverlet in pretty pastel colors of lavender and pink similar to the look of her sofa and other furniture. He could see around the tall bureau and bedside table and into the lush bathroom adorned with fluffy coral-colored towels. He checked under the bed, not that he expected to find Darius there or anywhere else in this place—for now. "Okay," he finally said. "Everything's fine."

But as he looked back at her face, she looked troubled. "Everything's not fine," she said.

His hackles immediately rose. "What's wrong?"

"I'm going to be lonely in here by myself tonight, especially after the stressful day we had."

Was she really going where he thought she was with this? He felt his body react in a manner that was completely inappropriate—and yet completely appropriate. He grew warm and felt an erection begin to grow. Really grow. "So you want me to stay with you?"

"Yes." Her tone was soft and almost pleading. How could he say no?

But notwithstanding where his thoughts had drifted before, could he say yes and risk her life and maybe his own, too?

"I understand what you're thinking," she said, and even looked down at his increasing arousal. "You don't need any distraction when you're trying to protect me. But what if we both really concentrate not just on what we're doing, but also on what we're hearing around us, and—"

He couldn't help it. She'd taken a step toward him,

and now he bent down and took her into his arms. "Bad idea," he whispered. "But—"

But when she grabbed his butt and ground her body tightly against his, how could he resist?

Madison knew she was being foolish. But she was so sexually aroused by this man that she simply had to do something.

Something wonderful. Or so she anticipated.

The hot encounter she envisioned and craved shouldn't take very long anyway. Not the way she wanted him to kiss her, touch her, sink into her, then move them both to completion. And she suspected that this hunk of a man wouldn't prolong their intimacy. He'd want it hard, fast and entirely, rapidly enjoyable, as she did. So they wouldn't spend too much time on their distraction…

She felt more desire than she ever had before. Her skin tingled. Her whole body hungered for more…now.

She'd backed away from Oren just a bit—just long enough to begin unbuttoning his shirt. He'd left his sports jacket over the chair in her kitchen as they ate, which of course she had noticed. Not that he'd revealed a lot of his body that way, but the shedding of any piece of clothing over dinner had been enough to tempt her, at least a bit.

"Oh, here," he muttered, finishing the job she'd started and dropping the shirt, and the slacks he removed, onto the floor. He stood there, his muscular chest and arms uncovered, in his gray briefs with the front extended, and Madison had an urge to drop to her knees, pull his shorts off and begin kissing him there.

But she didn't have the chance. Instead of just standing there, Oren moved toward her again, and soon her dress joined his clothes on the floor. And then her bra and panties. And then—

Then they lay on her bed. Oren's hands were all over her. Not to be outdone, she finally pulled his shorts down and grasped him.

He growled and grew closer yet, kissing her breasts, tickling them a bit with his facial hair, holding her most intimate area and using his fingers to stimulate her even more. She, too, began kissing him, there, also stroking him, wanting—

Fortunately, though she hadn't had a lot of reason to keep condoms here despite her engagement, she had a supply. She extracted one from the drawer at the top of the stand beside her bed and helped to put it on Oren.

She got what she wanted when he soon lowered her gently to the bed, pulled himself on top of her and entered her. And began moving in and out, slowly at first, then faster. As she moved in harmony below him, holding him close yet shifting her body to help provide the deepest and most delightful sexuality, she listened to his groans and her own. "Oh, Oren," she breathed— and felt herself reaching her climax at the same time he apparently reached his, since he inhaled deeply and stopped moving.

And she? She felt amazed—gratified and fulfilled and full of joy at this unique and wonderful experience.

Madison allowed herself to return to a bit of reality afterward. "That was...I can't even tell you how wonderful it was." She heard the hoarseness in her voice and felt her breathing begin to slow down.

"Now, just lie here for a while with me," he said, holding her closely against his hard, hot body. "We'll listen together for anything that shouldn't be around here."

Which made more reality crash down on Madison, but he was right.

And he had done exactly what she'd wanted—made incredible love with her. Probably for the only time that night. The only time forever, or at least until Darius Amaltin was caught?

Not if she could help it.

For now… Well, she soon realized she was falling asleep. Oren's breathing seemed deeper, too, but when she moved slightly so did he. "You okay?" he asked.

"More than okay." And then she wanted to know. "Will you stay in here with me tonight? I mean, we don't *necessarily* need to partake in any more enjoyment, but I'd love to have you near me, and we can both listen for…whatever."

"As long as I don't disturb you when I wake up and patrol the condo to keep an eye out for…whatever." His tone was light, despite the seriousness of what he was saying, and he pulled her closer against him once more, their bodies still bare and hot, and Madison felt stimulated yet again.

But she would restrain herself now.

"You definitely won't disturb me, whatever you do." Madison added a bit of suggestiveness to her tone just in case Oren wanted to have another go. But if he didn't, she'd certainly understand—and hope for more another night.

"That's fine, then." Oren tightened his arms around her. "I'll stay."

Okay, he'd wanted this to happen. Boy, had he. And what he'd gained was a reward far, far greater than he'd imagined. And he'd imagined a lot.

Had anything happened to endanger Madison when

he was lost in the delight of making love with this amazing woman? He didn't think so. He'd managed sometimes to let his mind escape the wonders his body was engaged in and think. And listen.

And then return to the ecstasy…

What now, though? He would continue to make certain she was safe.

Might they repeat this sometime? He could only hope so. Because, damn it all, right or wrong—he was falling in love with her.

Now, he let himself lie there holding Madison for a short while, then pulled gently away, albeit reluctantly.

"Are you patrolling?" she asked in a voice that suggested he'd awakened her.

"Yes," he said. "But I'll be back soon." He hoped. He also hoped he'd find no indication that Darius was anywhere around or that he even knew where Madison lived—although that was highly unlikely.

Still, Oren got up, dressed and conducted his inspection. All seemed fine, so he returned to bed and actually fell asleep with Madison's still-naked body against his. Fortunately, he'd put his shorts back on before lying down, and the warmth of her, her delectable curves, her sweet female aroma… Well, he managed to get some sleep without stirring up any more arousal. This time.

But closer to dawn, when he awakened for the fourth time, he decided he needn't resist any longer.

And their sex this time… Phenomenal.

Before he got out of bed, he found himself wondering what would happen once he'd found Amaltin and no longer had to be with Madison. He didn't want to think about that.

The next morning was pretty much the same as

they'd experienced before: cereal and coffee for breakfast, then heading to school.

But not really the same. The way they spoke to one another was even warmer, with a bit of suggestive humor thrown in. And they shared kisses before getting out of the car.

Oren accompanied Madison to her classroom, and that was a bit different since Bryce wasn't there that day. But Madison's brother called her at the same time they'd first seen him yesterday. At Bryce's apparent request, Madison put him on Speaker on her phone. "Just so you both know," he said, "I'm working today on a couple of cases. Oren, you were made aware of them. I've been given a lead on finding Len Davison, so I've got to follow up on it."

On looking more into what was going on in Grave Gulch, including the former demonstrations at the police station, Oren had heard of that situation beyond what they'd discussed with Interim Chief Shea. In fact— "Isn't that one of the killers who got away thanks to Randall Bowe playing with the evidence?"

"Yeah, the guy Brett talked to us about," Bryce replied. "That's one of his many misdeeds. But one good thing about Len Davison is that he's Tatiana's dad."

"Well, I hope you succeed with that lead and bring a killer down."

"Thanks from me and the rest of the FBI, buddy," Bryce said. "And I will be in touch. If there's anything urgent you need from me to keep Madison safe—"

"I'll definitely let you know," Oren concluded. He hoped he hadn't sounded any different to Bryce, now that he'd slept with the man's sister.

"Be careful, bro," Madison said. "Let's stay in touch."

After she hung up, Madison looked at Oren. "Guess I'd better get ready for the day," she said.

"Good idea. I'll go on my first patrol of the morning."

Which Oren did. He soon returned to Madison's classroom and sat in the back, as he had yesterday. And later went on further patrols.

Nothing that day appeared different from the prior days—except that several students approached Oren one at a time and said hi or otherwise tried to interact with him, which he found cute. These little ones certainly had charm. And definitely needed to stay safe.

When he could, Oren watched Madison interact more with the kids.

How would she be with children of her own? Their own?

Don't even think about that, Oren warned himself.

And when they started back to Madison's that night, Oren wondered if that night would seem the same as the prior one. He hoped so.

One possible similarity was that they could order another meal later from Bubbe's Deli.

And beyond? He ordered his mind to stay focused... even as he hoped there would be more distractions that night as well.

Chapter 18

Oren had been quiet on the drive back to her condo, so Madison let her thoughts loose as they cruised through the familiar Grave Gulch streets.

She didn't let herself get too excited about the possibility of spending another night with Oren. Due to practicality and professionalism, it most likely wouldn't happen again. The fact that all had gone well—amazingly well—this morning, no awkwardness, nothing, didn't mean they should take any further chances.

When she'd been with Alec—well, mornings had felt uncomfortable too many times, and Madison was always happy when they left for school. What if Oren and she enjoyed themselves that way one more time? Okay, she admitted to herself, she was beginning to care for Oren. A lot. In fact…well, she believed she might be falling for him. Hard.

Which probably wasn't a good idea. Oren's job was

in another town—and he'd undoubtedly be putting himself in danger frequently, even after things got resolved with Darius here.

A real relationship? He might disappear on her, die for real, the way her father had pretended. Which would be horrible.

Although… Oren did remain friendly that day, but she sensed some distance between them. What if he hadn't enjoyed himself as much as she had?

What if he didn't really like her as much as she was beginning to like him?

After all, he was there to guard her as part of his job, hanging out with her a lot, even at her school. And he did his job diligently.

But maybe a kindergarten teacher just wasn't his speed.

If so, then she would have to tamp her emotions down. *Way* down. She loved her job.

The right guy could be Oren. But only if the feeling was mutual. Or what if he wanted just something physical, not forever?

Enough. To turn her mind in other directions, she asked Oren about what they were going to eat that night.

She offered to cook but Oren said, "I think things went well enough last night. Are you okay with another dinner from the deli? We can order different food, of course, and I'll have it delivered again."

"Sounds great to me." And it actually did. She didn't need to pretend. She enjoyed cooking but she appreciated that she didn't have to now—plus, she enjoyed food from the deli. Besides, Madison appreciated seeing how close Oren was to his sister. And his love for his family only made Madison care for him more.

Oren said he'd call his sister once they reached Madison's place.

Then Madison thought about the phone call she wanted to make. She asked Oren if he thought it was okay for her to contact her mother and sister to learn if they'd been able to get together with her father, and if so, how it had gone. Oren insisted on their calling Brett again first, while they were still in the car, to get his okay. Good thing they did, since apparently the burner phone being used at the safe house had been changed. Brett gave Madison the new number.

They had just pulled into the parking lot of her condo. Oren chose a spot near the end of an aisle of the area for visitors, different from before. As always, he checked around first before helping Madison out of the car and walking cautiously to her unit.

Once they were inside, they discussed what they wanted for dinner, and both chose matzo ball soup and challah, plus a salad. Oren smiled and called Olivia. As he did so, Madison, sitting on her living-room couch near him, took the number Brett had given her for the latest burner and entered it into her phone.

Jillian answered. "Hi, Madison." Her tone was odd, Madison thought—soft and sad and somehow angry at the same time, though Madison wasn't sure how she could interpret that from two words.

A lot of questions crossed her mind, but she just asked, "Anything new?" Like, *did our dad actually get transported there today in protective custody to visit you?* Madison stared at the cream-and-gold pattern on the area rug on her wooden floor as if she could read answers there.

"Oh, yeah!" That sounded loud and upset. Madison prepared to ask what was going on, but Jillian continued. "Wesley Windham—yes, the former Richard Foster, our father—was brought here to visit today. And… well, it was so weird. He was friendly to me but remote with Mom. What he said sounded like a combo of apologetic, defensive and also cold, as if it wasn't all his fault. And before you say anything, I know it didn't start off being his fault, but…" she paused, then continued in a sorrowful tone "…how can someone go from not being your father for twenty-five years to suddenly being alive? Now I'm almost twenty-eight, and suddenly my dad is alive?"

"I understand." Madison wished she could hug her sister. "And I relate to all you're saying. I don't know how things will be among all of us when Darius Amaltin is caught." And with Oren and Bryce and even Jillian and others on the GGPD working on that, she felt he would be…eventually. Hopefully soon, before he could hurt anyone he'd been threatening. She raised her gaze and regarded Oren, who was also looking at her with an expression that seemed both curious and caring. She nodded slightly and looked toward the floor again. "But we'll stay in close touch and we'll…we'll learn more."

"Maybe." Jillian now sounded curt. "But the whole visit… Well, it was highly emotional, as I'm sure you can guess. Mom seemed somewhat glad to see him but angry and hurt, and she demanded answers he wasn't prepared to give."

"How about you?" Madison asked softly. "How did you feel, seeing him?"

"Mostly confused."

"How did you leave it?" Madison felt her body tense up. With all that emotion, would their father decide just to disappear from their lives again? Or…?

"He was only here for a couple hours, and then the

people watching him, apparently from the US Marshals Service like your bodyguard Oren, swept him away, heading back to whatever safe house they have set up for him in Kendall. We all kept things open as they left, hinting we'd do this again, if possible, but nothing absolute was discussed with the marshals—or with our dad. I just hope—" Her voice softened, then stopped.

"Hope what?" Madison urged. That they would get together again? That hopefully she could join them?

Or that their father would just leave their lives again and never return?

"I'm not sure," Jillian said softly. "I'm just so confused, and I mostly want the best for Mom."

"I know," Madison said. "I don't know what's best. I'm sure it's going to take some time to sort out."

Madison asked to speak to their mom, and Jillian agreed. But their conversation was short. "It...it didn't go the way I'd hoped, Madison," Mom said. "But I sensed that he still cared, that he was still being protective, and he indicated before he left that we'd see each other again."

That sounded somewhat different from what Jillian had implied, but Madison certainly wasn't going to make things any worse for their mother now. "Sounds promising." She tried to sound enthusiastic.

"Yes," her mother said. "But I have to say goodbye now. One of the nice people staying with us wants me off the phone. Let's talk again soon."

And Madison hoped they'd be able to. She hung up after also saying goodbye. Then she looked at Oren and gave a brief rundown of what her sister had said.

"Wow," she sighed as she finished. "I wish I could have been there, too. That wouldn't have made him act kinder to our mom, though. I feel awful for her, and for

Jillian. But if I'd tried… W-well, we don't know where Darius is, but there might have been more of a chance of his finding the rest of my family if he's actually doing a good job of following me without being obvious."

"True," Oren agreed, "but of course I hope not. Maybe, with so many people involved in protecting you, he's just backed down and not following through with any of his threats." But Oren's heated expression suggested that wasn't really what he was thinking. Maybe he was upset for her mother's sake, too. What a sweet, caring person he was.

"I can't help thinking more about my father and how he was with my mom," Madison found herself interjecting. "I'm really sad about it."

"Yeah, me too. After all he's done and all the time that's passed—Well, it's not really my business." But Oren looked deeply into Madison's eyes, and she saw even more anger there.

Which only made her care even more for Oren. She wanted to hug him. Tightly. And kiss him. Rub herself against his body. Oh, heavens. She was really falling for this man. Hard. Time to change the subject. "Will our dinner be here soon?" she asked. She didn't want to talk about the sorrow now percolating inside her.

"Yep," Oren said. In fact, his phone rang just then, and it was the delivery person. "I'll go out and get it."

And in a short while they ate the delicious dinner. Or at least Madison tried to eat. And she attempted to keep their dinner conversation light, and not focused on her family.

Soon, it was time for bed. Madison didn't want to become any more disappointed than she already was, so she just invited Oren to check her room while she finished cleaning up in the kitchen.

But when she headed toward bed, she found him still there. "I'd like some company again tonight," he told her hoarsely. "But this will only work if you understand—"

"I understand this is just a way for both of us to make a difficult situation easier to deal with. We'll both keep our senses aware of what's going on around us and stop if there's any indication of trouble. Right?"

"Right," Oren said, and Madison stepped into his arms.

Oh, yes, Oren thought the next morning as he showered and prepared for the day. Another day of protecting the woman he was slowly falling for. He'd reminded himself often it was a bad idea to get involved with someone on the job, as wonderful as sex with the beautiful, sensual Madison had continued to be.

He also reminded himself about his various relationships that had gone bad and told him he shouldn't really attempt to get close with a woman any way but physically.

But those reminders also prompted him to keep his mind and ears alert for Madison's protection, even as the rest of his body continued to enjoy what he touched and felt and experienced.

When he'd finished showering, shaving and trimming, and dressing, he joined Madison in her kitchen. He could only tell her, "Look, Madison, last night was great. Again. I'm not going to demand that we stop such wonderful experiences, but of course I'm concerned I'll miss—"

She put her index finger on his lips to stop him— and he couldn't help kissing its warm, sexy length. "As long as we spend nights together, we might as well enjoy them," Madison said, stroking his lips slightly with that finger. "But of course we both need to stay careful." The expression in her eyes as she looked him up and down made him want to drag her back to bed yet again, but he knew she was teasing him—but also still enjoying the reality of what they'd done.

"Sounds good to me," he said. "Especially the careful part."

"And the enjoyment part," she reminded him, and he couldn't resist taking her back in his arms. Too bad there wasn't time to follow through. She was on her regular schedule this school day.

Their breakfasts were now a routine, and soon they were on their way to her school. This day should be like the last couple, Oren figured.

Once again, though, Bryce wasn't in Madison's classroom. On Speaker, Madison filled Bryce in on her conversation with Jillian and their mother from the safe house, and Oren could hear his clearly frustrated reactions. He told his sister he wished he was there with her this morning. But he couldn't be. Once again, he was off on his real assignment, but the lead he'd been told to follow to find that serial killer Len Davison had gotten him nowhere so far. He was utterly frustrated that nothing had panned out yet. But he was determined to get the guy.

Oren was glad when Cora came into the room and Madison joined her at the front to go over what would go on that day, or so Oren believed. But he kept Madison's phone since they hadn't hung up. "Look," Oren said quietly, turning from Madison and continuing the call with Bryce. "Right now things are fine, but I want to be sure you'll be available to help if something happens and I need you to help protect your sister."

"Of course I will, but—"

"But you also have to do your job. I understand. Now, I've been considering what you're doing and that lead you're following. I've just got a few minutes before I need to start patrolling here, but let's discuss your strategy. We can continue talking about it later, if that makes sense."

"It sure does," Bryce said enthusiastically.

Then Madison continued her conversation with Cora, who now sat beside her at the teacher's desk. Though Oren doubted Cora would be much help if the wrong person entered the classroom before the kids did, she'd at least provide a distraction. Not that Oren wanted Cora, or the kids, of course, to do anything to protect Madison, or even potentially need to protect themselves. But at least he felt he could now leave and start his own brief patrol, including checking where the school's security guys currently hung out.

One way or another, Oren was going to make sure Madison was safe. That was more than his job now. He really cared.

Waving to Madison to make sure she knew he was leaving, Oren exited into the hallway, and was glad, but not surprised, to see Bob, one of the guys in the school's security detail, walking slowly by.

Since they'd introduced themselves before, Oren just said hi. "Everything look okay around here?" he asked.

"Yep." The guy must be approaching his senior years, considering all the lines etched into his face. But his body appeared solid, and Oren had no reason to believe he'd be anything but good at his job. "All okay with you?"

"Yes," Oren replied. "I'm about to get my first exercise of the day walking around here." He tossed Bob a smile that told him the reason for the walk wasn't just exercise.

"Well, you know where the security office is," Bob said.

"I do," Oren acknowledged. "And if you need anything from me, feel free to call." They'd previously talked and waved when they saw each other in the halls, but now Oren handed Bob a card, and Bob did the same to him.

"Great," Bob said. "See you around."

"Sure will." Oren saluted good-naturedly.

For the next half hour, he walked up and down the halls, mostly staying on the first floor, where the kindergarten room was. As he reached the back of the building he saw Principal Nelson exit her office. They traded morning greetings, and Oren continued on his way.

When he returned, the kids had started to arrive. Madison stood in front of her desk, bending to hold a conversation with the little girl she'd called Marti yesterday so her lovely red hair surrounded her face. They were talking about a children's book Marti held open, and Madison pointed at one of the pictures with the finger Oren had kissed earlier. A couple of other students stood nearby listening, including a boy named Buster, who held sheets of paper that appeared to have letters to copy on them.

Oren joined Madison briefly in the cafeteria at lunchtime but didn't eat his sandwich at the table near her since she had several students with her. He enjoyed watching the way she interacted with them informally here, unlike her more structured way in the classroom.

His prior wonderment of how Madison would be with kids of her own—*their own?*—flew through his mind and he again quashed it.

But his eyes mostly scanned where she sat and beyond to ensure there weren't people there who shouldn't be—one in particular.

They headed back to the classroom soon so Madison could finish her classes. Afterward, she hung out there longer to work on her lesson plans for the next day, Oren figured, since that was what she'd done before.

Later, he drove her back to her condo, again using roundabout routes to avoid potentially being followed. While they were on their way, Bryce called and asked to join them for dinner, and Oren was happy to agree.

The routine they'd been establishing was slightly different that evening, thanks to her brother. But this way, Madison had two protectors with her, which pleased Oren. A lot. The more, the merrier—and the safer. Even if he sometimes wished they were alone, just the two of them, for more intimate time.

Over dinner, Madison and Bryce had another discussion about their father and his visit with their mother and sister. "Yeah, I want to see him, too," Bryce muttered at Madison's question. "But sometime when he's with all of us and owning up to who he is—and why he left us for so long. He thinks he has an excuse, since his gunrunner's son is now after us, but there wasn't any kind of problem like that for all these years."

"Not to stick up for him," Madison said, "but he was warned by Louis Amaltin before he got killed in prison that there were a lot of colleagues of his ready to kill our father thanks to his testifying against him. They could have come after us, too, even when Amaltin was dead, so maybe there was some protection in mind when our dad stayed away."

"Yeah. Maybe." Bryce took a large bite of his sandwich and a swig of the beer they'd also ordered from the deli. Then he looked at Oren, across the kitchen table. "Well, I'm glad I'm working with you to protect my family, although I apologize for not having as much time as I thought I would. But I certainly appreciate what you're doing, Oren. And I'll do all I can to bring that Darius down. Still, seeing our father isn't exactly at the top of my priority list."

Not Oren's, either, despite his assignment. But Oren now despised how Wes/Richard had treated his kids—especially Madison.

"Please, Bryce," Madison said. She was sitting next to her brother. "You need to for Mom's sake, if she wants you to."

"I guess so, sis," he said after a moment, and the smile he sent to Madison appeared at least a little apologetic.

Oren was glad he wasn't involved with that decision, only the protection of Madison and her family—and, yes, her father, too.

Bryce left a short time after dinner.

And there they were, alone again.

Madison looked stressed, probably thanks to that discussion with her brother. Even so, Oren figured this was the best time to do his next patrol of her condo property that night. All seemed fine. No sign of Darius.

When Oren started back toward the condo, his phone rang. The ID indicated it was Brett.

"Hi, Chief," Oren said.

"Hey, you'll want to hear this," Brett said. "We got a call a few minutes ago from your buddy Darius Amaltin." That definitely got Oren's attention. "He said he knew our police department was now involved in attempting to protect the people he was after. He referred to them as Coltons and part of the family, acknowledged or not, of Richard Foster, who had helped to get his father killed. He told us to bug off, since he'd not only succeed in getting rid of them but also disappear after that, so we might as well stay out of his way, since he'd succeed no matter what we did."

"You're kidding," Oren heard himself say, realizing that no one would be kidding about anything to do with Darius.

"Nope," Brett said. "And though he called on a burner phone, there were background noises that gave us a good sense of where he was. Around a train stop not far from the safe house, apparently, though I don't know how he learned its location. I've got a team on the way to bring him in, but I figured you'd want to know."

"Thanks," Oren said. "Give me more detail about where he is. I may want to watch him being taken down."

"Sure. In fact, I'd really like to have you with us since you know what Amaltin looks like and you've seen him in person, although we do have copies of his ID photos."

"I'll see what I can do," Oren said.

Brett gave him the cross streets, then they hung up.

Good idea to leave Madison here alone? Well, if Amaltin was otherwise occupied, like in fighting off the police a distance from here, why not?

And Oren rethought what he would do next. He'd definitely like to see Darius taken down by the cops, too.

But that seemed too easy.

He could get the scoop about it later, if all went well. And if it didn't… Well, it would be much better if he hung around here with Madison.

And kept her safe.

Chapter 19

Madison knew something was on Oren's mind when he got back from his patrol of the area and shut the condo door carefully behind him. Something important, considering how his black brows that so matched his wavy hair were narrowed over his eyes.

"Everything okay out there?" She kept her voice light. Standing in her living room not far from him, she wanted to run right up and give him a big, soothing hug, no matter what he was thinking.

But if there really was anything wrong, a distraction wouldn't faze him, nor would it make him happy. Especially if he had seen danger.

"Didn't see any problems," he said, and Madison started to take a deep breath in relief but stopped herself. Something was definitely on his mind. "I'm ready for another beer, though."

"Sounds good." Madison turned to head to the kitchen. "But is there a reason?"

Hearing nothing over her shoulder, she turned to face him again. He appeared as if his mind was somewhere far away.

She nevertheless got a couple bottles of beer from her refrigerator, opened them and handed one to Oren. "So tell me what you're thinking about," she said, persisting.

Interesting. She'd never had a desire to learn what was on Alec's mind that way, to comfort him. But Oren? She'd do anything to help him feel better.

He sat down at the table and so did she. The swig of beer he took seemed shallow, but it appeared to soothe him somehow. "Okay," he said. "Here's the thing. Under other circumstances, I'd be off with Chief Shea and his troops in the GGPD somewhere else in town, maybe somewhere near the safe house. He invited me, in fact, since the police apparently received a call from Darius, who claimed to know where the house is and threatened to come after the people there. It came in on the station's main system and was recorded, so they've been able to go over it."

"Oh, wow." Madison, who'd been raising her beer bottle toward her mouth, suddenly grew stiff. "I gather they believed him."

"They didn't want to take any chances. Brett said a large group are on their way to track him down and take him into custody assuming he wasn't lying, although apparently the phone he used is another burner giving no ability to use GPS to track him."

"I hope they find him." Madison took a large swig of her beer. "Especially if he has any idea of where the safe house is. I certainly don't want him to find my mom and sister and start his threats—or worse—against them. But...you seem worried."

He shrugged, smiled at her and took another sip of beer. "I'd just love to be there when they take him down. But... Well, surprise, surprise, but I don't trust the guy. He told the cops something he wanted them to know. That doesn't make it true...and he's also putting himself right in their crosshairs."

"Of course not," Madison said. "But even so..." She got the impression that Oren somehow believed it. Or he wanted to find out the truth himself. Or what if he wanted to stay there with her? Could he be seeking to prolong their time together? She could only wish...

Maybe by going with the cops he'd help find Darius searching for the safe house. The safe house. Madison had hoped that Amaltin wouldn't find out about it at all, or if he did, that he had no idea where it was.

That might not be the case. And if so...

"I guess we'll learn tonight or tomorrow whether the cops find our buddy Darius." Oren took some more beer. "I certainly hope so, although I can't help being skeptical."

"Me, too." Madison had a thought. "And— Well, I have the impression you don't want to wait to learn the truth. That maybe you want to go along with the cops to check out the safe house area for any sign of Darius. Right?"

"Not really." But Oren's tone didn't exactly sound truthful, and his words weren't exactly a strong denial. "Although Bryce intends to be there, and Brett indicated he'd like me to be with them, since I'm more likely to recognize Darius than the rest of them."

"Then, go with them," Madison insisted. Not just because he wanted to, but also because it might help her mother and sister. "Please. Leave now. I assume Brett will bring you up to date about where he and the other cops are at the moment, since he contacted you in the first place. I can stay here, make sure all doors and windows are locked, including the building's front door, have my phone in my hand in case I need to call Bryce or you. Too bad I don't have a gun—but even if I did, I wouldn't know how to use it the best way possible. But I do have nice sharp knives in the kitchen. Darius can't be two places at once, so hopefully you and the authorities will find him, and they'll take him in, and I'll stay here nice and safe."

"I appreciate your offer." Oren stood. "And it sounds good. Too good. But if I agree, I'll get in touch with Brett and make sure he ups the number of patrols in this area. A lot."

"Fine." That made her feel a little safer, at least. "Go now, Oren." Madison spoke the words one at a time, making sure they sounded like an order. "I hate to have you hanging out with me when you clearly would rather be somewhere else. And the police chief wants your help. Plus, it'll benefit my family. And it's not like I'll be dashing about the schoolyard or somewhere that Darius could see me and come after me."

"But he probably knows where you live. And—"

"And I'll be locked in, and you'll be closer to him than I will."

Since Oren was already on his feet, Madison joined him, took his beer bottle from his hand and placed it back on the table. Now, if she only wasn't so worried about him.

"If you're sure..." he said.

"I'm sure. I'll even put your beer back in the fridge,

and we can drink some more before we go to bed tonight while you tell me how Darius was caught. Now go."

She was suddenly in Oren's arms. Their kiss was hot and hard—and Madison had a horrible thought that it could be the last one they'd share. Well, she'd be okay, carefully locked in here. But what about Oren?

"Go," she repeated, pulling back. "But please be careful." She looked up into his blue eyes as they regarded her with…well, it seemed like more than mere affection. Attraction? Heck, yes. And could that be gratitude? He had nothing to be grateful about. He'd been here for her since they'd met, and he was due for some time away from her, anyway.

And the time he'd be spending helping to bring down Darius could only be helpful to her, too. Even if he was endangering his life…and her heart in the process.

"Okay, but I'll stay in close touch. Keep your phone with you at all times. Do you have it now?"

"I will in a second." She hurried into the living room, where she'd deposited her purse on the coffee table. She pulled her phone out and waved it at Oren, who'd followed her in there. "See? And here." She pulled her condo keys out and gave them to him. "Now you can come in and out of this place whenever you want. So get on your way, Marshal."

"Yeah. In a minute." Madison felt a rush of further gratitude—and, yes, love—when Oren called Brett and asked him to beef up the patrols in her neighborhood, both patrol cars and cops on foot, even visiting her property. "He's on it," Oren said to her as he hung up.

He shoved her keys in his pocket and grabbed her yet again for a deep, quick kiss.

Then he left. She heard him rattle the door as he apparently tried the knob before he went away. She wondered if any neighbors would see him dash down the stairs and into the parking lot and question what that was about. Hopefully, they were all relaxing in their units.

Madison suddenly felt her body deflate. Damn, but she would miss Oren. And worry about him. And...well, she'd worry about herself a bit, too. Yes, she should be good and safe here, although she tried opening the door and also confirmed it was locked. This time of year, she never opened windows so she knew they were secured. She couldn't look out to see the patrolling police, but she'd no doubt they would be there. Oren had arranged for those patrols. He would protect her, even if he wasn't here.

She returned to the kitchen, sat down at the table and finished her beer. And kept her mind—and heart—on the man getting farther and farther away with each step.

Oren hurried down the hall to the stairway, ignoring his urge to go back and try Madison's door again. To make sure the woman he was coming to adore was safe, that no one could get to her. Or maybe open it with the key she gave him and go back inside.

But she was right. He hoped. He'd been asked by Brett to help bring the dangerous son of the gunrunner in, and he might have the unique ability around here to recognize Darius, although the guy probably looked like his ID photos that the cops would have access to.

But he was a law-enforcement officer, too. Bringing down bad guys was part of his job.

So was protecting the innocent...but wasn't Madison his responsibility, too?

Of course. And he'd arranged for more official protection in her neighborhood.

He hurried down the stairs, seeing no other building residents, which was normal. He opened the outside door, shut it and tested it.

He did a quick walk around the building and parking area. Of course he didn't see Darius. Maybe the guy had already been caught.

Getting into his car, Oren called Brett before starting out. "I'm on my way there," he told the interim chief. "But did you get him?"

"Not yet, but we've got patrols around the train station, near the safe house and more, including several in Madison's area. They'll be patrolling her street often, and at least a couple will walk around her development a lot." Which was exactly as Oren had hoped.

"Glad you're coming." Brett gave Oren directions where to meet up with him and his subordinates who also sought the suspect.

"Okay," Oren said. "I'm leaving now." He started his car and drove quickly through the parking lot and onto the street.

Where he pulled over by the curb—just for a minute, he told himself, till he convinced himself once more that he was doing the right thing.

Only that conviction didn't come. His heart—and his mind—were back at Madison's condo with her.

The officers apparently saw no sign of Darius or anyone they might think was him, or Brett would have let Oren know.

Sure, Darius had warned them he was heading toward the safe house.

Sure, the cops had recorded that call and heard a train in the background that helped them figure out where Darius probably was.

But the main word there was *probably*.

The idea of leaving Madison alone, even in a locked building, a locked unit, with lots of patrol cars going by as well as police on foot—but that Darius out there possibly playing games with the cops... Nope.

Maybe he'd feel bad later about not helping Brett.

Maybe Madison was completely correct, that she was safe there in her locked condo, especially since they didn't know for certain if Darius knew where she lived.

But Oren nevertheless turned the car around and headed back into the parking lot, taking the first un-designated space.

And headed back inside the building to personally protect Madison.

Not wanting to scare her, he called first rather than just unlocking the door to her unit and coming in.

She met him at the door. "I don't understand. Didn't they find Darius?" she said.

"I don't entirely, either," he admitted. "But—"

A loud noise echoed in Madison's bedroom. What the hell? It sounded like the window breaking...

Oh, yeah, he'd been right to come back. He wouldn't let anything happen to her.

What was going on? At first, Madison was irritated that Oren had returned. Surely she could take care of herself for a while, in her locked-down home.

But that noise—

She ran behind him to her bedroom, in time to see a man who could be that guy who'd run them off the road a few days earlier shout something unintelligible, grab the chair she kept at her computer table and bash Oren in the head with it.

Oren crumpled to the ground.

"What are you doing?" Madison screamed, not bothering to demand how Darius, who was supposed to be a distance from here near the safe house, had entered her condo. "Oren!" She ran over and knelt on the carpet beside where Oren lay, not moving.

"What the hell is he doing here?" was Darius's shouted reply. "I fixed it so he'd be leaving when I got here, and I even saw him drive away in his car."

"Well, he came back," Madison spat at him, wishing Oren responded. Hoping he was okay—or would be. She needed him to be. What should she do without him, her lover and protector?

He was definitely unconscious now. Or could he be pretending so he could leap up and subdue this guy? She didn't think so. She only hoped he was still alive. She stroked his head and its wavy black hair. He didn't move, and she had to prevent herself from crying. But at least when she touched his throat she felt a pulse.

"Get out of here," she demanded, glaring toward Darius. "The police are on their way." She wasn't lying about that, of course. Or she didn't think so. Brett had promised Oren to send some patrols.

"Yeah, sure they are," Darius scoffed. "I set things up with a call that would make them figure I was near the train station closest to where I think your family's safe house is—assuming my idea about it is right. But soon as I did that, I headed here, since it wasn't hard to learn where you live, my dear Madison. So here I am."

Madison had seen Darius Amaltin before, of course. Only for a few seconds and not close up. But she recognized him.

Mostly she'd noticed his eyes staring at them from his car as he tried to run them off the road on their way from Kendall to here and shoot them. Now, she saw those wild, dark eyes darting from her to Oren and back again. He looked midtwenties. He was skinny, had long medium-brown hair and wore a green-camouflage shirt over black jeans.

And why was she studying him like this? She'd want to be able to identify him later, after he was arrested, so she could testify against him.

Assuming she remained alive…but why was he targeting her instead of her dad or her other family? Was it just because he knew where she was? Not that she wanted any harm to fall on any of her family, not even her father.

Darius suddenly knelt on the floor on Oren's other side and grabbed his throat. "Your buddy's alive," he hissed. "Well, not for long. Gee, he could have lived, if he'd just gone to join the cops." He looked back at Madison. "But I want to take care of you first, and though he's breathing, he hasn't reacted to my touch so I figure he'll be out cold for a while. A good thing. You and I are going into the other room now." He rose quickly and yanked Madison's arm painfully, dragging her to her feet. "I'll make some calls, then you and I are leaving. Maybe we can have a little fun before I kill you."

"What? No! Leave me alone!" she shrieked, panicked. But Darius's grip on Madison was tight and she couldn't pull away. Why did he want to kill her? So her father would suffer the way Darius had when Louis was killed?

If only they were in her kitchen and she could grab one of those knives she'd mentioned to Oren.

If only she could help Oren…

Maybe she could dash off to the kitchen from the living room, which appeared to be where Darius was taking her. Why?

"Come on, dear Madison." Darius's tone seemed

mockingly warm. "I want you to be the first. We'll take care of it here."

They were in the living room now, and he shoved her toward the couch. She stumbled but managed to turn enough to wind up sitting on her sofa rather than falling to the floor.

Madison liked that couch, before. Especially since she and Oren had sat there several times talking.

When would they be able to talk again?

Would they ever be able to talk again?

"What do you mean?" she finally responded to Darius. "What will we take care of?"

"Oh, we're going to talk a little about why I have it in for your family, although I think you know about some of it, at least, thanks to your buddy Oren—and your wonderful killer of a father, Richard Foster, or whatever his name is now."

Darius had moved her coffee table away and put one of her armchairs in front of the sofa to block her from getting up and running.

"Okay," he said. "First, I need you to tell me exactly where that safe house is. Like I said, I have a general idea, but that's not enough. I'll have to find your father again, too, up in Kendall, but that will come later. I'll want him to doubly suffer by learning that all of you are dead first, before I kill him, too." His tone had been almost friendly before, but now he leaned down so his head nearly touched Madison's, and he grabbed her throat. "So where is that safe house?"

Madison began gagging. He released her slightly, maybe because he realized she couldn't talk that way. But even when she was back to near normal, she wasn't going to answer his question—not that she actually knew where the safe house was—so she pretended she still wasn't able to talk.

"Where. Is. That. Safe house?" Darius clearly wasn't giving up.

"I don't know," she managed to say, telling the truth.

"Yeah, right." He tightened his grip again, and Madison gasped. Was he going to choke her to death?

Did she have an idea where the safe house was? Not really. But she could guess…

He apparently planned to kill her, anyway. Why even give a hint of where she believed it was and make it easier for him to target her mom and Jillian, too?

She tried to stop focusing on him. How could she save herself?

How could she save *Oren*?

What was she going to do?

Oren was conscious. Just barely. But he'd been aware of Darius kneeling by him. Grabbing his throat. Choking him—in addition to the injuries he'd incurred when Amaltin slammed him with a chair.

He still lay on the floor, concentrating on his efforts to breathe. But Madison was with Darius. He had to go save her.

Assuming he could move.

At least he heard them somewhere down the hall. They hadn't left…yet. But Oren was certain Darius wasn't just going to hang around here indefinitely with Madison.

Why was Darius after her this way? Oren might have his suspicions, but he just hoped he would have an opportunity to ask Amaltin as he took him into custody.

Was she still okay? He heard her voice in the short distance, although he couldn't understand what she said.

She *had* to be safe. He wouldn't know what to do if that man had gotten his hands on her...

He moved slowly, hoping to rise so he could go help, ignoring his dizziness. Ignoring his pain. But he definitely wasn't strong enough to break into the room and confront Darius, even though Oren was still covertly carrying his weapon. Although...still lying there, he carefully rubbed his hand down his side toward the pouch where he kept his sidearm. And didn't feel it. Had it fallen out? Had Darius seized it? It didn't matter.

Damn! He felt naked, even more exposed. Terrified for Madison.

He needed help. And he knew just who he needed.

He pulled his phone from his pocket, and that wasn't an easy feat. He managed to look at it and made sure the sound was off. He kept looking at the door to the hallway to make sure Darius didn't appear from the room at the end, where Oren believed he was holding Madison. Quickly, Oren began typing a text message. To Bryce.

In Madisons condo, Darius here and has her. We need help.

In a few seconds he felt the phone vibrate and received the reply he'd hoped for: On my way.

Great. But of course Oren couldn't wait. He had to act.

As he attempted again to stand he grew dizzier—and the room disappeared.

Chapter 20

As calmly as she could, Madison had explained that the cops never told civilians where a safe house was, that she wished she knew. But she was actually glad, at that moment, that she didn't.

How long had they been there, she wondered now. Two minutes? Twenty?

She managed somehow to convince Darius to join her in the kitchen, and she pulled a beer for him from the refrigerator. Acted like his buddy. Like she understood what he'd gone through. Quivering inside, desperate to determine the best way to handle this—especially to help Oren—she'd encouraged Darius to give her his side of the story, why he hated her father so much, why he was determined to avenge himself against Richard Foster and all his family.

But where was Oren? Still in one of the rooms down the hall, most likely.

But was he okay? If he'd been fine, he would be here helping her…

And the thought that he wasn't made her frantic with worry.

At least while Darius was in here, he wasn't hurting Oren any more than he already had. But he clearly wasn't concerned about the marshal bursting in and arresting him.

That meant Oren must be badly injured. And although Madison had tried once to go in and see him, help him, Darius had made it clear she was to stay right there. Away from Oren.

With Darius.

If she wanted to remain healthy.

But what was she going to do? Oren needed help. He might even be *dying*.

Yet if she didn't remain alive, there'd be no way she could help him at all.

At least, as long as she stayed in the same room as Darius, the guy was almost cordial. He answered her questions about his father, who he claimed had been innocent, convicted because of Richard Foster's so-called lies, and his determination to kill that man's family as retribution.

And all the while, he was acting friendly, even as he urged her to tell the truth and let him know where the safe house was.

Which of course she wouldn't, even if she knew. She kept changing the subject back to his father. And so far, despite what she'd seen in him before, Darius kept his cool, didn't attempt again to choke the information he wanted out of her.

Yet.

But she couldn't be sure what would happen next.

How long he would let this go on before he did something physical again. Shook her, hurt her, or worse.

And she stewed inside, contemplating how she could physically retaliate against him. Like jump up, run to the drawers near the sink and pull out a knife to defend herself with.

But he was bigger. Probably stronger. And if she pulled out a knife, would she be able to keep control of it if he grabbed it?

It didn't help that she sat quite a ways from the sink. There were cabinets nearer where she was, where she mostly kept things for school: notebooks and even some reference texts she could look at for additional ideas.

Well, this couldn't go on forever—their discussion, his cordiality. And so she dwelled on how best to distract him…while still considering how she might arm herself.

So far, she hadn't figured it out.

"So now you know what it was like for me to have a dad in prison for just trying to make a living," Darius finally said, leaning over the kitchen table toward Madison.

Making a living as a gunrunner wasn't exactly admirable, but apparently Darius was okay with it as he described his childhood, twenty-odd years ago, with his father in prison…and then dead. The way he told his story was designed to make Madison feel sorry for him, she figured. And in a way she did.

She'd feel a lot sorrier for him if he hadn't tried to run them off the road and shoot them. If he hadn't burst in here and hurt Oren. If he wasn't targeting her entire family.

If he wasn't now keeping her prisoner. And if he didn't, apparently, intend to kill her.

"That had to have been so hard," Madison replied nevertheless, still trying to keep things calm.

"It was. I was so young. And I've suffered ever since, you know? So you have to understand why I want Richard Foster to pay for what he did."

"I sympathize," Madison said. "But will causing others to hurt really make you feel better?" she wheedled.

Darius stood up, shoving the kitchen chair behind him, and grabbed Madison by her throat, forcing her to stand, too. "Yes," he hissed. "It will. Now tell me where that damn safe house is."

Oren snapped awake again. Damn, but he hurt all over. Especially his head. It had been the target of Darius's chair-swing. But his shoulders and neck hurt, too.

Even so, he couldn't lie there any longer. He'd been here far too long already. He needed to rescue Madison.

Oren knew Darius still had Madison in the condo, outside this bedroom. He could hear their voices. He had no idea of Madison's condition, though. Physical or otherwise.

If only he didn't keep losing consciousness…

The hell with it. He couldn't stay here, not without knowing how Madison was.

His job was to protect her.

His life was to protect her. He had no doubt now that he'd fallen in love with the brave, determined teacher, appropriate or not.

This time when he moved, he forced himself to stand, grabbing the mattress for support. He took a couple of steps toward the closed door, unsteady at first.

But he had to get out there. Take charge. Bring Darius into custody. And he wouldn't necessarily need to do it on his own, although he had to be prepared to do so. He believed it had been a while since he'd texted Bryce. He had no idea where the FBI agent was now, but at least he was on his way. How long would it be till he got here? Who knew?

Oren didn't want to call 9-1-1 or anyone else now, since Darius would hear his voice. And he'd already held an important text conversation with Bryce.

The idea of having help on the way finally gave Oren the impetus he needed now that he was remaining conscious.

Time for him to get out there and do all he could for Madison. Bryce could show up any minute now to help. But once Oren got started, maybe he wouldn't even need Bryce's help.

Not that he could count on that, especially considering his current state. No, any help Bryce could provide would be critical.

But now was the time.

He'd act carefully, though, and not just because of his pain and unsteadiness. He wasn't sure exactly where Darius and Madison were.

Damn, but he was worried about her. Hearing her voice at least assured him she was alive, but in what condition? And for how long? This time, he managed to take a few more steps despite some residual dizziness. First thing, he opened the bedroom door a slit and waited. Darius didn't shove it open or come after him. He opened it farther and looked down the hall.

And heard voices again. They were in the kitchen.

It was time. He was moving. He felt stronger. Not his usual self, but at least a bit better.

He slid into the hallway, back against the wall, flexing his hands, and maneuvered slowly, carefully, silently, toward them both.

Yes, Darius was there with Madison. She stood facing the criminal, her back toward the door where Oren entered.

Darius, facing Madison, therefore saw Oren first. "You! I thought you'd be out a lot longer than this." Darius shoved Madison aside, his eyes even wilder than Oren had seen him before. He dashed toward Oren.

Who couldn't take time to wait. Not for Bryce or even his own thoughts to take control.

He'd been hit by one of the chairs and definitely injured. Those pieces of furniture therefore could come in handy.

Madison turned and called out, "Oren!" She moved as if to run over to protect him. But he grabbed the nearest chair and faced Darius.

Once their attacker almost reached him, Oren swung the chair at Darius's head.

And made the kind of hard, injurious contact he'd hoped for.

This time, Darius crumpled.

Oren wasn't about to take any chances, though. Bracing himself against the pain, he knelt on the hard tile and checked Darius's pulse. He was alive but didn't move.

Oren had had a pair of handcuffs in his pants pocket along with his firearm but didn't know where they were now. Darius might have swiped them along with the gun. He patted Darius down. Nothing. Worse—or better?—no gun. But Oren had to make certain Darius couldn't flee if he regained consciousness—or, more important, that he couldn't attack either of them again.

He looked up at Madison. "Does a schoolteacher happen to have any rope around? Or even a scarf that can be turned into a bond I can tie onto this guy?"

"I have scarves," Madison said, "but I'm not sure any of them can be twisted into a good rope. They're in my bedroom, but I don't think I ought to leave here right now."

"Oh, he's not conscious," Oren said. But he recognized that his own speech was somewhat fuzzy thanks to his injuries. He saw the concern on Madison's face.

"Good." She sounded skeptical—and frightened. How could she remain so beautiful, so determined-looking despite what was going on? "How about a cord from one of my appliances?" she asked. "My electric frying pan has one that comes off. Or even my phone charger."

"Sure," Oren said. He should have thought of that, or something like it. Obviously, his mind wasn't back to normal, even if he didn't fear losing consciousness again. "Let's give it a try."

"No way!" Darius suddenly came wide-awake, pushing himself up from the floor, shaking but definitely conscious. And apparently full of more strength than Oren.

He immediately faced Oren, teeth gritted, hands out, grabbing toward Oren's throat—just as the marshal heard the unit's door burst open and slam against the wall.

"Hey, Madison, I'm here," called Bryce as running footsteps sounded in the hallway. "Oren, you okay?"

"What the hell—" Darius shouted, turning slightly to look at Bryce as he appeared at the kitchen doorway.

Great timing, since the distraction allowed Oren to look around the kitchen for one of the cords Madison had mentioned.

"Get down on the floor," Bryce hollered toward Darius, his gun now aimed at the man who had started moving toward Madison.

She yanked open a drawer in a cabinet near the wall and pulled something out. A book, large and heavy-looking. A dictionary?

"Here, you horrible jerk!" she shouted, then smashed Darius's head with it, and the man who wanted to kill her and her family members tumbled back down to the floor.

Clearly unconscious again. Not that Oren was taking any further chances. "Electrical cord?" he demanded of Madison, and she grabbed the one used for her electric skillet. Oren bound Darius's hands behind his back with it, even though the guy didn't move.

"Glad to see you, bro," Madison said as Oren watched Bryce stick his gun back in the holster at his waist. He replaced the electrical cord with a set of handcuffs.

Madison went to give her brother a big hug as he said, "Ditto, sister. And you, too, Marshal Margulies. Hey, I expected you to have things better under control, guy."

All Oren could do was shrug. "Hey, what can I say? I was waiting for help from the FBI."

"And you got it." Madison had moved away from her brother, stepping over Darius's legs, and approached Oren.

This time, the hug was for him, and he reveled in it.

It was over.

At least the threat to the Colton family from the Amaltins was over.

But did that also mean that everything was over—including his bond with Madison? Because he hoped not. He could see so much more with her—a future, even. But would Madison feel the same way?

Chapter 21

I did it!

Oh, she'd had help, but Madison was thrilled that she was the one who had finally brought down the prospective killer of her family, Darius Amaltin.

With a weapon of her own choosing, too. Well, she hadn't been able to get to the knives she'd had in mind. But of course a teacher would use a nice, big, handy book. And it had worked well. Not that she'd tell any of this to her students.

Nearly an hour had passed, and now her condo was filled with members of law enforcement. Oren, of course, her wonderful brother, Bryce, and others were talking in her kitchen. They'd also called in Chief Shea, and Madison had learned that Brett and Bryce had been in touch—and her brother had let the cops know that they could leave the safe house, since Darius had set them up to go there when he came here to kill her.

Oren had taken a hit for her. He had been protecting her, as usual. And now he talked to the cops, letting them know his side, and therefore her side, of what had happened that night. He seemed okay now, thank heavens. Maybe not his usual strong self, but a whole lot better than he'd been.

A couple of officers had taken Darius into custody. He'd been well enough by then to go with them to the police station and not the hospital, although they'd said they would call a paramedic in to check him out. Her dictionary hadn't killed him, and she was glad of that.

At the moment, Madison sat on her sofa, waiting for whatever happened next. One of Brett's investigators had already interviewed her, so there was nothing for her to do but be patient. And worry. And grow sleepy, since her energy had been sapped by all that had gone on.

Then, it was truly over, at least for the night. Brett joined her, and he was smiling. His rugged face, beneath his red hair, looked relaxed. "Thanks for all your help, Madison," he said. "I'll head back to the safe house now and tell your mom and sister what's happened—and that they can go home. We'll eventually need you to testify when Mr. Amaltin is put on trial, and we may need more input from you before that, but I don't anticipate further danger in this matter. Let me know, though, if you think otherwise."

"Thank you, Brett. It'll be so good to have this all behind us."

Oren walked Shea to the door, while Bryce stayed with Madison. "We'll need to throw a party in celebration," he said.

"Maybe so." Madison hugged her brother, then he left. Only Oren remained in Madison's unit with her then, standing a distance from her in the living room. "Hard to believe it's finally over." His voice was cool, his expression relieved.

And Madison felt almost as if he'd shoved her to the floor. It was over. All of it?

She should never have let her emotions loose around him...

"I assume you'll let the marshals guarding my father know what happened."

"Of course," he responded.

"Will you be staying here for the night?" she asked, unhappy about her voice's raspy quality. She couldn't help it. She allowed her feelings to show in her longing look. *Please stay*, her mind pleaded. *I want you; I need you. Darn it all, I love you!*

His gaze seemed to mirror what she was thinking. "Of course," he said, "as long as I'm invited."

"Definitely," Madison replied, and he immediately came close and drew her into his arms. Their kisses helped her feel better. But when they stopped, she pulled away. "Do you feel okay now?"

"Still a little pain here and there," he said. "But I'm a whole lot better now that Darius is in custody at last—and can't hurt you."

"Or you," she responded with a smile, which he returned. Then she told Oren, "I've got to make a call."

She tried using the burner-phone number she had for her mother and sister, but it no longer worked. She wanted to talk to them, though, after they'd been informed by Brett, and by Bryce, too, about all that had gone on that night.

Fortunately, they called her a short while later. Bryce was with them. Her relatives all expressed how glad they were that she was okay and also thanked her for all she'd done to protect them.

They decided to get together for dinner the next night to celebrate. And, yes, they wanted to go to Oren's sister's deli again. Of course Madison had suggested it. She had come to care for Oren so much and wanted to get to know his wonderful sister more, too.

So that was finally settled, and Madison was delighted. She wanted to talk to their father, too, but Oren said she'd need to wait till at least the next day, and he would set it up.

Oren. They spent the night together, and she was thrilled. So maybe it wasn't all over. At least not yet.

Still, their night together was short. Too short. But sexy. For yes, they engaged in several highly heated encounters despite Oren's injuries, which he mostly ignored, except for an occasional grimace. Madison hoped she wasn't acting frantic, as if she wanted to get as much into this night as possible…in case it actually was their final night together since Oren's official duties, and therefore his official reasons to remain in this area, had ended. Of course that meant their relationship, such as it was, would have to end, too.

But the next day was Friday, a working day for Madison, so they rose as they had been doing since Oren began staying with her. Madison showered and threw on one of her usual school-day dresses, a teal one with a wide matching belt.

Oren didn't have to accompany her to school that day, so he didn't. Madison understood. But she also wondered if that was the first step of their distancing themselves from one another.

Still, she felt so relieved about the capture of Darius before he'd hurt any of them badly that she had a wonderful day of teaching, making sure all her students enjoyed their lessons as much as possible. She of course had reported to Principal Nelson first to let her know all was well.

Oren showed up at lunchtime just as Madison headed toward the cafeteria. She was thrilled. "So good to see you," she said.

"I just wanted to put you in touch with your father," Oren told her. Which also made her happy.

Though he looked around the empty room, then engaged in an erotic kiss with her, he didn't seem inclined to stick around after giving her the current burner-phone number Wes/Richard was using. Was the kiss a clue that he would spend a little more time with her before he left? She wanted him to stay in her life, but so far he hadn't given any indication he wanted the same thing.

She thought about Alec. At least he was local—but she had no desire to get back together with him.

After she'd grabbed lunch with some other teachers, Madison's conversation with her dad was brief, but he seemed really happy. "Good thing I didn't know what you were up to," he said. "I'd have worried a lot about my little girl. I was already worried about what that SOB Darius was up to regarding me and the rest of the family, but I never imagined you'd help to capture him."

She wondered what her dad had been told. And why he suddenly was calling her *my little girl*.

"I didn't set out to," she said.

"Well, I'll want to hear all about it. I hope to head to Grave Gulch soon, now that I don't have to stay in protective custody. I may still have some commitments around here first, at the bookstore. But I'll be there as soon as I can."

"Great!" And Madison meant it. Maybe she was too

optimistic, but she hoped, now that the pressure was off regarding their lives being at risk, that her mother and father would now get a good opportunity to get to know one another—again. And see what came of it.

Back to her classroom. Rather than teaching her full class, she'd worked out a session with only half a dozen students that afternoon, while Cora worked with the rest on basic addition. And Madison? She had her students, including Marti and Buster, each choose a picture book, and she read to them close-up so they could see.

Sweet kids. They reminded her of wanting children of her own someday. With Oren? She could hope so, but didn't feel optimistic that would happen.

Afternoon lessons were soon over, and the kids went home or to their day care for the rest of the day.

It dawned on Madison then that she didn't have a ride home. With all that had gone on, she hadn't yet gotten her car back.

"Of course," Oren said when she called him while alone in her classroom, sitting behind her desk. "I'll pick you up. And I've already checked with Brett. They still have your car at the repair shop near the station, but it's nice and safe and ready for you to pick up despite the dent still being there. We'll get it this afternoon and leave it at your condo. I'll drive us to the deli."

So she'd not only see Oren later that day, she'd get to ride with him. To talk to him.

He'd even eventually wind up with her at her condo, since he'd have to at least take her home after dinner.

And then?

Well, maybe Madison could seduce him. Invite him to stay in her life, which was what she really wanted.

But what did *he* want? She hoped she'd find out, and that she'd be happy with it.

She soon put everything away and went to the entrance of the school building. Sure enough, Oren was there, sitting in his car, waiting for her.

She slid into the passenger seat, stifling an urge to bend over the console to kiss him. He gave her a friendly-enough greeting but immediately got the car started.

"How are you feeling now?" she asked. "Last night was fun, and I know you've been driving today, but are you well enough?"

His brow furrowed beneath the black hair over his forehead. Was he in pain?

"I'm okay," he said. "Not perfect, but I've continued to improve all day, and I have been careful. I'm fine with what we've got planned for the rest of today."

She hoped so. She wanted to hug him, kiss the spots where he'd been injured, as she'd done before. Maybe more. But he was already cool toward her. Now that his job protecting her was over, was he determined to end their intimacy, too?

He soon got her to the large lot where her car was being held, not far from the police station. Brett wasn't there, but the guy in charge had all the paperwork as well as the keys, and Madison soon had her car back. They said they could take care of the dent when she was ready, too, and she said she'd be in touch. She'd contact her insurance company again first.

"I'll follow you to your condo," Oren said, which he did. Madison kept checking her rearview and side mirrors. He must be feeling okay, she figured.

Soon, she pulled into the driveway and parked in her designated space—no need to hide any longer—with Oren right behind her. He got out of his car and opened his passenger door for her since he would be driving to the deli. He looked straight into her eyes before she slid in, and her urge to throw her arms around him and kiss him seemed all-consuming.

But she saw no similar emotion in his friendly smile as he held out his hand to help her in.

She turned and blinked away the tears that rose to her eyes. She didn't want him to know how devastated she felt.

And yes, she did feel devastated and feared it would only get worse the more they were together...for now.

Well, the evening was just beginning. And it turned out delightful—but not because of any interaction between Oren and her.

Bubbe's Deli was busy, as usual. Her mom reached Madison first and threw her arms around her. "I'm so proud of you, honey! Bryce told us all about what happened yesterday. I'm so glad you're all right, and I heard you were the one who essentially captured the man who was threatening us."

"Well, it wasn't like—"

"Close enough." Oren's smile toward Madison made her feel all warm and gushy—and more hopeful than she'd been over the past few hours. Perhaps he wasn't so averse to being around her after all...

"I'll leave you all alone now," Olivia said. She was also smiling, and Madison also wanted to hug Oren's sister for owning this great restaurant.

"Thanks so much," Madison said. "I'm looking forward to my matzo ball soup."

Which made Olivia laugh. Nice lady, Madison thought, not for the first time.

And she had one wonderful brother, in many ways...

Okay, for this evening Madison wouldn't obsess over

Oren. He had helped to save her life, as he'd promised, and she'd even maybe helped to save his.

But that didn't guarantee a long relationship, no matter how much Madison had come to like the guy. *Like?* Heck, she'd already admitted to herself that she'd fallen in love, felt more for him than she'd ever felt for Alec. *This* was the type of forever she wanted.

But what did Oren think of her? She knew he was attracted to her, but did his feelings go any deeper than that?

He seemed to fit right in with her family here. They were chatting, and Madison was pleased that Oren sat at her side as had become their habit. She was eating her matzo ball soup, as was also her habit. Bryce was across from her, eating a corned beef sandwich, and that was what Oren and Jillian had ordered, too. Their mother, like Madison, was eating soup.

They all talked about what had happened the previous day—mostly to Madison and Oren, though those protected in the safe house had heard that the man who threatened to kill them was on the loose. Eventually, they learned that Madison had been involved in bringing that man down. Now, they cheered her, as well as Oren and the cops who'd been taking care of them.

"So I heard you went back to school to teach your students today as if nothing happened." Mom shook her head as she smiled at Madison.

"Of course," Madison said. "Life goes on. I've returned to my usual routine, and I assume Jillian and you will, too."

"Yep," said Jillian. "My normal routine."

"Boy, I don't envy any of you in law enforcement," Madison said, looking from Jillian to Bryce and then to

Oren. "All that potential danger from people who want to hurt others…and you."

"That's part of the fun of it." Oren winked at her.

Okay, she didn't like that idea of him being in danger. But at least he was lighthearted about it.

And his wink at her made her insides start fluttering again.

What would things be like that night? Would he stay with her after taking her back to her condo?

She'd wondered about that before and kept wondering about it as they finished their meals.

They all chipped in to pay the bill, although Jillian mentioned they needed to do an accounting sometime regarding previous meals mostly paid for by Oren. Tonight, Oren attempted to treat Madison—another good sign? Or was he just being a protective gentleman and a remote professional?

"I'm assuming you're staying the night with me again," Madison said as Oren drove them to her place. He didn't have a home here, after all—although she figured he could stay with his sister if he wanted to.

"Sure," he said, as he turned into the condo's parking lot. "If it's okay with you. I can sleep on the couch."

"Why not sleep in bed with me?" Madison said, forcing herself not to feel hurt at his rejection. That evening she'd occasionally seen him flinch in pain as he walked or sat down or rose. "I gather, from the way you've been wincing now and then, that your injuries from yesterday are still giving you some pain. Sleeping on the uneven sofa might make you feel even worse."

"Maybe so," he said. "Thanks. But just because we're in the same bed doesn't mean we have to…well, enjoy each other."

"Or," she countered, "even if we don't have to, we

can still probably have some fun, though we'll need to find a way that won't hurt you."

There was something about his not particularly happy smile after he parked and turned off the car's engine that made her be the one to wince—inside. What was he thinking?

He told her a little later, after they'd gone inside, watched a little television news and drunk some water, since they'd had wine with dinner.

"Time for bed," he finally said. "And, well, we've already discussed having some more fun there. But before you decide, I want to let you know I'm heading back to Kendall tomorrow to make sure all's under control there, and after that I'm returning to my job at the marshals office in Grand Rapids. So even though we've had a great time together, I don't want to lead you on."

Of course. That was who he was, a marshal. He'd been engaged in his job of protecting her while he was here, but now that was over. She'd allowed herself to hope he'd find a way to stick around, but apparently that wasn't what he wanted.

A wave of despair swept through her. But there was nothing she could do to change his mind.

So she made herself pretend to be blasé about it. "So I figured," she said. "But that doesn't mean we can't enjoy ourselves on our last night together."

"If you're okay with it," he said, "I am."

"But let me know if you feel any pain."

They were soon in each other's arms, and then they made their way to her room and her bed...

And Madison allowed herself to engage in the most wonderful sex possible that night with the man who had stolen her heart and was now about to break it.

She might as well enjoy one last time, she told herself. And she did.

But how was she going to go on without Oren in her life from now on? She didn't want to face that. But she would have to.

Chapter 22

Oren couldn't stop thinking about Madison as he drove toward Kendall. He'd had breakfast with her this morning, and of course she didn't have to go to school that day since it was Saturday. He'd done his best to keep her at an emotional distance, but there was no denying she'd crept into his heart.

He wondered what she'd do over the weekend. Probably go back to whatever she used to do on weekends before she'd first seen the man who turned out to be her father—and all the chaos that had erupted as a result. At least, whatever she'd done outside her then-fiancé's presence.

She didn't need Oren any longer. Sure, they'd seemed to be developing a relationship. But thanks to his prior experiences, Oren didn't believe in relationships. They nearly always seemed doomed to failure, so why take a chance?

He recognized that Madison cared at least a bit for him, as he did for her—well, maybe he cared a lot, but so what? They lived in different towns. Led very different lives. Had no chance at a real future together.

Which hurt. So much. But he would deal with it.

He'd already become too close to the subject of his protective assignment. Enjoyed it? Hell, yes. But that had to be the end.

Despite the tears he'd seen in her eyes as she said goodbye to him that morning.

At least she still had relatives in Grave Gulch, and none of them were hidden in a safe house any longer. If Madison hadn't any other plans, at least she could get together with one or all of them.

He'd passed the area where Darius had run them off the road a while ago and he'd let out an internal cheer. Darius would pay for that and for nearly murdering Nita the clerk—and all his crimes.

Now, Oren approached the final turnoff to Kendall. He intended to visit Wesley Windham one last time. Darius had been questioned, and no former associates of his father were known to be after Richard. He'd been the only one. Therefore, Wes no longer needed protective custody, Oren's or anyone else's. Still, Oren always liked to check on those who'd been under his protection one final time to make sure all was well with them. And he hadn't had to go far out of his way on his route to Grand Rapids.

It was late morning now, and Oren headed to the bookstore where Wes worked. He'd already called the guy, let him know he was on his way to say goodbye.

Wes. Madison's dad…

Okay, he had to stop thinking about Madison. He

could stay in touch with her, sure, just on a friendly basis.

And when he visited his sister in Grave Gulch? Would he visit with Madison then, too?

The idea sounded much too good—and much too complicated.

He soon entered the town and drove through Kendall till he reached the street where the bookstore was located.

And that boutique next door that sold wedding gowns.

So much here reminded him of Madison…

Enough.

He parked and got out of his car, then went inside the store. Wes was behind the counter talking to a younger man. "Hi, Oren," he said immediately after glancing in his direction. "Come over here."

He introduced Oren to the other guy, Reggie Blandi, who owned the store, a young fellow with lots of brown facial hair. He seemed delighted to meet Oren. "He couldn't talk about it before, apparently, but Wes has been telling me all about his background now—and how much he owes to you, Marshal Margulies."

"Just Oren," he told Reggie. Then he looked at Wes. "Do you have time to grab a cup of coffee?" And talk, of course, but that didn't need to be mentioned.

"Of course." Wes glanced at Reggie. "I assume that's okay, right?"

"Sure. No need for you to hang around much today or otherwise. I know you've got things to do."

The young man grinned and waved, and Wes nodded in the direction of the store's door. "So let's go," he told Oren.

There was a chain coffee shop across the street, and

Oren wasn't surprised it was the place Wes chose because it was so convenient. In just a few minutes they both had their orders, Oren's a large, regular black coffee and Wes a medium latte. They chose one of the half dozen unoccupied inside tables and sat down on two wooden chairs facing one another.

Wes started their conversation, leaning over his edge of the round table toward Oren. Having spent some time with Bryce, Oren now saw what Madison did—their resemblance.

"I've heard all about what happened in Grave Gulch," Wes said, "thanks to my most recent herd of protective deputies like you." He held up his drink as though offering a toast. "Here's to all of you. I appreciate it."

"You're very welcome. I'm just glad Darius didn't accomplish any of his highly nasty goals—like killing your family members first and then killing you."

Wes paused to take a sip from his cup. "And his father put himself in the position that wound up getting him killed. Anyway, I'm glad to see you here…but where's Madison?"

"Home in Grave Gulch." Oren felt his throat constrict as he thought yet again of possibly never seeing her again.

"But I thought… Nearly every time Madison and I spoke after you accompanied her there, I knew you were with her. And the way she talked about you, so fondly and more, well, I thought you were becoming a couple."

Oren inhaled deeply. "I…I do care a lot about your daughter. But what we had wasn't a relationship…I was protecting her. You certainly must understand that."

He was surprised when Wes half rose from his chair and glared at him. "Don't be me, you fool. If you care for her, go after her. Stay with her. I can't begin to tell you how much I've regretted not breaking out and going back to Verity before."

"You're not with her now," Oren pointed out, not wanting to think about any similarity between how he felt about Madison and what Wes had done with his life.

"No, but I hope to be. You know, when I visited them at the safe house…the moment I saw Verity again after twenty-five years, all my love for her came pouring back, but… Well, I'm determined to at least try to win her trust back, even though it might be impossible. Same with my children. But the risk is worth it. You know why I don't have to spend much time in the bookstore today? I've resigned! I couldn't leave while that idiot Darius was out there, but I'm heading to Grave Gulch later today to stay there and see what I can do to make myself part of my family again. But you…you don't have to do anything like that. You care for my Madison? Then go get her, Marshal."

Oren's heart sang at the very idea. But he couldn't even trust his own heart. And what did she really think of him? She let him go that morning, acting very nice and polite and accepting. Surely she wanted to move on with her own life…

Or did she? He had seen tears in her eyes. Or had he imagined it?

"You heading back to Grave Gulch with me, Marshal?" Wes pressed, swigging down the rest of his latte.

"Well, I can follow you back and make sure you arrive safely." That was the best Oren could do.

And on the way, he'd call Madison and let her know he was accompanying Wes to Grave Gulch. But would he get to see her?

He simply wasn't certain.

* * *

Really? Sitting on her living-room sofa while the contractors hired by the condo association fixed her broken window, Madison was on the phone with Oren.

His call had been very unexpected.

He let her know he'd followed her father on his drive to Grave Gulch, and they were just arriving in town. Yes, Richard—or Wes—was on his way here and hoped to talk to her mother. And maybe her and her siblings, too.

Wow! Her family was finally coming back together after so long apart.

But Madison couldn't focus on that now. Oren had decided to come, too, to make sure her father arrived here safely. Even though there were no threats anyone knew of against him now. No more Darius.

So why was he really coming? To see her? He'd made it clear he wasn't interested in pursuing anything further with her, so he had to be accompanying her dad back to town, to make sure there were no more threats to his life or his family. That must be it. Oren was, once again, just doing his job.

She had to ask. Shaking her head, drinking some water from a bottle she'd gotten out of her refrigerator, she said, "Am I going to see you while you're here?"

"Would you like to?" he responded.

If he'd been there, she might have kicked him. Or not. He was probably still sore from his injuries, but he surely knew how she felt.

"Yes," she said forcefully. "I'd like to see you." And then she decided to go for it. After all, she hadn't been sure she'd ever talk to him again, let alone possibly see him. "Oren, in case you haven't figured it out, I really care for you. And not just because I enjoy you in bed, or I'm grateful for all you did to protect me. And those feelings have nothing to do with my former fiancé no longer being in my life, in case you're wondering. But I...I need to know how you feel about me."

She could picture him with his scowl of concentration as he drove, although he did shoot her frequent smiles when she was sitting beside him.

Did she really want to know how he felt about her?

Well, she'd already asked.

"This is better said in person," Oren began, and Madison clutched the phone. Was he going to admit he wanted nothing more to do with her? She braced herself, preparing to tell him that was how she really felt, too. Assuming she could lie that well. "But... Well, I do want to see you when I'm in Grave Gulch, although I don't know where this will go. I don't think I'm ready to get involved with someone who's fresh out of a relationship, despite what you said, someone I was just working to protect..." He hesitated, and Madison shut her eyes.

Was this going where she thought? And did he even want a family?

Well, she loved him. And she'd be willing to see how things went if they actually got together.

Wouldn't she?

He hadn't resumed what he was saying, so she had to prompt him. "So how do you really feel? What do you want?"

"I love you, Madison. But—"

She felt her mouth open, her body tense. She didn't know where the *but* was going, and Oren didn't continue. "I love you, too, Oren," she responded breathlessly, hopefully, despairingly. "But—"

"But I'm not sure we can go anywhere," Oren finished.

"I get it," Madison lied. That's when her phone started to ring with a second call. She glanced at it. Jillian was calling. Good. An excuse to end this painful conversation right now. And to take it up again later? Maybe in person? All she said was "Hey, Oren, sorry. I have to get off this call. I've got another one coming in that I have to take. Can I call you back later?"

"Of course," he said and immediately hung up, leaving Madison feeling heartsick even as she answered the call from Jillian.

"Hey, Madison, did you hear?"

Madison suspected she knew what her sister was talking about but asked anyway. "Hear what?"

"Our father just arrived in town. He's at Mom's now. He'd apparently called to say he was coming, and she got in touch with me to let me know since we've stayed in even closer contact since that safe-house thing. Anyway, she said she'd confirm it after she'd had a chance to talk with Dad. I'm calling him that in the hopes that he really will be acting like one of the family now. Which I gather he is. Mom wants Bryce, you and me to come to her place for dinner tonight. Dad'll be there. Are you available?"

"Oh, yes. I wouldn't miss that for the world," she said, relieved to be discussing something other than Oren. "I can't assume all will go well, but I'll at least want to be there for Mom."

"Great! Unless we hear otherwise, we're supposed to be there at six. Okay?"

"See you then." Madison felt highly excited as she hung up. Were things going to improve now for Mom? For the rest of them?

What would they all really think of Wes Windham—uh, Richard Foster? Hopefully, he'd at least let them know what name he intended to go by from now on. He'd come back from the dead, and his feelings must still persevere for him to want to see them and their mother now. That appeared to be true love—but was that really what she had with Oren?

She continued to sit there and think. She'd said she would call Oren back. Though he hadn't sounded particularly excited about the idea, she decided to do so.

To stay in touch with him as long as she could.

After all, he'd admitted he loved her. But was that just some kind of soft excuse to supposedly make her feel better as he exited her life? He'd told her he couldn't be involved with her.

Before calling Oren again, though, she had to go talk to the guy who'd finished fixing her window. She looked the area over and thought it looked fine but hoped the condo association would have someone check it out, too. "Thanks," she said to the guy and handed him a tip.

And sat down again after seeing him out.

Her life might never return to what it had been like before she'd seen her father in Kendall, but at least it was taking small steps in that direction.

Taking a deep breath, she called Oren.

She heard noise in the background. "Where are you?" she asked.

"At the police station in Grave Gulch. I'm going to be meeting with Brett soon to get his update and to thank him for his help."

"Thank him for me, too," Madison said and then grasped for what she should say next.

She didn't have to. Oren was the one to speak. "Look, Madison, I think we need to talk. In person. Could you meet me for dinner tonight?"

Her heart sank, even as a tiny shred of hope swam through her. "Sorry," she said. "I've got a family dinner planned—with our father, at our mother's house. I'm really excited, and curious about how it will go."

"Well, I'll probably still be around tomorrow, although till I'm done talking here I won't have much idea about my schedule. I'll call you if I'm available, and you can let me know if whatever I can do works for you."

That sounded as if he was inching his way away from her. Not making getting together with her a priority, despite how he allegedly felt about her. And she wasn't going to settle for a lukewarm relationship again.

Trying to hold back the sorrow she felt, she attempted to sound normal.

Happy.

"Okay," she said. "I'll wait to hear from you tomorrow."

And when she hung up, she was glad the worker was no longer there to see her cry.

He'd had a sudden urge to see Madison that night. Heck, he had a constant urge to see her all the time.

But she'd brushed him off despite admitting she cared a lot about him, too—even loved him. Sure, her reason for not seeing him made sense. She'd be getting together with her family.

Without him, of course. But in a way he also wished he could be there to see what happened once Wes joined the group and would most likely try his best to start mending fences.

But for now…

Yes, he'd followed Wes the entire way to Grave Gulch, and right now Oren was parked in a lot near the police department, since Wes had decided to ask Jillian to accompany him to her mother's place. Probably to act as some kind of buffer if Verity wasn't as pleased to see him as he hoped. Wes had gone inside already, and Oren wasn't certain when they would head to Verity's. Maybe they'd already left.

Oren considered going inside and talking to Brett but decided he'd better make his plans for the evening first. He obviously wasn't going to be staying with Madison that night.

Hopefully his sister would let him stay at her place.

Rather than calling first, he headed to Bubbe's. It was midafternoon, and Olivia was likely to be there. In fact, she was there nearly all hours, even on weekend days like this, although she did choose times to take off each week and leave the place in the hands of trusted staff.

She wasn't behind the counter but walking down the aisle toward it. Toward him. Customers filled the booths and tables that she walked by, even at this hour of the day, and Oren was glad his sister's business remained so successful.

She raised her hand to wave at him. "Why, hi, bro," she said as she reached him. "I thought you'd left town for a while."

"Well, my intention was that it would be for a long while—like, I was heading back to Grand Rapids."

Her face scrunched into a frown. "What do you mean?"

He cocked his head. "I mean to go home, where my job is."

"But… Hey, come into my office, Oren. I've got some questions for you."

That didn't sound good. Oren figured his nosy sister intended to ask him about Madison. Well, he'd at least be able to ask Olivia if he could spend the night at her home. And discuss Madison? He hoped not.

He followed her up the stairs behind the counter and through the door into her office.

"Okay, Oren. What's the story between Madison and you? I know you haven't known her long, but when I've seen you together, I've seen something really good starting there. Am I wrong?" Her eyes glared at him.

"Well, I'm attracted to her, sure. What sane guy wouldn't be? But she was my assignment, and that assignment is over."

"But the attraction is still there, right? How strong is it?"

Hell, Olivia was his sister. He could be honest with her. "Pretty damn strong," he acknowledged, looking down at his hands on his lap. "We've both even admitted that we care a lot for one another." No need to mention love yet.

"Then, have you at least invited her to come with you?"

"She's a schoolteacher here, Olivia. You know that. She wouldn't come with me. Assuming I wanted her to. And she just ended another serious relationship."

"But you want to be together. I can see that and hear it in what you're doing. So…find a new job here. Grave Gulch has a good police department. Or maybe your office could use a presence here. You at least need to check. Even if this is new, don't give up on it just yet. Explore what you feel for Madison."

"But—" He brought his gaze up and glared at his sister. "You're telling me to get into a full-fledged relationship with Madison, right?"

"Right. Assuming you care about her as much as you appear to."

"Okay, I do. But that could lead to marriage, and—"

"And marriage can be a good thing, at least for some people. Look, stop living in the past and looking at how you hadn't found the right woman before. Look toward the future. Potentially with Madison. If she's the right woman for you, don't let her go. Got it?"

"I hear you," he said. And damn if he didn't find what she said to make sense. A lot of sense. It allowed him to start being truthful to himself. And the truth was— "Is it that obvious?"

"That you really care about Madison after knowing her even for so short a time? Hell, yes. Go for it, bro."

"I'll think about it," he said. And of course he already was.

"You do that. And more."

"Meanwhile… Well, can I stay at your place tonight? One way or another, I'm not heading back to Grand Rapids tonight now."

"Fine with me," Olivia said. "But think about the place you've been staying all the other nights since you arrived here."

He did think about it. A lot, as he gave Olivia a hug, kissed her cheek and thanked her.

He left Bubbe's Deli then, his mind swirling.

And trying to focus on what he wanted to do next.

Chapter 23

It was wonderful, Madison thought.

She was in her mother's kitchen as Verity, with assistance, prepared dinner for all five of them: Jillian, Bryce and Madison, and now their father, too.

A roast was cooking in the sizable oven in the especially lovely kitchen. Everyone chipped in. Madison was helping Jillian put a salad together. And Bryce and their father were peeling potatoes that they would boil and mash in a while. All of them were working on the shining granite counter that ran down the center of the kitchen.

Unsurprisingly, Mom kept popping over to check on the potatoes' progress—and to talk to Dad. The two of them seemed to be getting along phenomenally. Now that they were together again, did they feel the love they'd once had?

Would they stay together now? Marry?

That seemed a bit much after all this time, but Madison hoped things went the way Mom really wanted them to, whatever it was.

The smell in the kitchen was delightful. And Madison was really enjoying being with her family members.

Even so…

"Are you okay?" Jillian scooted over closer to Madison. "You seem…well, quiet." She paused. "Where's Oren tonight?"

Madison grabbed another head of lettuce and began pulling it apart, pretending to concentrate on it rather than what Jillian had brought to mind. "Actually, I'm not sure," she finally said, as coolly as she was able.

"Is he in town now? Or—"

"Yes, as far as I know he's in Grave Gulch tonight. He followed Dad here from Kendall to make sure he arrived safely." Madison kept her voice low so their father hopefully wouldn't hear her—and possibly participate in this part of the conversation.

"Then—"

Madison looked at her sister. "I don't want to talk about him, Jillian," she said softly, hoping no one else was listening. "Not now. We can talk later. I… There's a lot going on in my head about him. I'd like your sympathy, but not now."

"Sympathy? Then…okay, we'll talk later." At least Jillian's voice was soft, too. And having a caring sister to talk to might help Madison get through this night, and the following ones, with at least a bit less emotion. She'd only known Oren a few days—she couldn't really love him, surely. This would pass…but she would most likely need compassionate company. Madison was certain she'd lost Oren. Not that she ever really had him, other than as her protector.

And lover. Her wonderful lover…

Okay. She had to pay more attention to the salad, or she might fall apart here as much as the lettuce that was being torn apart.

"Good job," her mother said a few minutes later as Madison and Jillian combined the salad ingredients in the large wooden bowl in front of them. "Let's all go into the dining room and start with the salad while the roast, potatoes and veggies continue cooking." Mom had also started steaming some broccoli in a pan.

Madison followed Jillian into the dining room and sat between her sister and brother, across the table from their parents.

Their parents. Together…

This was definitely an emotional night, in many ways, Madison thought. She didn't have much of an appetite, but she managed to start eating her salad, even enjoying it.

And she attempted to eavesdrop on what her dad was saying. "I don't think I need my undercover name much longer, if at all, so I'll probably go back to my real name, if the authorities say it's okay. And if that's okay with you." He looked at their mother's face, and the smile on it seemed so warm and loving that Madison felt her insides grow warm.

Well, maybe two people at this table were looking at a happy ending, even if she wasn't.

She sighed and took another bite.

But they also discussed where their dad would live while he was in Grave Gulch. It sounded as if he'd stay in Kendall at first and visit often to spend time with their mother—and also look for a place to live.

Maybe eventually—soon—at their mother's.

And as they were discussing Grave Gulch and what it was like these days, Madison's phone rang.

It was Oren, so of course she answered. She stood up from the table and walked into the hallway to talk so she wouldn't disturb anyone.

"Hi, Oren," she said, knowing puzzlement sounded in her voice. "Is everything okay?"

"I hope so," he said. "Could you come outside for a minute? I'm in front of your mother's house. There's something I want to discuss with you before I leave."

Her heart sank. Well, at least he was saying goodbye.

She waved at her family. "I've got to check on something outside," she called and then went to the front door.

She walked onto the front porch before seeing Oren standing at the side of the lawn under a dim pole light. She headed there.

Her heart started racing as she saw him. He was so handsome. And like it or not, he had hold of her heart.

Though this might be the last time she saw him.

As she neared him, she said, "What's wrong, Oren? Is there anything I can do to help?"

His smile was wide—but there was something about it that suggested worry. "Nothing's wrong, Madison. Not yet, at least. But yes, there's definitely something you can do to help."

She stopped right in front of him. "What—" And then she gasped as Oren dropped to one knee on the grass in front of her. He held a small box in one hand that he held out to her.

"Madison Colton, I love you. I want to be with you forever, here in Grave Gulch or wherever. Will you marry me?"

No need to think. Never mind that she had just exited an engagement. That had been with a man she'd liked but hadn't really loved.

But Oren? "Oh, yes, Oren. Yes!" She held out her hand, not for the ring but to touch him, touch his arm, be in contact with him.

But he opened the box and pulled out a lovely ring with a large diamond surrounded by smaller ones in it. He reached out, and Madison put her hand in his.

The ring fit as perfectly as if he'd measured her finger beforehand. Maybe that was another thing marshals did as well as they somehow kept track of the people they were protecting...

And as Madison threw herself into his arms, against his wonderful, hard, sexy body, she heard some noise from behind them.

Her family was cheering, yelling "Congratulations!"

But Madison didn't want to talk to them. Not yet. She drew even closer to Oren, threw back her head and said as closely into his ear as she could, "And I love you, Oren Margulies."

Damn. After his discussion with his sister that had focused him on how he really felt about Madison, he had become certain that he wanted to marry her. To spend his whole life with her. To have kids with her.

He'd wanted their commitment to begin immediately. That was why he had bought that ring.

And hoped her answer would be the positive one it had been.

As a result, Oren certainly had planned to spend the entire night of their engagement with the wonderful woman who had become his fiancée hours ago, and he had accompanied her home. But it was late now, and he'd just pulled his car into the dark parking lot behind Bubbe's Deli, parked in his usual employee spot that wasn't far from one of the dim lights mounted on the building. He grabbed his weapon as he exited the vehicle.

And was glad to see others in the parking lot, too: several cops in uniform, one with a K-9. They came over to him, and he immediately showed his ID. They advised him that their interim chief knew he was here.

Olivia had called him. She had stayed long after closing the place to go over some things in the books, she'd told him, her voice shaking. "I've been robbed," she cried. "Can you—"

"I'll be there in a few minutes," he'd told her. "But have you called 9-1-1?"

"Yes, and a couple of officers are already here."

"Good. You do as they tell you, and I'll see you soon."

Of course the call had interrupted an absolutely wonderful session between Madison and him in bed. His gorgeous, naked fiancée was sitting up, her red hair mussed, holding a sheet around her. "What's wrong?"

He told her as he got dressed in his suit. He needed to appear official, even though his main reason for being there would be to take care of his sister.

"Can I come, too, to help Olivia? She'll be my sister-in-law soon, after all. And what happened sounds so horrible."

"You'll stay right here," Oren commanded. "I don't want to have to worry about you, too." He left soon, after giving Madison, now wearing a robe, a deep, loving kiss and promising he would return as quickly as possible.

"Stay safe," she'd told him and kissed him again.

And now he was here. He hurried to the front door and entered the deli, which was full of more cops. Some of them were collecting fingerprints around the checkout counter.

Olivia was sitting at one of the tables near the front with several cops surrounding her, including Brett, with Ember sitting beside him. Oren hurried over there.

"Olivia, what happened?"

Though there were tears in her eyes, she managed to smile grimly at him. "Hi, bro." Her voice was trembling. "I may be able to show you a little of what happened if these wonderful police who showed up so fast can get footage from some of my neighbors' security cameras."

Good. If that worked, they should be able to identify whoever it was.

And in fact, Brett stood up and joined Oren, Ember at his side.

"I'd like you to contact Bryce. I have his number, but it would be better if you called. And he might be very interested in what happened here."

Curious but wanting to cooperate fast, Oren immediately walked away and called Bryce. The guy sounded groggy at first, till Oren finished his quick explanation of what had happened. "I don't know why the chief thought the FBI would be interested, but—"

"I'll be right there," Bryce said.

After they hung up, Oren returned to his sister's table and asked her to elaborate on what had taken place. He held out his hand, and Olivia put hers in it. Brett remained at the table, but the other cops had risen to patrol the inside of the restaurant, even though it sounded as though the perpetrator had left a while ago.

Olivia talked first about closing time, the customers who'd been there and dawdled a bit. "It was late, and I was alone, of course, going over the books. This man suddenly burst in. He had a gun, and I was terrified." Her voice hitched with emotion, and Oren, looking into her blue eyes, waited till she could talk again. And strangely, she wound up smiling, though sardonically. "Would you believe he demanded a corned beef sandwich?"

"Hey, that sounds good to me, too." Oren lifted his brows, kidding, of course, but hoping to lighten things up even more for his sister.

"Then, come back when we're open."

"Got it."

Olivia continued. The guy had left after eating the sandwich she'd of course put together for him, but that wasn't all. "He made me grab all the cash I had in the register, plus from my purse. He left with hundreds—but I can't complain too much. He didn't hurt me. Only... Well, he said he really liked the corned beef sandwich, so he'd be back to try the pastrami. Or kill me, I don't know."

Damn. Oren asked her a few questions, then talked to Brett a bit. Yes, the cops here now on patrol, including K-9 officers, were looking for the guy.

And the detectives on call that night at the station had already gone over the security footage. "You were very lucky, Ms. Margulies," Brett told Olivia. "It turns out your visitor is known to us—too well. He's a serial killer, in fact. Name of Len Davison." He looked at Oren. "That's why I thought your FBI connection would be great to bring in here."

Olivia nodded. "I thought he looked like the images that have been circulated everywhere, but I didn't know for sure. I was too scared to think straight."

Bryce entered the deli then. "Hey, tell me about that robbery here." He turned to look at Olivia. "Are you okay?"

She stood up. "I…I think so. But—" She said to Brett, "He's a serial killer? And he said he'd be back?" She sank back down on the chair. "Maybe I'm not so okay, after all."

She clearly needed some cheering. This seemed a good time for Oren to relay his news to her. "Well, you were certainly okay before, when I was here yesterday. Smart, of course. Inspirational."

Olivia looked up at her brother. "What are you talking about?"

"I proposed to Madison tonight…and she accepted."

Olivia screamed happily and rose again and threw her arms around him. "That's fantastic! Congratulations, Oren." She stepped back and scowled at him. "But you didn't tell me."

"I was going to bring Madison here tomorrow—uh, today—to surprise you. I still might, though it won't be a surprise. And will you be opening later?"

"I—I don't know." Olivia looked from him to Brett to Bryce. "Would it be okay? Although, I'm sure this is a crime scene." She choked a bit. "He said he'd be back for more." She was clearly shaking.

"Let's hope he does come back," Bryce growled. "So we can catch him at last." But he took a couple of steps toward Olivia, hugging herself in obvious fear, Oren thought. He was about to chastise Bryce when the FBI agent said, "I'm going to hang out with you, Olivia, till he's been captured, whether he's caught here or somewhere else. Well, consider yourself in my protective custody till we get this resolved, okay?"

"O-okay," she stammered, then looked at Oren as if wanting his okay as well.

He gave it. He had full faith in his future brother-in-law.

"And yes," Bryce said, "after we do our crime scene investigation, like checking any security footage, dusting for prints and whatever else makes sense as we go along, you should open the deli today, both for your own peace of mind and because it might attract Davison back sooner."

A while later, after further discussions with the cops patrolling the area, who'd not found Davison, Brett said he was going to leave. "We'll have patrols around here all night and into the day, too. And we'll count on the FBI's services here as well."

"Good," Bryce said.

"And I'll be back here during the day," Oren told Olivia. "With my new fiancée."

Olivia's squeal wasn't frightened; now, it was just excited, Oren was glad to note. "I can't wait! But don't make it too early. I may even get some rest tonight, and I'll have to help clean the place when the police say it's okay." She glanced at Bryce. "And I guess I may have company then, too."

"Right," Bryce said, nodding. "Unless we're lucky and catch the guy tonight."

"I hope so." Oren shook hands with Bryce, then walked out the door with Brett and his dog. Something had been on his mind to talk to Brett about. "By the way, since I've gotten engaged to a local girl, I'll probably want to stay around Grave Gulch."

He felt sure his parents would understand if he moved here to be with his future wife. They'd probably even visit here more to see Olivia, too. Still, that remained uncertain. But he had introduced them to Madison via a video call, and they seemed delighted.

Madison and he had also promised to visit them soon.

"Sounds good," Brett said.

"Not sure if the Marshals Service will have a job for me here, though—but how about the Grave Gulch PD? Do you think I could come work for you?" Oren continued.

Brett turned under the dim light in the parking lot. "Let's talk about it when we're both wider awake, okay? Maybe we can find something here..."

"Excellent!" Oren exclaimed. They shook hands, and Oren headed for his car.

He drove to Madison's as quickly as he could, then used the key she'd given him to get in.

Unsurprisingly, she was in bed, but not sleeping—not deeply, at least. She sat up immediately when he entered her bedroom and turned on a lamp beside the bed. "You're back," she said. "I'm so glad. Is your sister okay?"

"A bit scared, of course, but she'll be fine," Oren said. Especially with Bryce watching over her to make sure her assailant didn't return and hurt her. "But how about me? Aren't you going to ask if I'm okay?" He'd sat down on the edge of the bed and was now staring down at her with a pretend frown.

"Aren't you? You look fine to me. In fact, you look delicious."

They were suddenly in each other's arms, and their kiss was definitely delicious and more. He could hardly wait to show his fiancée off to his sister. But right now, he was glad he was home safe, in the arms of the woman he loved, the woman who would become his wife. This was where he needed to be—now and forever.

He held Madison tightly against him. "I love you, Madison."

"And I love you, Oren. How about we prove it to each other again?"

"Oh, yeah," Oren said and stood again to pull off his clothes.

* * * * *

Check out the previous books in
The Coltons of Grave Gulch series:

And don't miss the next book

Available in December 2021 from
Harlequin Romantic Suspense!

#2159 COLTON 911: SECRET ALIBI
Colton 911: Chicago • by Beth Cornelison

When Nash Colton is framed for murder, his former lover, Valerie Yates, must choose between proving his innocence and putting her mother's fragile mental health at risk. As they fight to rebuild their relationship, they must learn to trust each other—and find the person trying to kill Nash.

#2160 DROP-DEAD COLTON
The Coltons of Grave Gulch • by Beverly Long

FBI agent Bryce Colton has dedicated the past year to finding serial killer Len Davison. When Davison becomes obsessed with Olivia Margulies, Bryce believes the man may be within reach. But the obsession turns dangerous, and Bryce takes the ultimate risk to save the woman that he loves...

#2161 THE LAST COWBOY STANDING
Cowboys of Holiday Ranch • by Carla Cassidy

Marisa has been waiting to kill a man who kidnapped her. When she hires Mac McBride to care for an abused horse on her ranch, she thinks there might be some good in the world after all. But Marisa's past isn't finished with her—and Mac may not be enough to protect her.

#2162 MATCHED WITH MURDER
by Danielle M. Haas

When multiple murders are connected to users on Samatha Gates's dating app, Detective Max Green knows she'll have information he needs. Neither of them expected Samantha to become a target—and now she has to share her secrets with Max to find the true culprit.

HRSCNM1121

SPECIAL EXCERPT FROM

ⒽHARLEQUIN
ROMANTIC SUSPENSE

*When multiple murders are connected to users on
Samantha Gates's dating app, Detective Max Green
knows she'll have information he needs. Neither of them
expected Samantha to become a target—and now she
has to share her secrets with Max to find the true culprit.*

Read on for a sneak preview of
Matched with Murder,
Danielle M. Haas's
Harlequin Romantic Suspense debut!

Samantha dropped her head in her hands. "I had the
same thoughts. I called the Department of Justice this
morning, and the woman I spoke with said I needed to
speak with the warden. I didn't get a chance to call before
Teddy stormed in. But I...I can't believe Jose is behind
this."

Max stared at her with hard eyes and an open mouth.

She wrapped her arms over her middle, not knowing
how to explain the conflicting emotions Jose still stirred
in her gut.

"I have to go." Max strode toward the doorway of the
kitchen that led to the foyer, his strides fast and furious.

She staggered off the stool and followed behind him
as quickly as she could. Her mind raced with a million
possibilities. Her bare foot touched down on the wooden
floor of the foyer.

Crash!

She whipped her head toward the broken window that faced the street. Glass shattered to the floor and something flew into the newly formed hole.

"Get back!"

Max's yell barely penetrated her brain before he scooped her over his shoulder and ran in the opposite direction. He reached the carpeted floors of the living room and leaped through the air. They crashed behind the couch and pain shot through her body.

Boom!

A loud explosion pierced her eardrums. The lights flickered and plaster poured down from the ceiling. Max's hard body crashed down on her. Silence filled the heavy air and Samantha squeezed her eyes closed and waited for this nightmare to end.

Don't miss
Matched with Murder *by Danielle M. Haas,*
available December 2021 wherever
Harlequin Romantic Suspense
books and ebooks are sold.

Harlequin.com